D0385213

DEEPER WATERS

Also by Mary Morgan

The House at the Edge of the Jungle

Willful Neglect

DEEPER WATERS

MARY MORGAN

Thomas Dunne Books
St. Martin's Minotaur New York

THOMAS DUNNE BOOKS.
An imprint of St. Martin's Press.

For information, address St. Martin's Press, 175 Fifth Avenue, New York, N.Y. 10010.

www.minotaurbooks.com

Library of Congress Cataloging-in-Publication Data

Morgan, Mary.
Deeper waters / Mary Morgan.—1st ed.
p. cm.
ISBN 0-312-29035-7
1. Indians of North America—Land tenure—Fiction. 2. Washington (State)—Fiction. 3. Indian students—Fiction. 4. Law students—Fiction. 5. Islands—Fiction. I. Title.

PS3563.O81724 D44 2002
813'.54—dc21

2001058492

First Edition: June 2002

10 9 8 7 6 5 4 3 2 1

For Richard, Charlotte, and Rowland,
who succeeded in life despite a mother who wanted to be a writer

ACKNOWLEDGMENTS

I'd like to thank Richard Morgan, J.D., who helped me with some of the legal issues in this book, and especially for uncovering a particular circuit court decision for me. My sincere thanks also go to Ruth Cavin, senior editor at St. Martin's Press, who stuck with the project, and to Anna Cottle and Mary Alice Kier of Cine/Lit Representation, who've given me much wise advice over the past years.

These are much deeper waters than I had thought.

—*Sir Arthur Conan Doyle*

PROLOGUE

IT WAS DARK ON THE BEACH, ONLY A HAZY MOON GLINTING fitfully through the clouds. And silent, except for the small slapping of waves. Deserted. No one walks on a Northwest beach on a dark February night, the air cool and damp, the mist clinging to one's face; when I was a boy, exploring alone, it had always been summertime, with lingering remnants of sun in the western sky. But this night, the seductive sound of surf had lured me out of the house, down to the water's edge, compellingly close.

I'd brought a flashlight to light my path, but once over the driftwood piled just below the house, I switched it off. A gleam of phosphorescence at the water's edge and the moon's faint reflection showed the way, but now there was an eerie quality to the long stretch of beach, the sand disappearing into the darkness, everywhere so quiet. No crying of gulls, no thrumming of boat engines, just the trudge of my feet on the shingle and the sucking of the waves, as though the secretive world of the undersea were out there, watching, holding its breath.

Other people lived along this beach, total strangers only a few days ago when I first set eyes on Edward's Bay. The new and fragile strands of acquaintance were already beginning to tangle and knot, complicating our separate lives, but it was the reflections in the shining water and the swirling current round the end of the spit that had so delighted me. It was irresistible to have salt water this close to my back door, to have the sound of surf to make my sleep peaceful and dreamless.

The beach stretched before me, fading into the night. I could see only a few yards ahead. Flotsam and jetsam and sea wrack slopped at the edge of the water, rising and sinking, and there were rocks I didn't recall from the daytime, long black logs that hadn't made it as far as the high-tide mark. Except, as I peered ahead, my heart suddenly thumped and lurched. The shape lying directly in my path wasn't a log. Or a rock. I hoped, as I drew reluctantly closer, that it would turn out to be a seal, because dead seals sometimes wash up and lie stranded on the sand for all the world like a human being.

I switched on the flashlight. Stood very still, the sand clutching at my feet.

The shape was not a seal. Or a log. It was, unmistakably, a human being. Face downward on the sand, arms flung wide in a gesture of submission, clothes sodden with water, cold and wet to the touch. Cold wet flesh. A dead human being.

And as the narrow beam of my flashlight flickered over the back of the head, the spreading arms and hands, the legs and feet strewn at unnatural angles, my heart lurched again, sickeningly. I knew who it was.

I shut off the flashlight quickly, as if that would somehow make reality go away, as if it could be wished away, a trick of the mind. I stood rooted to the spot for a long time, my feet sinking deeper into the sand, unable to think or react, staring down, wanting the shape to move, to prove it wasn't dead after all. Couldn't be. Someone alive so recently couldn't be dead. Not here, not alone on this cold dark beach.

But there's no mistaking death, that awful inert flaccidness of the limbs, that sinister weight pressing flesh back into an expectant mother earth. I looked away, up to the lights of the houses along the beach, back to the shape on the sand, at last switched the flashlight on again, walked around the trailing legs and directed the beam of light on the face. I dreaded what I might see. I knew how crabs and sea creatures could nibble at dead flesh.

The face was quite whole. Utterly recognizable. Strands of black seaweed clung like a veil of mourning across the wide forehead, over the high cheekbones, and into the once firm mouth. Now the mouth gaped open against the sand, as though trying to eat it, as though hungry for the taste of it. The eyes, thankfully, were closed.

Kneeling down, I took hold of one icy hand. It was dreadfully cold and limp, the fingers already beginning to stiffen, curling upward as if in a final plea. After the first wrenching shock of recognition, my heart filled with terrible regret for a life that had been so full of promise and now was gone forever.

Only today we'd talked together. Only this morning. Just a few hours ago. Now a lifetime ago.

ONE

EDWARD'S BAY HAD CAPTIVATED ME THE FIRST MOMENT I LAID eyes on it. A low curving finger of land thrust out into Puget Sound. The water was dazzling all around, the houses built so close to the shore that their reflections floated, mirage-like, in the shining, placid water. Among the shallows, blue herons bent long necks in search of prey, and the only sound was the lapping of tiny waves at the edge of the sandy beach.

A miraculous place, peaceful, yet not lonely.

"Just go look at the house, Noah," Bigelow Harrison had said. "You'll be doing me a favor if you'll live in it for a few months. It's sitting there empty, costing me money. It doesn't do to have property sitting empty."

So I'd taken the ferry from downtown Seattle on a quiet Friday at the office and driven to Edward's Bay. And once I saw it, so sunny and serene and beautiful, I was hooked.

The house that Bigs Harrison was offering for a nominal rent was brand new, without the stamp of anyone else's personality on it. The smell of fresh paint, the gleaming finish on the floors, were intoxicating to someone who'd lived too long in a tired old house, among too many trees. It was a relief to be away from trees. In the Northwest, the overbearing evergreens suck the meager light from the sky, and only moss grows beneath them.

From the living room, no other houses were visible, the view wide and open along the sandy spit, out across the sound to the Cascade Mountains. But from the street side, the neighboring houses were near and companionable; they had sand and driftwood for yards, no lawns to mow, no trees for shade. Above a few windows, canvas awnings stretched in anticipation of summer, and here and there a few bare-branched saplings were staked, hopefully. In February in the Northwest, there's usually no need for shade, but on that particular February morning at Edward's Bay, the sun struck shards of brilliance off the water, and I had to shield my eyes from the glitter.

Bigs Harrison had come to my rescue I couldn't live in Springwell any longer. The events of the past months had left a sour atmosphere, a bad taste in the mouth, and the time had come to move on. Move on! God, it was good to be able to say that! Edward's Bay gave me a sense of rebirth and renewal, of life and vigor. It held no memories. It was exactly the right place to start over.

The telephone was connected. I picked it up to call Bigs. "This is Noah. I'll take the house. The location is fabulous."

His laugh was cynical and familiar. I'd known Bigs a long time. "Location, location, location," he said. "That's what the realtors say, isn't it? I can't understand why those houses didn't sell in a flash, but I guess they'll all go by summer. So don't make yourself too comfortable, Noah."

They didn't sell in a flash because none of them was priced under half a million dollars. Even in the red-hot Northwest market, half a million is no small potatoes, especially with a ferry ride to consider. But for me, the new practice in downtown Seattle meant I could walk to the ferry, and Edward's Bay would be perfect. Perfect!

"So it's mine, Bigs? From this moment on?"

"Just put a check in the mail, Noah I guess I can trust you."

In that instant, I decided to stay in the house that very night, even if there was no furniture, no bed. A sleeping bag would suffice. I'd slept in far worse places than the floor of an empty bedroom. Tomorrow, Saturday, I'd begin to move in properly.

"Thanks, Big." I was grateful. "I owe you."

He cleared his throat noisily. "Hey, Noah, no sweat. Glad to help. Things have been rough for you these last couple of years. I want you to know I'm rooting for you."

That surprised me. Bigs Harrison, a dyed-in-the-wool Northwesterner, from old lumber money, could be difficult to deal with. We'd had a few disagreements over his property developments. But I was out of real estate regulations now, into the more stimulating world of defense law. Bigs and I wouldn't have to disagree over anything anymore.

I was about to put down the phone when he cleared his throat again. "There is one little problem you could help with, Noah. Later. When you've settled in."

I paused. "What little problem is that, Bigs?" Of course, warning flags should have gone up immediately, but I guess I wanted to ignore any problems.

He laughed again. "No biggie, Noah. Enjoy the house. It's a great spot."

"Great! Thanks again, Bigs."

I checked around the house. The water wasn't turned on, but everything else seemed to be working—lights, stove, refrigerator. Down in the clean bright basement, so unlike the dark and dusty basement of the old house, I found an inlet valve, cranked it, heard a satisfactory gush of water into the tank; with a little more searching, I located the circuit breakers and flicked on power to the water heater. Already the house felt like my own.

Upstairs, the stark white paint and the bare smooth walls made me think I wanted to keep everything just the way it was, shining and uncluttered. Total simplicity. No baggage. One sofa for stretching on in front of one TV. One bed for sleeping in. Alone, unfortunately.

I decided, then and there, to try to buy this house from Bigs. I could search for months, years, and not find anywhere like Edward's Bay, the fresh salt smell, the beach a few yards away. So maybe the house was ridiculously large for one person—it even had a hot tub built into the deck—but the absurdity of having it all for myself pleased me. Sinful luxury.

I went down the steps from the deck, crossed the sparse patch of sandy grass, clambered over the heap of driftwood at the property line. Beyond the driftwood, the beach sloped gently from a line of seaweed at the high-tide level and was littered with clam shells, small rocks, and fresh logs. A huge container ship came looming out of the sunshine, filling the horizon, and from the opposite direction, a small green tugboat chugged low on the water, pulling a pair of barges in its wake. Traffic like this had to pass here every day. Riches indeed.

Strolling along the beach to the end of the spit, round the corner where the tide ripped, I came to the inner curve of the spit, inside the bay. Here the water was green and still, the beach sandier and smoother, the houses facing into the headland opposite. A completely different feel from "my" side. I preferred "my" side. In the middle of the bay, in a small wooden dory, a lone fisherman was setting pots, and I watched for a while as he bent over the gunwales, dropping a pot, lifting an oar, sculling to a different spot, repeating the maneuver in a slow timeless fashion. Setting pots for crab, no doubt. Something about his shape and his movements made me think he was Indian. I knew the village above Edward's Bay was on the Quanda Indian reservation.

No one else was out and about, and there were remarkably few signs of life in any of the houses. I wondered how many were, in fact, sold. I knew very little about this development of Bigs's, only that he'd built it in partnership with another contractor. Developing raw land always seemed risky to me, as I was not a gambler, though there's no getting away from the fact that a lot of money can be made at it. If one doesn't go broke first.

The inside beach eventually curled back into the mainland at a point where a couple of unfinished houses stood, raw and skeletonlike, no one working on them. Turning, I retraced my steps, and when I was halfway back to the end of the spit, someone at last appeared out of one of the houses. A young woman with a bundle of blankets in her arms. It was reassuring, in a way, to see someone else. There was an odd dreamlike quality to the empty beach and to the deserted houses, as though time were standing still, as though no one really lived there.

The woman stepped carefully around the logs, noticed me, and then stood motionless, the blankets clutched close to her body. She raised a hand to shield her eyes, and the sun glinted on her dark shiny hair. Perhaps a stranger wandering the deserted beach was alarming to her; if she lived here, she'd know everyone who belonged.

I called out. "Hi, there. I'm just moving into five-twenty-one. The gray house with the white trim."

A huge shapeless jacket overwhelmed her, made her look waif-like and fragile. She was probably still in her twenties, with dark thick-lashed eyes and smooth creamy skin, but the bones of her face were almost too defined, shadowy hollows beneath her cheekbones, as if she didn't get quite enough to eat. She kept staring at me, suspiciously, without speaking, as though unused to talking to people, as if she wasn't going to speak at all. Then she said, "So we'll be neighbors. I live in the house behind."

She spoke with an accent I couldn't quite identify, very English, yet unlike any English accent I'd heard before. The house behind was cedar-shingled, as new and raw as mine. Not as if a family lived in it.

"You live in a great spot," I said enthusiastically.

She shifted the bundle in her arms. "It's far too quiet, if you ask me. Too isolated. Just Indians around," she said and waved one hand toward the boat in the bay. "They seem to think this is still their property."

We both turned to look at the fisherman. He looked right back, caught in the action of dropping another pot, rope in hand, frozen in still frame. I thought I'd resent it, too, if someone built over what once had been my land.

"Anyway," the woman said, "there's nowhere to take the baby."

Where else would a mother want to take a baby except to this sunny, peaceful beach? It seemed like paradise to me. But I didn't have children of my own, so what did I understand about mothers and babies? However, I understood enough to express a polite interest in the contents of the bundle.

"A boy?" I ventured, brilliantly deductive about the blue blankets. "How old?"

It seemed to be the right question because she smiled at me then, as if making up her mind to trust me, and in an instant her face was no longer waiflike, only warm and friendly, mouth curving, dark eyes glowing. She folded back the edges of the blankets, exposed a thistledown head lolling against her shoulder in sleep, and held the baby in the sunshine, an idealized picture of motherhood and childhood. An unexpected pang of envy caught in my throat.

"Christopher," she said. "That's his name. He's seven months old. Actually, he's not very well."

"I'm sorry," I said, inadequately. He looked perfectly fine to me.

"Just a little cold. No big deal. But I thought we'd catch some rays while it lasts. You know how fickle the weather is around here," and she settled herself on a smooth rounded log, the baby on her knee, and unwrapped more of the blankets. "I'm sorry if I was abrupt just now. It's such a surprise to see anyone. Usually there's no one else around during the daytime."

If my first exploration of the beach was anything to go by, she probably didn't find much company around Edward's Bay. "Where is everyone?" I asked.

She shrugged. "Oh, working, I suppose. Doing their own thing. Whatever it is people here do all day."

"If I lived here," I said, "I'd be out on this beach all the time." I laughed. "But, of course, I am going to be living here, aren't I? Got to get used to it."

"After a while, you'll just take it for granted," she said, in the funny accent, but I thought I'd never take a place like Edward's Bay for granted.

"Well, got to be on my way," I said. "Got to catch the ferry." I liked the sound of the words, "catch the ferry." "My name's Noah, by the way. Noah Richards. I hope your baby's better soon."

As I started away across the sand, she called after me, "And my name's Sarah. Sarah McKenzie. Stop in for a cup of coffee sometime. Anytime. I'm always home."

I looked back at her, the sunshine gleaming on her dark hair, on the baby's blond head, the water dancing around and about them, blinding me.

"Thanks," I said. "After I'm moved in, I will."

Sarah. A good solid uncomplicated name. My mother's name.

Her accent inevitably reminded me of Daphne Carlsson, my friend Chauncey's English wife, both of them left behind in

Springwell. Daphne and Chauncey were the only things I'd miss about Springwell.

I climbed over the driftwood, up to the deck, and into the brand new house for one more satisfied look, and promptly forgot about the woman and the baby on the beach. There were plenty of other matters to occupy my mind.

TWO

MY NEW OFFICE WAS IN PIONEER SQUARE, WITHIN A CLOSE walking distance of the ferry terminal, in a handsome stone-and-brick building from around the turn of the century, with high ceilings, creaky wood floors, and old-fashioned sash windows that still opened. If I felt fortunate about the house and Edward's Bay, I felt even more fortunate about the office and the association with Charlie Forsyth.

Charlie and I went back a long way, to student days at the University of Washington. He'd stayed at UW for law school while I went off to UCLA, and then we'd lost touch; even after I came back from California, we hadn't been in contact. But I knew about Charlie's career, of course. Everyone knew about Charlie Forsyth, the glamour-boy attorney, high-profile defense lawyer, brave—or reckless—enough to defend notorious cases and clients. And when caught Charlie's interest, of course. He could help with it, he said, and I needed all the help I could get. But the gift for me was that I'd no longer be alone. Single-handed practice had definitely not been my bag.

That Friday afternoon, Charlie wasn't in the office. "Having lunch with Annie," Sibby told me, disapprovingly. "He'll be miserable when he gets back."

Annie was Charlie's soon-to-be ex-wife, and Sibby was our paralegal, a breezy, skinny woman of thirty-something with lots of mascara on her eyelashes and a set of metal braces on her teeth. Sibby was frighteningly efficient and never less than cheerful, and she wore such silly short skirts one could forgive her almost anything. But I was curious about the braces. Charlie told me she was having her teeth straightened to persuade a reluctant boyfriend to marry her, but the condition of teeth seemed an inadequate reason for marrying or not marrying someone.

The rest of the office staff consisted of Beth and Grace, who were quiet and self-effacing in comparison to Sibby. They answered the phones, managed the filing system, ran the errands, and kept the books; temps came and went, depending on the workload, plus a couple of investigators on call for emergencies. It all seemed to work reasonably well, certainly with good humor and remarkably little friction. I'd been there a couple of months now, and Sibby, unlike my former legal secretary, hadn't once called me Mister Noah or instructed me on the best way to run a law practice.

"I found a great place to live," I told her. "Over near Seawards. I'll be a ferry commuter from now on. No more damned freeway every day."

I'd gotten to loathe the freeway drive up and down to Springwell, the constant jams and backups. As I waxed enthusiastic about Edward's Bay, the very sound of it was so entrancing that I couldn't wait to get back there, fearful it might have vanished like the mirage it had seemed at first sight.

Sibby scooted backward and forward on her rolling chair, entering data in the computer, rattling papers, accomplishing half a dozen things at once as usual. When I finally ran out of superlatives, she glanced up briefly from the screen.

"Sounds great, Noah. Too good to be true, if you ask me. There's got to be a snag somewhere. There usually is, isn't there?"

"Oh, Sibby! Don't tell me that's how you feel about life."

She flashed her shining braces at me, shrugged her thin shoulders.

Charlie eventually arrived back from lunch, suspiciously loquacious. He'd probably had at least one glass of wine to get through the meeting with Annie, and one problem with Charlie was that he shouldn't drink at all. A single glass of anything and he was off on a tear. At least, nowadays, he recognized it, unlike those long-ago student days. But his divorce, like all divorces, was proving to be stressful. It baffled me why anyone would want to divorce Charlie, an empathetic kind of guy, but who ever understands what goes on in other people's marriages? I kept out of it as much as humanly possible, though the pending divorce was the reason Charlie needed a new associate. Annie, it turned out, had taken up with Charlie's former associate, one sure way to break up a professional relationship.

Thank God he didn't want to talk about Annie now. What he mainly wanted to talk about was some woman who planned to sue her company for sexual harassment. I listened as he explained the sordid details at length.

"So what do you think, Noah?"

"Sounds fairly unpleasant. But I'd have to talk to her before I could give you a decent opinion."

Charlie smiled. He had lots of very white teeth and crisp black hair that was just beginning to turn gray at the temples. The dusting of gray made him look even more distinguished, older and wiser, and could only stand him in good stead in the courtroom, but the gray reminded me how many years it was since we were at school together.

He said, approvingly, "That's right, Noah. Never let yourself get rushed into an opinion." He handed over his preliminary notes and asked me to think about it.

We did, in fact, have plenty of work for the time being: a pending battery and assault, the appeal of a rape conviction, a shoplifting charge against the daughter of one of our more prominent citizens, several DWIs, two personal injury suits. The usual messy cases that clog up the court system, of no great account unless one of them happens to be your own personal problem. It was all fairly low-class stuff, the kind of legal scut work my former colleague, my late and puritanical father, would almost certainly have disapproved of. To tell the truth, so did I, in a way. But it was a definite step-up in the zest level after the wills and probates and real estate deals I'd been churning out in Springwell. Already I'd appeared in court twice, exactly twice more than in the past three years, and if those appearances gave me restless nights beforehand, at least they proved stimulating and rewarding. Stimulating because I had to think on my feet and rewarding because our clients got off on both occasions and even paid their bill.

I told Charlie about Edward's Bay.

"Good!" he exclaimed. "About time you extracted yourself from that one-horse town."

He meant Springwell, of course.

It was past six-thirty before I remembered the sleeping bag. I raced to the sporting goods store on First Avenue, bought the first one that came to hand, and barely made the seven-thirty ferry. There were far more cars waiting in line than I'd reckoned on; my car was almost the last vehicle squeezed into the cavernous belly of the boat, immediately before the flashing red gate lowered. But, it was Friday evening, when people took off for the Olympic

Peninsula for the weekend. In future, I'd make sure to leave the Saab in the park-and-ride lot on the other side.

I climbed to the top of the ferry, the metal decking groaning beneath my feet, the wind blowing hard in my face, and watched the lights of downtown Seattle glitter and fade into the night. Catching a ferry wasn't going to be quite as simple as driving the freeway, but it was going to be a hell of a lot more fun. There'd be time to read the morning newspaper, set myself up with a latte. I'd be another downtown worker bee on the early boat from Seawards, returning, if lucky, on the six o'clock run. Some evenings I'd catch a later ferry, go to the opera or the theater. The possibilities seemed endless and diverting.

The trouble was there was still no one to share those diversions. Lauren Watson, my nurse friend from Springwell, might have come to the opera with me, but she'd gone home to Minneapolis. Temporarily, I hoped. But it had already been three months since she left, and when I thought of Lauren's flecked hazel eyes and her insecurities, I wondered whether she really would return to the Northwest and to me.

But for now, listening to the thrust and rumble of the huge diesels, the soft bumping against the pilings as the ferry edged into the dock at Seawards, I was determined to enjoy this new way of life, the clanging and bustle as the ramp lowered, the sporadic revving of engines, the impatient flashing of brake lights as the cars waited to unload. A long stream of red taillights disappeared like fireflies into the darkness, and I almost forgot to swing off the main road to the supermarket in Seawards, so engrossed was I in my new life.

But once at the house in Edward's Bay, unpacking the grocery bags in the kitchen, the decision to stay that night seemed precipitate. The sound of surf beyond the deck was just as alluring, the new and shining kitchen with the new and shining appliances just as pleasing, but now the house felt naked and empty, and I was spotlit under the kitchen's fluorescent lights. There were no blinds or drapes to shield the world inside from the outside; the windows were mere black holes that sucked the light outward and allowed anyone to watch my comings and goings. It wasn't that I was nervous. Just overexposed, unprivate, on view. After all, I was unaccustomed to neighbors.

Switching off a few lights so the kitchen was less of a stage set, I poured a glass of wine and set about fixing dinner. It was late and I was hungry, but soon it became evident I'd done a less than adequate job of stocking up. I'd purchased milk and coffee, a bottle of wine, a skillet for the steak, a couple of cheap glasses, a few plates, and a corkscrew, but had managed to forget a bowl for mixing the salad and even a knife and fork to eat the steak with. I contemplated the untossed salad, the uncooked steak, the meal that was so blindingly simple a few moments ago, and was uncertain what to do next. Eat with my fingers? Go back to the grocery store? Find a neighbor to lend me some utensils? A foolishly trivial and taxing dilemma.

Lights were burning brightly enough in a couple of adjacent houses; some of my neighbors were home, it appeared, yet it didn't seem such a smart idea to go knocking on strangers' doors on a dark February night. I certainly didn't want to drive five miles back to the supermarket. Then I remembered the young woman I'd met on the beach. Sarah. Sarah McKenzie. At least we'd been introduced. If I walked down the street between the houses, perhaps I'd recognize her place.

As a last resort, there was always the tavern up in the village, though it sure looked very much like a last resort.

The road between the houses was tarmacadam, more like a suburban street than a bulwark against the sound, but the air was fresh and salt-laden and the night so quiet that the thumping surf beyond the houses was quite distinct. The road soon ended in a cul-de-sac, and I reached it without seeing anyone or picking out Sarah McKenzie's house, so I turned around and headed back the way I'd come. Suddenly, almost blinding me, a bright burst of light lit up the dark street around me and a voice called, "Hey, isn't that Noah Richards?"

The light streamed from an open door, and though the shape in the rectangle of brilliance was indistinct, the odd accent was instantly recognizable.

I called out, "Yes, it's Noah. Is that Sarah? Do you have a knife and fork I could borrow?"

"A knife and fork?" She sounded amused.

I groped at the fence in front of her house. "I forgot to buy cutlery. No knife and fork, no dinner. Not unless I eat it with my fingers, and I don't fancy that, somehow."

"I should think not," she said and laughed. "Come on in."

The light still dazzled me, but its path led through a gate in the fence and up to an open door.

"How's the baby?" I asked, when I got to the door.

"The baby?" she echoed, as though she'd no idea what I was talking about.

"You said he wasn't very well this morning."

"Oh, yes, that's right. But he's okay now. Asleep."

She held the door open and smiled the toothy friendly grin of the morning. As I stepped inside her house, I hardly recognized her, tried not to stare. In the morning, she'd been disguised under that shapeless jacket; now she wore slim wool pants and a thin jewel-colored sweater that clung softly to rounded breasts. Her skin glowed creamy and soft under the kitchen lights, and the dark hair swung on her neck like thick silk. It was quite a transformation.

Inside, her house was much like mine, obviously built by the same hand, bare white walls and shiny surfaces and wide windows, a minimum amount of furniture, just as I'd imagined mine should be. Sarah McKenzie was obviously an extremely tidy housekeeper. There was an almost unnerving lack of clutter, no pictures on the walls, no books or newspapers lying around, no evidence of anything occupying her, not even a radio or TV playing.

"You haven't eaten dinner yet?" she said. "It's rather late, isn't it?"

"I caught the seven-thirty ferry, stopped to do a bit of shopping. It took longer that I'd thought."

She rooted around in a drawer, produced a couple of knives and forks. "So, you work in Seattle?"

"In Pioneer Square."

"Oh, then you must be an artist? Or maybe an architect?"

Pioneer Square is one of the cultural crossroads of Seattle, with low-rent studios for artists, upscale offices for architects. And lawyers. "No," I said. "Not an artist. Or an architect, unfortunately."

It's hard to know why I'm reluctant to tell strangers what I do for a living. After all, it's nothing to be ashamed of. "An attorney," I said.

Sarah McKenzie gazed at me thoughtfully, much as others seem to when they first hear of my trade. Perhaps everyone gets looked at in the same manner, doctors or police officers or fashion designers. Who knows? I tried to think how I looked at other people on first meeting. Did I size them up as she seemed to be, assessing me, weighing some secret pros and cons?

"Anything else?" she asked. "Tea? Sugar? Milk? A glass of wine?"

I smiled and shook my head. "Thanks all the same, but the steak's ready and waiting. Can I take a raincheck on the wine? But tell me about your accent. Where's it from?"

"Well," she said, "I'm a Kiwi." As though I should know what that meant.

I thought about it for a moment. "A small fuzzy green fruit?"

She laughed. "A New Zealander. That's what we call ourselves Kiwis. I don't really know why, come to think of it. The kiwi is a rather stupid bird that doesn't fly. Not at all like New Zealanders."

"New Zealand! You're a long way from home."

And as though the sun had gone in, the corners of her mouth pulled down and her eyes darkened. "Too right, mate. A bloody long way."

"So what brought you all the way to the Northwest?"

The corners of her mouth drooped farther. "Oh, the usual story. A man."

But there was no evidence of a man in that tidy house. Apart from the baby, of course.

I put my hand on the doorknob. "Well, thanks again, Sarah. I'm glad you opened this door at that precise moment. I might have been forced to go to the tavern. Frankly, it doesn't look too appealing."

Her eyes brightened immediately. They were a deep rich brown, the lashes thick and dark. "Oh, but the Eagle's Nest is marvelous! Full of the weirdest characters. It's on the Indian reservation, you know." In the morning, I'd gotten the impression she didn't particularly care for Indians. "It reminds me of Maori places back home. And the drinks are cheap. I usually go on Saturday night. It's pretty lively then. Got to do something for entertainment around here. It's as dead as a doornail otherwise."

I said, inconsequentially, knowing I should leave, "I've always had a romantic view of Indians."

She looked doubtful. "Then you should like it around here. This is Indian land, they say. They think it was stolen from them."

"Stolen?"

"Oh, another one of those disputes over treaties and things." She waved a hand, dismissively. "I don't know who's in the right and who's in the wrong, but a lot of the locals have got their knickers in a twist about it. Luckily, it doesn't concern me too much. This house isn't exactly mine."

"You're renting, too?"

"Sort of."

"I'm renting from a friend. But I'm thinking of buying the

house. How could one find anywhere better than Edward's Bay?" I opened the door. "I'll have to check out the Eagle's Nest. Goodnight, Sarah. Thanks again."

"Goodnight, Noah Richards," she said and remained in the doorway as I went down the path. I looked back and waved, and then she shut the door and the street was plunged into darkness once more. I wondered if she was alone and, if so, why. An attractive young woman, a baby, a comfortable home. Though God knows, life doesn't consist anymore of one man, one woman, one happy family.

I could see the neon signs at the tavern glowing on the hill above Edward's Bay. What I'd said about Indians was true. I was brought up on tales of Chief Joseph and Sitting Bull and Chief Seattle, and have always been fascinated by things Indian, considered them a noble, proud, and persecuted people. Even as a child, I had a degree of bleeding-heart sympathy for them because they'd been royally screwed. Except what else is new? Who hasn't been screwed some way or other at sometime or other? But in my mind's eye, there lingered a persistent image of this country as it must have been before the white man came upon it, pristine and empty, nature and man in harmony. If only I could have seen it then, before roads sliced through the forests, before houses were built all over land like Edward's Bay. Before there was an Edward to stamp his European name on such a delicate sliver of ancient land.

I took the borrowed knife and fork back to the empty house, cooked the steak, finished off the bottle of wine, went out in the cool night to gaze at the water for a few contented minutes, and then rolled into the sleeping bag on the bedroom floor. I fell asleep dreaming how Sarah McKenzie's silky hair would feel under one's fingers, what those rounded breasts would look like without a sweater covering them.

THREE

AT NINE O'CLOCK THE NEXT EVENING, SATURDAY, I DROVE past the tavern at the edge of the village. It sounded even more lively than Sarah McKenzie predicted, a hideous cacophony of heavy rock exuding from it, a wild thumping that almost visibly bent the gimcrack walls. Not my type of music. Not my type of tavern. I drove on by.

I'd been up at the old house in Springwell, and the day had grown late. Despite those self-made promises to start completely afresh, I ended up bringing things from the old house to the new one, such as the knives and forks and dishes I lacked. And Oriental rugs. The rugs looked much more desirable than when I'd lived with them every day, and so I rolled a few up and stuck them in the trunk, not sure whether it was an eye for the beautiful or mere backsliding. I spread them on the shining bare floors in the house at Edward's Bay, admired the soft colors and fine wool, and then grew weary of the game of setting up house.

What I needed was a beer. And a bit of company. High time to meet my neighbors, even if it was a bit of a stretch to imagine the occupants of the half-million-dollar homes at Edward's Bay hanging out at a place like the Eagle's Nest. But I knew one who might be there. Sarah McKenzie.

The village and the Eagle's Nest were up on the headland, only a few hundred yards away. A fresh breeze from the north blew in my face as I strode purposefully up the hill, the Big Dipper hazy overhead, Puget Sound a dark void on the other side of the houses. As the road climbed from the flat of the spit, a distant ferry came into view, a slash of slow-moving yellow on black water, and at the top of the hill, at the beginning of the village, the neon signs of the tavern gleamed cheerily in the darkness.

The Eagle's Nest was a low wooden one-story building, not in the best of repair. It had once been painted an optimistic red, but now the paint was peeling, and the whole rickety structure had a definite tilt to one side, as if it might keel over at any moment. When I pushed at the battered door, a blast of amplified sound hit me right in the face, and only the seductive lure of a cold beer and a bit of company persuaded me inside.

There was a surprising amount of company inside the Eagle's Nest. Through the layers of cigarette smoke and general murkiness, it was just possible to make out a large horseshoe-shaped bar, surrounded by a mob of large bodies; beyond the bar, a pair of pool tables were islands of brilliance in the gloom, green baize and colored balls lit up like a Hopper painting. The tables and chairs scattered around and about all seemed to be occupied, while against the walls, fading into the gloom, were more large shadowy figures. The source of the amplified racket was at the distant end of the room, spotlit on raisers, a band of sorts, long-haired youths twanging on electric guitars, banging on drums. No one appeared to be listening. The whole place was thunderous with the din of the band, the clacking of pool balls, the roar of shouted conversation and laughter. But it was a friendly enough noise, and though it was hard to imagine where all these people had come from, at least they weren't sitting at home, glued to their TV sets.

I elbowed through to the bar for a beer, fought my way back out again and leaned against a frail upright in the middle that may have been a main support for the rest of the structure. I didn't lean too hard. Peering through dimness and the crowds, I saw no sign of anyone who looked the least like Sarah McKenzie, and soon the cigarette smoke was stinging my eyes, the blast of amplifiers assaulting my ears, and I began to wonder what on earth I was doing there. The Eagle's Nest wouldn't have been my first choice. Above the bar, containers of pull-tab cards filled the spaces to the ceiling, and a couple of huge TVs flickered overhead; it was impossible to tell whether the sound was on or off. Around the edges of the room, video machines flashed and whined, and the plywood walls, or what I could see of them, were plastered with beer and cigarette ads and handwritten admonitions. No Credit. Don't Even Ask.

But the Eagle's Nest was obviously the local gathering place. The locals appeared to be mostly male and mostly Indian. This was, after all, Quanda territory.

Just when I knew I couldn't tolerate the band for another second, there came a final shrieking chord and the lead guitarist shouted into the mike, "Taking a break now, ladies and gentlemen. Back in twenty minutes." The crowd whistled and catcalled, and a blessed silence fell over the room. Except it wasn't silence, of course. The laughter and roar of voices continued unabated.

In the lull, a voice called out. "Hey, there, buddy. You holding up the joint? There's a seat here."

At a nearby table, a heavyset man in a jeans jacket, long hair tied back in a ponytail, was beckoning to me, crooking his finger, indicating the empty seat beside him. A stranger, of course, because I knew no one in Edward's Bay. I glanced around to see who else he might be signaling to, but he grinned and nodded his head, and patted the empty chair. The gesture was both welcoming and authoritative. Intrigued, I pushed through the crowd.

He stood up to shake my hand and towered over me. He had a great barrel chest and bulging belly, thick coarse skin, narrow black eyes. My hand disappeared inside his, his palm rough and calloused, the grip surprisingly gentle.

"Wayne Daniels," he said. "You looked lonely there, all by yourself."

"Noah Richards. First time I've been in here."

"We knew that." He laughed, the sound rolling out of the depths of his chest. "We know everyone who comes in here. Sit down. Make yourself comfortable." He waved at the other occupants of the table. "Meet Billy and Albert and Jay and Frank."

The men nodded and stared at me without expression, neither welcoming nor unwelcoming, as though the presence of a stranger meant nothing to them. On the opposite side of the table, two of them wore black Stetsons with feathers stuck in the band, the brims shadowing their faces so their eyes were hidden. I sat down and raised my glass. "Cheers."

Wayne Daniels leaned on the back of my chair and breathed down my neck. He snapped his fingers at a passing server. "Get this gentleman another beer. What'll it be?"

My glass was still half full, but I didn't argue. "Heineken. Thanks."

"Least we can do for a lonely visitor," he said and slid his bulk into the chair next to mine.

"I'm not exactly a visitor," I said. "I just moved in down at Edward's Bay."

"Didn't think you'd have moved into the village," he said and laughed again. Around the table, six pairs of eyes fixed on me as if waiting for me to say something significant. I had nothing significant to say. I looked around.

"Is it always as lively as this?"

"Saturday night," Wayne said. Each time he spoke, the others nodded silently, in unison. "The Eagle's by way of our tribal headquarters, you might say."

I noted again the preponderance of Indian faces. "Am I intruding? Is that what you're saying?"

"Hell, no, Mr. Richards! This here is public property. Everyone and anyone's welcome. No, we just like to gather for a bit of chitchat now and then, just like ordinary folks."

"Bit difficult with that band, isn't it?"

"You don't like our band? Boys from the village, you know."

"No offense. It's just that I'm not so fond of rock. I'm more into . . . well, classical music."

The men stared at me with that curious immobility I'd noted in the few other Indians of my acquaintance, the ability to remain perfectly still for long seconds without speaking or changing expression, a disconcerting trait that could stand a courtroom lawyer in good stead. After a few more seconds of challenging silence, Wayne shouted his baritone laugh and slapped me on the shoulder. "Classical music! I'll be damned."

His companions echoed his laughter, shifting ever so slightly in their seats. If this were a tribal meeting, Wayne Daniels would surely be chief.

"So, Noah Richards, what do you do for a living?"

For another moment, I hesitated. "I'm an attorney."

The little group froze into attention.

"An attorney, eh? So what's your specialty?"

"No real specialty," I answered truthfully enough. The hodgepodge of cases with Charlie Forsyth didn't qualify as a specialty. "Just a jack of all trades."

"Not a prosecutor or anything?"

"No. Not a prosecutor."

Leaning closer, Wayne peered down his big fleshy nose. "What then? Real estate? Wills? Divorces? Taxes?"

"Defense law."

Somehow he seemed to approve of that. He said, "I got a nephew learning the law. At St. Benedict's. Going to specialize in Indian treaty law."

St. Benedict's, a private university on the eastern side of the state, was known for offering generous minority scholarships.

"Treaty law?" I said. "Well, that makes a lot of sense. He'll have enough to keep him busy for the rest of his life."

There was more silent nodding from the group and a few more moments of beer drinking and silence.

"So, Mr. Richards, you bought one of them fancy houses down at Edward's Bay?"

If Sarah McKenzie hadn't alerted me to the Indian claim to Edward's Bay, I might have wondered about all the questions. "I'm thinking of it. I'm only renting at the present."

The harassed server came by with a slopping tray and clapped another bottle of Heineken in front of me. Wayne dismissed him with a peremptory snap of the fingers. "Put it on the tab, okay?"

"Your good health, gentlemen," I said, and each man at the table lifted his glass, solemnly. Now I'd accepted a drink, I couldn't get up and leave right away, even if I'd wanted to. In any case, there was nowhere to go, except back to an empty house. But when the time came for the band to return, I wasn't sure how much of it I could take.

Wayne Daniels leaned closer again. "So what do you do for entertainment round Edward's Bay, Mr. Richards? Not much classical music out here on the peninsula. You got a family?"

"No," I said and left it at that. "I guess fishing is my main entertainment. Any good spots locally?"

"Fishing, huh? That's my trade, you might say. For most of us Quanda. Used to be great salmon runs off the point. Not so good anymore. But then nothing's so good anymore, is it?"

"When I was a kid," I said, "my father could leave work at the end of the day and catch a salmon for dinner. No sweat. Now, of course, it might take all day to find a single fish. Too bad."

"And what did your dad do?"

"When he wasn't fishing? He was an attorney, too."

Wayne shifted his backside in the hard chair, gazed intently into his glass. He said, not so casually, "I'd think about it, if I were you. Buying a house on Edward's Bay, I mean." Then he said, "Maybe you should talk to my nephew," and he gestured to the Stetson hat wearers on the other side of the table. "Mr. Noah Richards. Meet Mr. Jay Bishop."

One of the men leaned forward, touched the brim of his hat with his index finger, and placed his right hand palm upward on the tabletop, an openhanded gesture. "Jay Bishop," he said. "Law student."

I tried not to stare too hard at him over my beer, but I was taken by surprise. Until that moment, the other occupants of the table had faded into the background, allowing Wayne to do all the talking, offering no opinions of their own. Hardly what to expect from a law student. All the men seemed to recognize my surprise and watched with interest as I put down my glass and grasped the proffered hand. Then he removed the shadowing hat, as if there was no longer any need for disguise, and I could see he was a good deal younger than the others, more Plains Indian than Coastal Indian, his features defined and sharp, high cheekbones, long upper lip, hawklike nose. His hair hung over his shoulders in two long braids, very black and glistening, as though it was oiled. The whole of him glistened, shining coppery skin, eyes black and sparking, a defiant and challenging look to him, as if he was expecting an argument from the world. He was wearing the same jeans jacket and T-shirt as the rest of the men at the table, but there was an indefinable air of superiority about him, arrogance almost.

"Happy to meet you, Mr. Bishop." I said. "So, when do you graduate?"

He smiled, his teeth gleaming. "June."

"This year? Nearly done? Where are you going to practice?"

He shrugged. "Wherever they'll take a radical Indian."

The laughter exploded out of Wayne Daniels. "Radical. It's a tribe, you know."

I looked from him to the law student. "So tell me. Is there some problem about buying a house on Edward's Bay?"

Jay Bishop rested his elbows on the table, brought his face nearer to mine, and stared into my eyes. "Maybe yes, maybe no. Maybe I'll come and talk to you about it. You got a card?"

Taking my wallet out of my back pocket, I placed one of my new business cards on the table, and they all leaned forward to stare at it, as though checking to make sure I really was who I said I was. Jay Bishop picked up the card, held it between finger and thumb, examined it, fixed me again with the bold hooded eyes.

"Defense law, eh? I've heard of Charles Forsyth. Maybe I will come and see you."

"You don't need to come to the office," I said. "I'm right down there on the spit. Number five-twenty-one."

"Perhaps I'll come and see you before I go back to Spokane," he said, which wasn't what I expected. I'd have guessed it was the office and Charlie he'd want to see, rather than me. "Maybe even tomorrow."

"Tomorrow'll be good. I'll be at the house all day, moving in."

Taking the card out of his hand, I scribbled the address and phone number at Edward's Bay on the reverse side, handed it back and Jay Bishop tucked it into his own wallet. Then from behind me came the ominous whine of an electric guitar, and I glanced over my shoulder to see the band trailing onto the stage, gathering up their instruments, vibrating the guitar strings, riffing the drums.

"Oh, oh," I said. "I think I'm outta here. I don't have the stamina for your local music." I drained my glass and stood up. "I'll say goodnight to you gentlemen. Thanks for the company. The drinks are on me the next time."

The truth was that I was glad of an excuse to leave. There'd been a wariness to the long slow encounter with Wayne and his cohorts, not at all relaxing, somehow challenging and testing.

Wayne stood up, too, put his hand on my shoulder, weighing the flesh as opposed to slapping it. "Good to have met you, Noah Richards," he said, as though some sort of test had been passed. On the other side of the table, Jay Bishop saluted casually. "See you tomorrow," he said.

I jostled my way to the door, the band warming up noisily behind me, looked round one last time for Sarah McKenzie. The band deterred me from searching any further. Just as I reached the door, a hand came from nowhere and thumped me on the back, and I turned, half expecting it to be Sarah, except the blow was too hard, and too heavy for a woman. From the shadows against the wall, the familiar figure of Bigs Harrison loomed out at me. Bigs Harrison, ex-client, new landlord, larger than life, in his usual red suspenders, plaid flannel shirt, and ruddy weathered face. He was grinning idiotically, a ridiculous cigar clamped between his teeth, his eyes screwed up over the smoke.

"Bigs! What the hell are you doing here?"

There was absolutely no reason Bigs Harrison shouldn't be in Edward's Bay; after all, he'd been building here for months, but to me, Bigs belonged firmly in the context of Springwell.

He circled the cigar in his lips and swayed gently on his feet, his words slurring over one another. "Checking on my property, Noah. Checking on things in general. How's the house working out?" He inclined his head toward the table I'd just left. "See you've been making friends."

"Edward's Bay seems a friendly sort of place all round, Bigs. Are you staying down here?"

"I might be. Or I might be going back to Springwell Depends."

"On what?"

"On whether I can see to drive the damn truck or not."

"My advice would be to stay put, Bigs. I'd offer you a bed except I don't have one. But you're welcome to the floor."

He rubbed the side of his nose with a thick finger and put on a silly voice. "Jolly nice of you, Noah. But I wouldn't want to intrude," and he grinned the foolish grin again. "I got a place to stay, anyways. My cousin's. You met my cousin? My cousin Ralph?" Lurching around, Bigs peered into the haze. "He was right here just a second ago. Where the hell's he gone? He's a neighbor of yours, you know. Lives just down the street from you."

I thumped Bigs on his upper arm. It felt like steel. "Take care, Bigs. Please don't drive. The house is great, by the way. We must talk about it."

"I'll make you a good deal on the house, Noah. Just for you, of course."

The door was within my grasp, no more than a few inches away, and I was almost out of it when Bigs said, "Hey, here he is! Hey, Ralphie, meet my old buddy Noah Richards from Springwell. He's a good guy. He's renting the house down the street from you."

I wanted out of the Eagle's Nest by now, out of the noise and the smoke, and didn't need to meet anyone's cousin, but I shook Ralph's hand anyway, of course. He looked more like Bigs's twin than his cousin, just as tall and beefy, same thick skin and thinning hair, deep-set eyes, prominent frontal bones. The main difference between Ralph and Bigs seemed to be that Ralph was more sober. And not in such good humor.

"Saw you powwowing with them Indians," Ralph said. "Let me give you some advice. You want to keep away from them. They're a load of damn trouble."

I pushed at the door. "I assure you they weren't causing me any trouble," I said. "Goodnight."

FOUR

OUTSIDE, THE AIR WAS COOL AND BLESSEDLY SMOKE-FREE. I took a grateful gulp of it, then heard the band blasting into a new number, and stepped hastily out of earshot. The door opened again, and Bigs came staggering out, Ralph on his heels.

"Hey, now, Noah!" Bigs called. "No need to get on your high horse. Ralph's just trying to put you straight, that's all. Some things you should know about, that's all, when you live around here. Me and Ralphie's partners, you know, not just cousins, and them Indians are giving us shit, that's the truth. A guy like you, Noah, you've done me favors in the past; you could help out with the problems, if you wanted to, now, couldn't you?"

Of course! Bigs's little problem! I'd been slow to put two and two together. I opened my mouth to tell him to forget it, shut it again. He was doing *me* a favor, after all, letting me have the house.

"I've given up the real estate stuff, Bigs. It's defense law now. You need me to defend you in court, I can do that." Pulling my wallet out again, I pushed a card into his hand. "Pioneer Square, Bigs. Nice office. Nice area. More upscale than Springwell."

"You gave your card to them Indians," Ralph said.

I stared at him. "I give my card to whomever I damn well please."

"Now listen, Ralphie," Bigs said, "Noah could be very useful to us. You know we're going to have to get us a lawyer."

"We don't need a lawyer who's too friendly with the Quanda. We need someone who's on our side."

"That young guy," Bigs said, swaying alarmingly from side to side, "the one with the braids. He's some sort of lawyer, you know. He's stirring them up."

"Not now, Bigs. Talk to me in my office. Anytime."

"Anytime ain't going to cut it," Ralph said. "It's getting serious around here. We got a neighborhood meeting tomorrow. You want to know what's going on, come listen." He pulled a crumpled and folded piece of paper out of the inside pocket of his parka, thrust it at me. "Noon."

It was too dark there in the parking lot to read the printing. "What's the meeting about?"

"About fishing treaties, of course. About the damn Indians claiming all the damn fish. About tidelands and this shellfish harvesting nonsense."

That wasn't quite what Sarah McKenzie had said. The Indians are claiming the land, she'd said. Bigs and I had been involved in land issues before. We'd battled with the state over wetlands on a development up near Springwell, and we'd lost. Or rather Bigs had lost because he dug in his heels and refused to jump through the necessary hoops, and permission to build had been refused. I hadn't been able to persuade him to cooperate with the powers that be. Bigs was not a cooperator.

"Come to the meeting," Ralph insisted. "That way you'll find out what's going on. Aren't you interested in what's going on?"

Of course, I was interested. Why wouldn't I be interested in another of the running feuds over ownership of places such as Edward's Bay, a beautiful piece of the Northwest world that I was thinking of owning myself? I didn't want to fight with Bigs. Or Ralph, come to that.

"Sure. I'd like to come along," I said and stuck the flyer in my jacket pocket.

Ralph seemed to lose the unreasonable hostility and grinned at me instead, so that the two of them, Bigs and Ralph, were grinning and breathing beer over me, enfolding me into their camp.

"That's the fella," Bigs said and thumped me on the back again, almost knocking the breath out of me. "Knew you were a good guy, Noah."

As they drove off, Ralph in the driver's seat, thank God, Bigs raised a hand in farewell, and I was suddenly sure he was in financial trouble. He might have inherited a pot of money from the family lumber business, but he'd taken a bath on the property up near Springwell, the development that never became a development. How much more had he dropped on Edward's Bay? How many dry wells could he drill?

Behind me, the tavern door creaked open again, emitting another blast of metallic rock to pollute the night air. Someone called, above the throbbing, distracting noise, "Noah?"

The accent was instantly recognizable. Sarah McKenzie. She came across the parking lot toward me, in the same overwhelming jacket she'd worn on the beach.

"You were in there all the time?" I said. "I looked for you."

"You did?" She seemed pleased. "I was over in the corner, playing darts."

For some reason, the idea of her playing darts surprised me. "I didn't look far enough, I guess. I was driven out by the so-called music. Don't tell me you really like that noise?"

She sighed a little. "But it's better than staying at home, isn't it? Especially on a Saturday night. And I'm quite good at darts, as a matter of fact. I play a couple of rounds with the guys, and someone always buys me a beer. It's a bit of company."

A bit of company? She was searching for the same thing I was? We stood together in the parking lot for a moment, and the red and green neon signs flickered on her face, tingeing her skin into a decadent pallor, emphasizing the hollow curves of her cheeks. There was an odd but attractive chameleon quality to Sarah McKenzie. Waiflike, lost, and lonely on the beach; in the house, glossy and groomed and housewifely; while now, in that garish neon glow, she'd a world-weary air, a middle-of-the-night fatigue, as though she'd been living it up at some big-city nightclub. Not playing darts in a run-down country tavern. Something of a mystery about her. Why did she go alone to a place like the Eagle's Nest? Where was the baby's father? How could she afford to live somewhere I wasn't too sure I could afford to live myself? Why was her house so alarmingly bare and empty?

She came a step closer. "I was wondering if I could beg a ride back down the hill with you, Noah? I walked up."

"So did I. We'll walk back together. Women shouldn't wander around in the dark by themselves. Anywhere."

She laughed, not unkindly. "That's very gallant of you, Noah."

"This isn't New Zealand," I said firmly and took her arm. It was quite impossible, of course, to imagine anything sinister happening to anyone in this peaceful tranquil place.

"Yes," Sarah said, a little coolly, "I do happen to know this isn't New Zealand," and eased her arm from my hand.

We set off down the slope of the road, the sky dark above, the moon hazy among thin clouds, past the last houses of the village. The houses were run-down and shoddy, just like the tavern, nothing picturesque about their state of disrepair, a pervasive whiff of neglect about them, as though no one really cared. Not at all like the houses on Edward's Bay. "The village is a bit of a dump, isn't it?" I remarked.

Sarah stared around, almost as though she'd never noticed the village before. "It certainly could do with some tidying up," she said, tartly.

Which made me wonder again about her house, its almost unnatural, compulsive cleanliness and tidiness. Which was better—or worse—sterility or squalor?

"How long have you lived here?" I asked.

"Here? In Edward's Bay? Just a few months. But I've been in the States four years altogether." She was silent for another moment; then she blurted out, "Four years too long, if you ask me." The words erupted out of her suddenly, as though she'd been storing the resentment up, waiting for the right moment to express it, and when I looked at her, she was coiled in a defensive ball, shoulders hunched up around her ears, hands strained deep into the pockets of her jacket. If I'd touched her, she'd be tight like a drum. Her patent unhappiness distressed me.

"But if you dislike it that much, why not go back home? Or move somewhere you do like?"

She stopped in her tracks, her face a pale oval in the faint light, her eyes dark and mournful. "Easy enough to say, isn't it? If you don't have a soon-to-be ex-husband who won't let you leave the country with your own child. Or even allow you to go and live in another state, for that matter."

"Ah, I see." Of course. That explained everything.

She gazed at me steadily for another second. "Do you? Do you have any idea how it is to have to dance to someone else's tune?"

But I didn't want to hear about it. Like Charlie Forsyth's divorce, I didn't want to be involved. There had to be at least two sides to the argument. Even the thinnest piece of paper, the Chinese say, has two sides to it. No absolute right or wrong to any of it because marriage is such an infinitely complicated matter. Thank God, I never had to handle divorce cases. Wills and estates and malpractice cases, and now defense trials, were complicated enough for me.

I didn't have any words of comfort to offer Sarah McKenzie. For a few minutes, we continued walking in silence. Then she said, "Oh, I suppose it's not so bad. Not really. I have a lovely baby, and I'd have died for a house like mine once upon a time. And I suppose Edward's Bay *is* rather beautiful. It's just that now and then I get homesick, you know how it is?"

But I didn't know about homesickness either. Once I'd ached to be back in the sunshine of California, but nothing had prevented me from returning to California if I'd really wanted to.

"Tell me about New Zealand," I said. "I've never met anyone from there before."

Once again, I'd pressed the right button. Her smile flashed suddenly, and she straightened her shoulders, flung her hands out of her pockets. "Volcanoes, fjords, beaches, mountains. You name it, New Zealand's got it. My family has a farm, a small holding really, not too far from Auckland. Near the Bay of Islands. Have you heard of the Bay of Islands?"

I wasn't sure I had. To me, New Zealand was nothing but a distant dreamlike country on the edge of the world, overrun with sheep and rugby players. It was hard to recall the names of any other city besides Auckland. Christchurch? Wellington? That was about it.

Sarah said, "Now it's *really* beautiful at the Bay of Islands," and the longing was evident in her voice. "Almost tropical. The sun shines all the time. And wonderful waters for sailing. Do you sail, Noah?"

"I did, when I was a boy. On the lake near our house. But it was hardly tropical. Nowhere around here. I can see why you miss it."

"When I look back, I wonder whatever made me leave. Here I feel lost, adrift, you know. People don't take care of each other here. It's every man for himself. The survival of the fittest." She was almost talking to herself now, as if she'd forgotten anyone was with her, worrying the rag of nostalgia, a little desperate, a lot unhappy. "We had horses, and we could ride along the beach for miles and miles. Horses are big in New Zealand, if you know what I mean." She laughed, a small uncertain sound, as if she'd almost forgotten how to laugh. "Horse shows and gymkhanas and dressage competitions, point-to-point-meetings, ordinary racing. Lots of thoroughbred breeding. Yes, people love their horses in New Zealand."

"Ever been to the racetrack here?" I said. "I used to valet park at Longacres, the old racetrack in Seattle, when I was a student. I never let my parents know. My father disapproved of gambling, believed it all crooked and dirty. But if someone had a win, they'd tip like crazy. Helped with expenses. Since then, the old track's been pulled down. I've never been to the new one."

Sarah said, "It was a dream of mine to own a racehorse. That must be the most exciting thing in the world, watching your horse win a big race."

"And what if it loses?"

She laughed again, more confidently. "Only optimists should own racehorses," she said, and I thought, that's my problem, I'm not enough of an optimist. Not just about horse racing. About life in general.

I was thinking of saying, "We could go to the track together," because it would be fun to throw a little money away, watch the scene, size up the jockeys and the horseflesh, but I thought about it too long, let the moment pass. I was too slow, too tentative, too unsure of my way in the new and complicated world of asking someone out. I wanted to be casual and didn't quite have the casual touch.

We reached the bottom of the hill where the road turned to run along the spit. "So," I said, a variation of the question I'd asked before in the house, "what made you leave?"

"Well, you see, if you grow up in New Zealand, you have to go round the world before you settle down. So . . . I went round the world."

"And ended up here?"

"So far," she sighed.

Down on the flat now, on the tarmacadam street, we went past my house, a single porch light shining on the white paint, the whole place spanking and gleaming even in the darkness. I admired it surreptitiously as we went by. As we approached Sarah's house, I asked suddenly, for no particular reason, "Who's baby-sitting for you?"

It was a relief when she said, "A neighbor kid. Her parents only allow her to stay till eleven o'clock. That's why I had to leave the Eagle's Nest just now." A relief because I'd had a sudden, ridiculous, and totally unfounded suspicion she might have left the baby home alone. I can't imagine what gave me that idea. Her air of desperation, I suppose.

We stopped at the picket fence around her house. Sarah unlatched the gate and paused for a moment. "Come on in," she said. "Say hello to Christopher."

I hesitated again. It wasn't that I didn't want to go in with her. Beneath the shapeless jacket, Sarah McKenzie was curvy and available. Or I wanted to believe she was available. I also knew very well she was the reason I'd gone to the Eagle's Nest in the first place. The beer and the company were just an excuse. But now I held onto the fence, my fingers skittering across the sharp points of the pickets, as if the decision to go inside with her was momentous, as if it would determine some future, long-term or short-term, right there and then. "Say hello to Christopher." Something committing in it. And she did have a husband, even if he was soon to be an ex-husband. I'd walked that tightrope before, liking someone else's wife too much.

Sarah said, "Just for a few minutes. Then I have to take the babysitter home."

Which presented an immediate, convenient alternative to going inside. "Why not let me take the baby-sitter home? That would be easier, wouldn't it?"

She wrinkled her forehead, as if assessing my trustworthiness. I must have passed muster because she smiled and said, "Why, Noah, that's very kind of you. If you're sure it's not too much trouble. Then I wouldn't have to put the baby in the car."

"No trouble," I assured her.

But as I jogged back to get the Saab parked outside my new house, somehow trouble was exactly what I sensed, tingling up my spine and along the nape of my neck.

FIVE

THE BABY-SITTER TURNED OUT TO BE A PERFECTLY ORDINARY teenager with braces on her teeth like Sibby. She was waiting by the front door with a pile of books in her arms and an earnest expression on her round face as though to convince us that she'd been studying hard all evening.

Sarah said, "You'll show Mr. Richards the way, won't you, Gretchen? He's new around here."

Gretchen ducked her head and didn't look at me. "Okay, Ms. McKenzie," she said, swallowing the "Mizz" as if it didn't come naturally. "Thank you, Mizz McKenzie. Thank you, Mr. Richards. It's not very far."

Sarah held the door open for us and said to me, sotto voce, as we went out, "Stop in on your way back, Noah."

As I ushered Gretchen down the path, I glanced back over my

shoulder. Sarah stood in the doorway, her shape outlined, the light a tempting halo around her head. I thought that stopping in on my way back wouldn't be such a smart idea. Keep this on a neighborly basis. "I reckon I'll turn in when I get back, Sarah. It's been a long day. See you around, okay?"

"Okay," she said, closing the door, and the light disappeared abruptly. Gretchen and I were left in the blackness of the night.

Gretchen wasn't a garrulous child. When I asked where she went to school, she answered perfunctorily. "Smith High." She sat nervously on the edge of the passenger seat and directed me along twisting tree-darkened roads, to a left turn a couple of miles away. There were no streetlights anywhere, only the headlights illuminating the conifers pressing in on either side of the road.

"You baby-sit for Mrs. McKenzie often?" I said, to break an awkward silence.

"Sometimes," Gretchen replied and pointed to a claustrophobic dark brown house hardly visible among all the trees. She jumped from the car as soon as it pulled up, as if she couldn't wait to escape from me, and as I watched her scuttle into the safety of her home, I wasn't sure who was more relieved, the nervous girl or me. Making a U-turn, I slid back the way I'd come, and yawned, suddenly tired, as if the day truly had been long. Tomorrow morning, I'd lie in the sleeping bag until late, explore the beach, put the new house to rights.

But as I reached the bottom of the hill and turned into the quiet street, I was startled to see a wild figure running toward the car, caught in the beam of the headlights, hair streaming behind, white twisted face. It was a moment before I realized the figure was Sarah McKenzie, a familiar bundle of blue blankets in her arms. I barely had the chance to get the car door open before she was calling to me, her voice high and frantic.

"Oh, thank God you're back! The baby! He stopped breathing. Oh, Noah! Help me."

I leapt from the car in a panic Sarah stood in the middle of the road, pumping the bundle up and down in her arms, wailing over it. I snatched the coverings aside, and to my horror saw the baby lying limp in his mother's arms, his small face deathly white, blue-tinged around the lips.

"My God! Did you call 911?"

She didn't answer, just stared down at the child; then she thrust the blankets away from him, threw him against her shoulder, and thumped him on the back. Hard. Once, twice. For a heart-stopping moment, nothing seemed to happen; then all of a sudden he coughed and spluttered and sucked air noisily, his mouth opened wide, and he began to scream, a piercing shriek, high-pitched and ear-splitting, a blessed sound in the quiet street. His eyes screwed up and his face turned pink, and in a moment, he seemed quite normal, as though nothing had ever been wrong with him. But for that endless few seconds, it was as if my own breath had stopped and started again.

"Oh, thank God!" Sarah was sobbing and laughing at the same time. "Oh, God! I was so frightened."

I said again, "Did you call 911?" I had absolutely no idea what to do about a baby who'd stopped breathing.

"No," she said and moaned, as if in pain. "I should have, shouldn't I? But I panicked, Noah, just picked him out of his crib and ran outside with him. Oh, that was stupid, wasn't it?" She rocked the baby backward and forward in her arms, the classic mothering motion, peered into his face, up at me. "I should take him to the hospital in Seawards, shouldn't I? Get someone to check him out. Someone to tell me he's really all right now."

"I'll take you," I said, relieved to have something definite to do, not just stand around uselessly. "We can be there in fifteen minutes."

We were there in less than fifteen minutes. There was very little traffic on the roads, and I drove at high speed, rocketing around corners, much faster than the limit. I kept asking, "How is he now?" because I couldn't see the baby. He was tucked into the blankets on his mother's lap, but he seemed safely and quietly asleep, Sarah crooning to him under her breath. My gut cramped at the fearful responsibility of caring for a baby; how fragile and tiny they were, how delicate and precious.

By the time we arrived at Seawards, Sarah seemed quite calm and under control, much more than I was. She directed me up the hill, not far from the ferry dock, and the sign for the emergency room came glowing out of the night like a beacon of hope. Obviously, Seawards Hospital was another community hospital for a large rural area, like St. Mary's at Springwell. I careened to a stop outside, and Sarah was out of the car in a flash, running inside, looking neither to left nor right.

My own panic hadn't completely subsided, and I had to sit in the car for a few moments, breathing deeply, waiting for my heart to slow before following Sarah through the doors. It wasn't easy to get inside. A uniformed guard behind a window wouldn't let me pass until I gave him my name and my reason for being there. "I brought a woman and her baby," I said, but he insisted on her name and the name of her child, made me show my driver's license, and though I understood it was his duty to keep the inner sanctum safe from marauding strangers, the ritual made the hospital feel like a dangerous place.

The emergency room at Seawards Hospital seemed to consist mainly of curtained cubicles on either side of a central hallway, the whole place calm and reasonable enough, as though everything, whatever it was, was under control, not dangerous at all. But to me, the calm felt unnatural, unreal. I tracked Sarah to one of the cubicles where she was perched on an uncomfortable plastic chair, the baby wrapped in his blankets on her lap, his face pale and smooth, alabaster-like, long eyelashes lying on his soft cheeks, the fuzz of thistledown on his head. A beautiful child.

"You'd never know anything was wrong with him," I said.

Sarah sighed and clutched him closer.

Without warning, the curtains were pulled aside with a flourish, and a doctor came into the cubicle, white coat rumpled, doughy face bored and tired, the inevitable stethoscope around his neck, "Hi. I'm Dr. Hayward. What's the problem?"

Sarah started to explain and she laid Christopher on the examination table, like a sacrifice. He stirred and opened his eyes, periwinkle blue, blank with sleep, gazed without understanding at the stranger prodding at him, opened his mouth, and howled piercing cries of protest. The doctor's hands were swift and practiced. He slid the metal stethoscope gently over the small heaving chest, the round belly, but now the baby was really screaming, and soon the doctor scooped him up and handed him back to Sarah.

"I can't find anything wrong with him," he said, and looked at me. "Are you his father?"

Sarah interjected, quickly, "No, his father isn't in the country. Noah's just a friend." She peered down at the baby, still screaming in her arms. "Are you sure he's all right? Aren't you going to do any tests?"

The doctor rubbed his face, wearily. "There are no signs of airway obstruction. Or anything else wrong that I can tell. We'll keep him here a couple of hours for observation; then, if he's still okay, you can take him home."

Sarah's eyebrows shot up, her voice high with indignation. "You're not even going to X-ray him? Not even take some blood?"

He frowned. "We don't like to do unnecessary tests on a healthy infant." He began explaining the pros and cons of blood tests and the probabilities of a diagnosis, and I thought it time to make myself scarce; medical examinations are something intimate, not for the ears of a passing stranger.

Beyond the curtained cubicles, the double glass doors led back to the outside world, and I sidled through them, away from the glare of fluorescent lights, away from the danger of blood and guts being spilled in front of me. Hospitals made me nervous. As I lurked in the shadows outside the emergency room, a steady stream of cars arrived, people in trouble, a youth with a blood-soaked towel to his head, a man groaning and retching and clutching his gut, a woman crying loudly. Through the glass doors, I saw a nurse scurry into Sarah's cubicle and come out with the doctor, and after a while, when nothing else seemed to be happening, I went back inside, through the same rigmarole, as if the guard hadn't seen me just a half hour before, as if he wanted to punish me for skulking outside.

In the cubicle, in the hard chair, Sarah rocked the baby against her breast. He was asleep again, fitfully, stirring in his sleep, blue eyes half-opening and then closing again.

"They're going to take an X ray. Noah, you don't have to stay. We might be here for hours."

"I can't leave you here in the middle of the night. How would you get home? Anyway, tomorrow's Sunday. I can sleep late."

"But you look terrible," she said. "As though you're sick yourself."

I made an effort to smile. "I'm sort of allergic to hospitals."

She frowned. "Does anyone like hospitals?" Then she looked at me more carefully. "Are you quite sure you're feeling all right, Noah?"

I tried to shrug it away. This wasn't the time or place to explain why I happened to dislike hospitals so much, why they made me sweat every time I entered one, why I got this cramping in my gut. Sarah McKenzie had enough troubles of her own. But she was frowning at me as though she wanted to know, as though she needed to be diverted from her own problems, and so I told her.

"The thing is," I began, "my wife . . . Janet . . . had leukemia. They tried everything, you know, everything. Chemotherapy, a bone marrow transplant. But she got that host-rejection reaction. She was so sick, so weak. I couldn't do anything for her, just sat and watched her fighting, fading away . . . And now, as soon as I step over the threshold of a hospital, smell the smells, hear the intercom . . ." I shook my head.

Sarah stared at me, mouth slightly open, dark eyes melting.

"Oh, Noah. I'm so sorry." She was silent for a moment, that same expression of pity and concern on her face I'd grown accustomed to seeing when people heard the story. One more reason I didn't care to repeat it. "So," she said at last, simply, "it was especially kind of you to come with us."

She didn't pursue the subject, and I was grateful for that.

We sat together for a while, without speaking, listening to the intermittent bustle outside the curtains. But the night was very long. It passed in a blur, up and down endless hospital corridors, to Xray, to the path lab, then back to the cubicle, waiting and more waiting. Eventually, the doctor returned to inspect the X ray, listen to Christopher's chest once more, and pronounce him fit to go home. Sarah was given a raft of instructions—to be careful about feeding, to call the next day—at last, in the dead of night, we were released from the confines. It was three A.M. by the time we got back to Edward's Bay. God knows how Sarah was feeling, but I was blurred with fatigue after the hours of anxiety.

We spoke very few words on the way back, but when we pulled up outside her house, Sarah leaned across from the passenger seat and kissed me on the cheek, a small brushing grateful kiss.

"Noah, thank you, thank you. Whatever would I have done without you?"

I reached a hand out to touch the baby's face, pulled back, afraid of waking him. "As long as he's okay. Poor little tyke. I hope you both get some sleep now."

"They didn't seem very concerned, did they? I won't be able to sleep a wink. I'll be awake for the rest of the night."

I watched as she went into her house, saw the lights go on, and was only thankful I didn't have to be awake for the rest of the night. I circled the cul-de-sac, parked outside my house, hardly conscious of unlocking the front door, rolled into the sleeping bag on the bare floor. I thought I'd fall asleep immediately, but as soon as my eyes closed, the sight of that baby's face, so white, so still and silent in his mother's arms, kept coming back to haunt me. Somehow I'd sensed trouble, but I never imagined it would be trouble for that poor little baby.

SIX

IN THE MORNING, WITH THE ALARM THAT CAN COME AT THE edge of sleep, I awoke in a jerking instant, all my nerve endings alerted. Wakened, not by the pale morning light filtering through the uncurtained window, but by a sudden dimming of it, as though some light bulb had gone out. Blinking up from the sleeping bag on the floor, I saw the window pane was blocked by something. A head. Someone was staring into the room, looking down at me. Fingers rapped on the window, and I sat up abruptly, exposed and vulnerable and slightly ridiculous, caught in an undignified position. Adults shouldn't be discovered in a sleeping bag on the floor.

My eyes focused on the shape of the head in the window. On the Stetson hat on the head.

"Damn!" I'd completely forgotten about Jay Bishop.

Rolling hastily out of the bag, I pulled on my pants and stumbled to the front door. Jay Bishop was propped casually against the uprights of the porch, thumbs hooked in the pockets of his narrow jeans, hat tilted over his eyes, surveying the street.

"Fancy property all right," he said. "Pity it's built on Indian land."

I didn't succeed in stifling a yawn. "Want some coffee?"

In the kitchen, he assumed the same relaxed and elegant attitude against the refrigerator door, expensive leather boots crossed at the ankles, not one sign of tension in all his long body, watching silently while I ground coffee beans, fumbled filter paper into the machine, poured in water. "Sorry I can't offer you a seat," I said. "No furniture yet."

"So I see. Nice place though. Mind if I look round?"

"Help yourself." It would be a relief not to have him watching me with those hawklike eyes. "I'll bring the coffee out on the deck. It gets the morning sun."

When I carried the coffee outside, there wasn't much sun. This was, after all, February, and such sun as there was, was already high in the sky. I looked at my watch and was amazed to find it was almost ten o'clock. "I was out rather late last night," I explained, as if there was a need to explain. "I don't usually sleep until this time."

Jay Bishop was leaning on the rail, staring out at the sound. He turned his head, and the hazy light reflected off the water into the narrow dark eyes, on the wide slit of mouth, the gleaming copper skin. He smiled knowingly. "Oh, yeah? Well, I guess Edward's Bay can be a pretty entertaining place."

Entertaining? Was he kidding?

I handed him a mug of coffee. "So what is it that you do around here that's so entertaining?"

He grinned. "Salmon fishing. Crabbing." He took a swig of coffee and laughed aloud, throwing back his head, the muscles of his face and neck engaged. "And then there's always bird watching. That's a good sport."

Bird watching hardly struck me as Jay Bishop's type of sport. Though what did I know about him? I felt thick and sluggish, newly roused from a very short, very deep sleep, as though only a few seconds had elapsed since crawling into the sleeping bag after the long anxious night. Even the soft sheen of the water was too bright for my eyes. I needed dark glasses to shade them, or a hat like his, and I was acutely conscious of how wide awake Jay Bishop seemed in comparison to me. But the coffee was hot and black and helped jolt me into a semblance of wakefulness. I swallowed a mouthful, wondered how the baby was this morning. If Sarah was coping.

After a moment, Jay said, "Let's go down to the beach," and he stepped lightly off the deck, leaping with sure footing over the driftwood. He settled his spine against a log, stretched his long legs in front, tipped the black hat farther over his face. Totally at ease. I followed slowly, sat on a log a few feet away, sipped the coffee in silence, grateful for the silence. For a chance for the caffeine to work some magic on me.

We sat quietly for a while; then Jay scooped up a handful of the sand, held it in his palm as though weighing it, opened his fingers, and watched it trickle away. "See that?" he said.

"Sand?"

"Gold. Pure gold. All those creatures living beneath it. Clams, Razors and butter clams, geoducks. A whole world of goodies. And half of it belongs to us."

"Us?" But, of course, I knew who he meant.

"Did you realize, Noah Richards, that there's another appeal about shellfish rights in the ninth circuit, even as we speak? They're going to find in favor of the treaties, of course. Fifty percent of the shellfish. Same as the salmon. And when they find in favor of the treaties, they'll also be finding in favor of the tribal claim to this land. Edward's Bay is tribal land, Noah Richards. No one else has the right to build on it."

I looked away from him, down along the spit. All was quiet

and empty, despite today being Sunday. The tide was almost at its lowest, small waves slopping sluggishly against the wet sand, the water a dull slate gray, no breeze to ruffle its surface. The usual debris was left behind by the tide: seaweed, flotsam and jetsam, logs of all shapes and sizes, some freshly cut and still oozing resin, some ancient and worn by the salt water into odd sculptured shapes. Below the driftwood heaped at the high-water mark, lower down on the shingle, an occasional clam jetted water high into the air so the sand appeared alive. Which it was, of course. A whole world teemed beneath our feet. Not only clams. Each rock hid a host of tiny shelled crabs that scuttled away if their hiding places were exposed, and there were also sea anemones and chitons, sand dollars and starfish and mussels. Out there, beneath the deceptively metallic surface of the sound, another mysterious universe went about its business, killer whales and harbor seals, salmon and crab, octopus and squid. Someday, one of the orca pods that cruised the inland waters from north of Vancouver Island down to Commencement Bay would come past here, chasing after salmon and seal. Someday, I might get a glimpse of the great black-and-white whale bodies rolling and breaching in flashing splendor.

"Is that what you came to tell me?" I said. "That Edward's Bay really belongs to the Quanda?"

Jay tilted his head back against the log, closed his eyes. "You know what Chief Seattle said? About the earth?"

"Chief Seattle is supposed to have said a great many things."

"He said, 'The earth does not belong to man, man belongs to the earth.' "

"So this land can never belong to anyone?"

Jay's mouth stretched in a sort of smile. He didn't open his eyes. "But if it belongs to anyone, it belongs to the Quanda."

I was awake enough now to protest. "That's having it all ways. Either it was sold by the people who believed they owned it, or it wasn't anyone's to sell in the first place."

"Or it was stolen from its rightful owners."

"Is there some treaty? Some written proof of ownership?"

"It is written. Usual and accustomed grounds and stations."

There was a familiar ring to that phrase, but I couldn't exactly place it. I stared over at him, at his head resting against the bleached wood, the high cheekbones and jutting nose beneath the black shadowing hat, the long braids hanging over both shoulders.

"Tell me. How do you get away with the braids in law school?"

He opened his eyes, grinned. "My first exercise in fighting discrimination."

I laughed. "Tell me something else. You're not Quanda, are you?"

"I'm Indian."

"And thus all Indian causes are your cause?"

"Of course."

He was so certain of himself, so self-assured. It was tempting to try and sharpen my dulled wits on him, puncture a little of that arrogance.

"Is that why you took up law? To fight their fight?"

He shifted his backside on the sand. "The Indian hasn't had weapons to fight his battles for more than a century and a half. Arrows and bravery didn't work against the white man in the nineteenth century. But this is a different century, a different time. Lawsuits and treaty rights are the way to win the battles today." He caressed the sand at his side, almost lovingly. "If this land belongs to anyone, it belongs to the Quanda. They'll get it back. Together with the shellfish rights. You seem like a decent person, Noah Richards. That's why I'm telling you not to buy property here. You'll lose it if you do."

After a moment, I said, "You know what Crazy Horse said?"

Jay lifted his head and gave me one of those long silent stares. "You're asking *me* what he said?"

"Crazy Horse said, 'One does not sell the earth upon which the people walk.' "

"That's right!" For a moment, he was almost animated, half-rising to his feet as though unable to keep up the pretense of cool anymore; then he sank down again, quickly, squatting on his haunches. He carved a sign in the wet sand with one finger, and the sign, whatever it was, was quickly obliterated by the water oozing from the sodden sand. No mark lasts long on a damp northwestern beach. "That's exactly right, Noah Richards. The land was nobody's to sell."

I swallowed another mouthful of coffee, cold now, unpleasant. "Surely you're confusing your arguments. Anyway, it's going to be tough to make that stick in the twenty-first century. If you'd made that argument a hundred years ago, it might have been different, but now you're talking about an impossible unraveling of the fabric of the country, of the whole concept of the United States of America. It's too late for that now. However, it's decent of you to warn me about Edward's Bay. After all, what do you know about me?"

"Wayne took a fancy to you. I trust Wayne's instinct."

"He's really your uncle?"

"All Indians are related."

"And all Indians are related to the land?"

"Precisely."

There was more silence for another moment; then I said, "You're only a third-year law student. How come you think you know so much?"

He smiled the cultivated enigmatic smile again and, as though trying to impress me with a certain mystique, with his state of being Indian, said, "I am wise with the knowledge of my forefathers."

I drained my coffee mug. "Each and everyone of us has forefathers, but most of us need to spend a great deal of time on the books when it comes to the knowledge and practice of the law of the United States of America. And whatever you think, you're part of the United States. Tell me. Are you working on this with someone?"

In my own third year of law school, I'd interned at the attorney general's office in California, working up a piece of state legislation, perhaps not too significant, but one which had left a stamp on the state forever. It was a heady experience for a young law student, and no doubt I'd been equally as arrogant then as this young man was today. But now I couldn't quite remember who was appealing what in the fishing and treaty rights issues in the state of Washington—was the state appealing against the tribes or vice versa? These fishing disputes had been going on for so long they'd become background noise. I didn't intend to expose my ignorance about the status of the appeal to a third-year law student, but it was a pretty good guess that Jay Bishop wouldn't be working for the state on this one.

"Who are you working with? A private law firm? Is it a class-action suit?"

Jay turned his own mug upside down, emptied the dregs into the sand, watched them filter away almost instantaneously. "Plenty of people are interested in the honoring of those treaties. Isn't that what we are taught to believe, that one's word is to be honored? Isn't that what this country is supposed to be founded on? Law? Honor? Contracts?"

"That still doesn't tell me who you're working with."

He smiled the secret self-satisfied smile again and rose easily to his feet, thigh muscles flexing under the close-fitting jeans. He stood in the way of the light, casting a shadow on me. I squinted up at him.

"Just take my word for it," he said. "I know things. Don't buy property here."

"Well, I appreciate the words of warning. I'm not certain I can afford it anyway."

"Believe me when I tell you they're going to be tied up in the courts for ever."

"They?"

He rearranged the hat on his head, and his white teeth gleamed under the shadowing brim. "I think you know who I mean. By the way, if ever you're interested, I could mention your name to people who like to work with someone of . . . shall we say . . . liberal tendencies."

I laughed aloud, amused by his chutzpah. Not even qualified yet and here he was offering to find me a job. "Thanks," I said. "But you do know 'liberal' is a somewhat contentious word, don't you?"

He grinned again. "Especially in Edward's Bay?"

"I don't know about that. I haven't been here long enough to delve into the political cast of my neighbors."

"No? But perhaps in Springwell? You see, I've heard about you already, Noah Richards. About that case in Springwell. I hope you get her off. But it's going to be tough."

I hope I hid my astonishment. I could hardly believe the details of Angel Ambrose's case had spread as far as the campuses of eastern Washington. I said, "Charlie Forsyth's got a good record on such cases."

Jay remained standing in front of me for a moment longer, as though waiting for me to reveal the secrets of the defense. His cocksure attitude amused and irritated me at the same time. This time I outwaited him.

"Perhaps 'empathetic' is a better word than 'liberal,' " he commented eventually. "Whatever. Now I'm off fishing. To catch a salmon, maybe. Take it back to my roommates in eastern Washington."

"Good luck," I said. "You'll need it. Salmon are very scarce these days."

He handed back the mug, touched the brim of his hat, stuck his thumbs in the corners of his pockets. "Yes, empathetic," he said. "I prefer that word."

A soft gray rain started to fall. Jay looked up at the sky.

"Good fishing weather," he said. "See you around, Mr. Richards," and he strolled off down the beach as though he really did own it.

His lean figure melted into the gentle haze of rain, like a wraith, a ghost. The ghost of Indians past. Or perhaps the ghost of Indians to come.

SEVEN

THE ANNOUNCEMENT FOR RALPH HARRISON'S MEETING WAS on fuchsia paper with heavy black lettering and multiple exclamation marks: Urgent! Before It's Too Late!! Protect Your Property Values! Indians on the Warpath Again!! The address was right here at Edward's Bay. I should have invited Jay Bishop to come along.

A protest meeting with its inevitable rancor and hyperbole wasn't the best way to spend a Sunday. Sundays are for hanging out, for replenishing the mind and soul before the onslaught of Monday, and as I had to eat breakfast standing up because there was nothing to sit down on, it would have been smarter to ignore the meeting and go find some furniture instead. But I'd learn something about my new neighborhood. About my new neighbors.

I picked up the phone to ask after Christopher, realized I didn't have Sarah's number. I'd call in on the way to the meeting. It was hard to believe he'd recovered so quickly from such a terrifying episode. I'd heard of sleep apnea, of course, but thought it an affliction of middle-aged men. What would have happened if Sarah hadn't found him so soon? Would he have started to breathe again, spontaneously, or would he just have lain there until he was found . . . what . . . dead? A mysterious crib death? I'd never sleep again if I were Sarah.

A few minutes before noon, I set out for the meeting, counted the houses along the street out of idle curiosity. Thirty in all, including the two unfinished ones, more on the outside curve of the spit facing the sound than the inside curve facing inland. It wouldn't be long before I knew who belonged to which house, what they did for a living, what their interests were; such close proximity made it inevitable everyone must know everyone else's business.

The houses were built at varying angles from one another, an attractive enough feature that ensured a degree of privacy, but from the street side, in the daylight, Edward's Bay looked more like suburbia than beach, an ordinary upscale residential development, two-car garages, instant lawns, neat shrubbery. The impression of houses floating, mirage-like, over the water was quite lost from the street. How much had this development cost Bigs and Ralph Harrison? A hundred and fifty thousand per house? More? Less? I no longer had a secure handle on building costs, but at, say, a hundred and fifty thousand each, thirty houses would run to four and a half million dollars. Bottom. A tidy sum to invest on spec. And from whom had they bought the land, if, as Jay Bishop claimed, the Quanda had title to it? Had Bigs and Ralph known there was going to be a problem? I doubted it. No one would be foolish enough to risk millions of dollars on disputed land. So, the dispute must be recent. Tribal sovereignty, tribal status in general, were slippery issues, and I wasn't at all certain the Quanda were an official tribe. They had a reservation, but did that make them a tribe?

Once again, there was surprisingly little activity around and about the houses. It was a little mystery to me where the inhabitants were all the time. They certainly hadn't been evident on the beach when Jay Bishop and I were there. In one driveway, a man washed his car; at another, a woman planted small and fragile seedlings into bare earth, watering each one with care. The man waved as I passed by; the woman ignored me. I hadn't seen Sarah's house in the daylight before and wasn't absolutely sure which was hers, but the picket fence and the brick path looked familiar, and the front door stood ajar, like an invitation, so I went up the brick path and knocked on the door. After a moment, Sarah came to the door, black hair tousled around her pale face, the hollows below her cheekbones more distinct.

Tactlessly, I said, "You look beat. Didn't you get *any* sleep?"

Shrugging her shoulders, she clutched at the doorjamb as if in need of support. "I bet I do look horrible. I feel horrible, to tell the truth. I sat up all night. Or what was left of it. I mean, could you have gone to bed and to sleep? I kept dropping off, but every few minutes I'd wake with this terrible start, as though something awful was happening. As though I'd forgotten something important. Christopher slept perfectly peacefully, of course. Out like a light. Didn't wake until eight o'clock. Want to come in and see him?"

She opened the door a little wider.

"I'm on my way to this neighborhood meeting." I showed her the flyer. "You're not going, I suppose?"

She made a face. "They're always having those meetings. I don't need to get involved with anything like that, even at the best of times. People get so worked up, don't they? Surely there's enough land and water and fish for everyone. It's like the hysteria about cutting down trees. As though one could possibly get rid of the millions of trees around here in a hundred years."

"A hundred years might just about do it," I said. "How long did it take for the passenger pigeon to disappear? The buffalo? The salmon?"

"Oh, dear." She sounded weary, disappointed with me, as though she'd caught me in a politically correct act. "Don't tell me you're one of those conservation nuts."

"I believe we have to take care of this poor little earth. It's all we've all got, isn't it?"

Sarah folded her arms and sighed. Her persona was different today, older, tired, depressed. A night without sleep will do that.

"Conservation isn't what that meeting is about, Noah. People round here think organizations like the Sierra Club, the Nature Conservancy, are a joke. No, the meeting's about the Indians. Everyone's anti-Indian round here. Don't go to the stupid meeting, Noah. It'll only make you bad-tempered. Stay and have some lunch with me."

Once again, I turned down an invitation from her. "I've only just had breakfast. And to tell the truth, I want to hear what they have to say. Out of curiosity, if nothing else. Whose house is this?"

Sarah peered at the flyer, flinched at the lurid colors. "That's the Harrisons'. He's one of the developers of this estate. I don't really know them. People aren't so friendly in Edward's Bay. They keep to themselves. This isn't a proper neighborhood, you know. Not the kind I'm used to, at any rate."

The wistful echo was back in her voice.

"Listen," I said, "after the meeting, come help me choose some furniture. We'll go into Seattle. I need everything. Chairs, tables. You name it, I haven't got it."

Immediately, her face lit up, as if I'd given her a gift, and she flashed the wide toothy smile. "Hey, I'd love that. Spending someone else's money is so much more fun than spending one's own. But I'll have to bring Christopher, you know."

"You couldn't possibly leave him at home, could you? I mean, only last night . . ."

Sarah gazed at me thoughtfully, as she had the first time we met. I didn't tell her the idea of carting a baby around daunted me. Babies were altogether outside my province, especially sick ones.

"We can make the one-thirty ferry," I said, and was glad I'd got around to suggesting it.

Cars had been drifting down the street and now were jammed into the circle at the end, parked two or three deep in adjacent driveways. In front of the Harrisons' house, the buzz of voices from inside was quite distinct. I edged through the open front door, into a hallway crowded with people in Sunday best, as though they'd come straight from church. They clutched cookies and polystyrene cups in their hands and seemed deep in conversations that had nothing to do with fishing rights or Indians. I heard one young woman say to another, "He's just a little tyrant, you know, has to have his own way about everything . . . ," and a tall man said, "Just beyond Possession Point. Must have been a twelve-pounder at least. . . ."

The atmosphere was more like a neighborhood kaffeeklatsch than a protest meeting. Maybe Sarah McKenzie had got it wrong about the friendliness of her neighbors.

The people in this house could have been from a different country than the people at the Eagle's Nest, just a few hundred yards away; these folk showed strong strains of a Viking heritage in their light eyes and spare, rangy height. Much of the blond hair was peppered with white, and most of them looked liked retired blue-collar workers, their clothes neat, not flashy, comfortable but not affluent. They smiled vaguely at me as I squeezed past, flattening themselves politely against the walls "Coffee's in the kitchen," a woman with very blue eyes told me. "Meeting's that way."

The woman pointed to another room, out of my direct sight, where a single male voice was raised above the general hum of conversation. I gradually eased my way from the hallway into the other room. It was a large room with a high ceiling and lots of windows, and it also was full of wall-to-wall bodies. I wedged behind a sofa with its back to one of the picture windows, and the view from the window took my breath away—the curve of the spit, the rushing currents round the corner, the shining waters of Puget sound, the inner bay delineated by soft green headlands. The sound stretched away to the glistening mass of Mount Rainier, Seattle's downtown towers insignificant smudges below its bulk, as though the whole world of Edward's Bay belonged just to this one house. I was astonished that this view was so much better than the one from the living room of my house, which until that moment I'd considered unbeatable.

Reluctantly, I turned to face the room.

The speechmaker stood in front of the fireplace. He had white hair, a white golfing cap with "Olympic View Golf" embroidered in scarlet letters above the peak, white shoes, yellow pants, a green polo shirt. As if he'd just wandered in from the golf course. Below the white cap and white hair, his face was red from the effort of making himself heard. "What I'm saying," he was saying, "is all of us round here pay more than our share of property taxes. Even those of us who live up on the headland are assessed at prime waterfront rates, and you all know how exorbitant those are. And now the Indians are telling us they want half the shellfish beds. That the tidelands really belong to them, even though we bought them fair and square. So I say, let them pay the bloody taxes. Until then, they'd better keep their damn butts off my property, or I'll be out with a shotgun to let them know exactly who has title to these tidelands."

There was a faint scattering of applause, muted and halfhearted, as if these sentiments had been expressed before. I leaned down to ask a woman sitting on the sofa in front of me, "Who's speaking?"

She swiveled her neatly permed head around, stared up at me. "Walter Drummond," she said tartly, as though it should be perfectly obvious who he was. "You know, lives up there on Saddlers Way." She gestured toward the headlands above the bay. "And who are you?"

"Noah Richards. I just moved here."

"Then you'd better listen," she said briskly and sounded exactly like my mother.

Someone among the crowd, someone I couldn't see, spoke up. "If the tribes win this appeal, we'll be back to square one. They'll have the right to walk all over our beaches and take half of what's there. And who's to say what's half? Are we going to have to count the damned oysters and clams? Who's going to count them? Who's going to pay for it all?"

A man stepped forward on the other side of the room, a lean man in a plaid shirt and worn jeans. "Jack Partridge," he said. "Bay Oysters." There were murmurs and rustles in the room, as though they all knew who he was. "Took me years to build up my oyster beds. Didn't touch them myself so they could grow and increase. Now I'm told someone who did nothing has the right to help himself to half. Coming in, ruining my years of hard work. I'll be damned before I see that happen."

Another man, his face as red as the first speaker's, the veins at the side of his neck bulging, shouted, "A man's property is his property. Bought and paid for."

There was another scattering of applause. A young man who didn't look or sound like a northwesterner—dark slick hair, khaki pants, boat shoes—said, "No use losing our heads at this point in time. We're not beaten yet. For one thing, the verdict hasn't been handed down, and even if it goes the wrong way, the state will appeal and appeal. No one's going to be able to come tramping on our land."

"I saw one this very morning. Cool as a cucumber. On the beach. Looking as though he owned the place. One of them Indians. Tramping past my house."

"Anyone has the right to walk between high water and low water," the young man said, quietly, reasonably. I wondered if he was an attorney.

I heard the familiar voice of Bigs Harrison. "We can't let them come in with these jumped-up claims. Ever since the Boldt decision they've been more and more uppity, claiming this and that, salmon here, clams there, fifty percent of this, fifty percent of that."

A hiss of approbation ran among the crowd. I knew the Boldt decision was almost certain to be raised, a decision, handed down in the seventies, upholding the tribal rights to half the harvestable salmon and steelhead in the state of Washington. It had been—and still was—wildly unpopular with the majority of the citizens of the state. Particularly fishermen. But I also knew the shellfish claim had to be a little different because shellfish generally lie in tidelands, on land people believed they owned. Or at least assumed went with their property, like these houses here, built so close to the water's edge that the tidelands were their backyards.

Then I realized it wasn't Bigs who'd spoken, but his cousin, Ralph, standing across the room from me, arms folded tight across his chest, the light from the window behind me in his face. A pretty young girl with dark curly hair and pink cheeks stood beside him. Ralph and Bigs not only looked alike, they sounded alike, something I hadn't been so aware of last evening in the noisy tavern. I looked around for Bigs but couldn't see him.

The young man spoke calmly again. "We've been having these meetings for months. As I see it, there's nothing to be gained until the ninth circuit hands down its verdict. We can always appeal the appeal, get a dispute resolution."

Definitely an attorney.

Ralph pushed his way to the front of the crowd. "Our corporation—that is, Bigs and me—are looking to hire ourselves an attorney to deal with the Quanda. It's more damned money out the window, of course, but we got to protect our interests. We could all join together, a class-action-suit type deal."

"The interests of your corporation aren't necessarily the interests of the individual property owners around here."

Ralph thrust out his chin. "We're all in this together, don't forget. It's us against them. They put a claim on your tidelands, what'll you do about it?"

"We got to protect our property values," the woman on the sofa said. I couldn't see her face, but her voice sounded scared and worried. "It's all we've got, most of us. Anything devalues it, we're all in trouble."

Another round of applause rippled in the room. It was all too obvious there was a yawning and almost certainly unbridgeable gulf between Jay Bishop's views and the views of the people assembled here.

"I say wait until the appeal decision about the shellfish. Indians lose that, then we're okay."

"They'll sue again. They seem to have unlimited funds. Where does it all come from?"

"Gambling."

"Cigarette sales."

"Making money for being Native American."

"Want to be Americans and want to be separate."

"Want everything."

The meeting was degenerating into anti-Indian rhetoric that I didn't need to listen to. But I thought it interesting that Ralph hadn't openly stated the Quanda were claiming the land the houses were built on. Was their claim legitimate? I had only Jay Bishop's word for that. And what did the Quanda plan to do about it? Tear the houses down? Reach a monetary agreement? If so, with whom? The state? The Harrisons as the developers? The property owners? If the experience of other states was anything to go by, much energy, passion, money, and time could be expended on a dispute like this.

I sidled out from behind the sofa. It was easier to get out than to get in, the large warm bodies parting like butter, and suddenly I found myself at the forefront of the room, almost face-to-face with Ralph.

"Why," he said, "here's someone who can probably tell us exactly what the Quanda are up to."

His words fell into one of those odd little silences that come over a crowd. All eyes turned on me.

"Mr. Noah Richards," Ralph said. "Attorney-at-law. Just moved in. Number five-twenty-one. Already on intimate terms with our local Indians."

"Sorry," I said. "I know nothing more about any of this than any of you. Probably less. I just came to listen. You invited me, remember?"

"Are the Quanda your clients?"

This was Ralph Harrison's house, and one doesn't pick arguments with people in their own homes, but he seemed to be spoiling for an argument, his attitude belligerent again, as though I'd roused his antagonism in some way. The problem with protest meetings is that people get all worked up, just as Sarah McKenzie predicted.

I tried a smile. "If they were, I'd claim attorney-client privilege. I'm here merely as a local resident," I said and continued toward the door. "You know Bigs is an old friend of mine."

The girl standing beside Ralph, with the uncomfortable expression of a teenager whose parent is about to embarrass her, put a hand on his arm. "Dad, please. Let's not get into any more arguments."

He glanced down at her, a parental mixture of exasperation and affection in his eyes, opened his mouth to say something more, snapped it shut. "Sorry," he said—whether to me or to her I wasn't sure—and I took the chance to slip out without further confrontation. The truth was that I was sympathetic to both sides. The truth was that the land was quite likely stolen in the first place and the present owners had bought it in good faith. Sorting it out couldn't possibly make all the parties happy.

In the hallway, people were still standing around drinking coffee and munching cookies, ignoring the meeting. "Anyone happen to know where Bigs Harrison is?" I asked.

A man and woman looked at me, at each other. "Bigs? Went crabbing, didn't he?"

"Crabbing?" I said. "Isn't he interested in what's going on here?"

The woman had curly soft hair, and she smiled sweetly at me. "Tide's low, young man, and you know what they say, time and tide wait for no man. Or the crabs. Anyways, we have this sort of meeting every few weeks. Bigs isn't missing anything new."

"Yeah." The man hitched at his pants. "Bigs's got enough sense to cut out now and then."

"So these are regular events? How are they going?"

"Well, just trying to keep ahead of them, you know."

"Them?"

The man screwed his eyes up and peered down his nose at me. "The Indians, of course. You new around here?"

"Just moved in."

"You'll learn," he said. "You'll learn."

EIGHT

SARAH, CHRISTOPHER, AND I RODE INTO SEATTLE ON THE TOP deck of the ferry, sheltered from the wind in the sun lounge. The yellow tinted windows made the sky appear full of brilliant sunshine, so there was a feel of summertime to our little outing. The baby, heaped in a carrier on his mother's shoulders like a miniature jockey, wore a purple woolly hat on his lolling blond head, and his mother wore the big jacket that swamped her into the fragile look. When the ferry reached Seattle, she drew in a deep breath. "Thank God," she said. "Back in civilization again."

Like a child, she stopped to stare into every shopwindow, as though she'd just come in from a remote part of Alaska, and she kept exclaiming over all the changes in the city. There were certainly plenty of changes. Seattle was in the process of being reinvented, new condos along the waterfront, more high-rises in downtown, a new baseball stadium, parks, and sidewalks.

"Don't you ever come into town?" I wanted to know. "It's only a half-hour ferry ride away."

"It's like this, Noah. By the time I get Christopher fed and changed and in the car and drive to the ferry and park the car and take him out of the car, or wait in the line with the car, it's time to feed him again. And change him. Etcetera, etcetera. It's all too much trouble." She sighed dramatically, "I expect it'll be easier when he's older."

The amount of effort to maintain one small child certainly sounded like a hell of a lot of work. "But I think you should get out more, Sarah. I can't believe it's good for you to be alone with the baby all the time."

"No," she said and sighed. "No. You're probably right."

Before, I hadn't wanted to hear about Sarah McKenzie's problems, but now I was curious, despite myself, about her husband "Out of the country," she'd told the doctor at the hospital. Which could mean anything, of course. There could be no husband at all. There was no good reason for this slight wariness about Sarah McKenzie, nothing to put my finger on. She seemed open enough, yet I had the vague sense of something not ringing quite true. The same prickly feeling I'd had last night. And look what happened then.

At first, I watched the baby compulsively, every sigh and mutter, but after a while it was easy to forget there'd ever been anything wrong with him. He slept most of the time, very quietly, fuzzy purple head nestled into the carrier on his mother's back, and soon I hardly noticed he was there.

Sarah threw herself into the furnishing project with serious energy, plumping cushions, poring over fabrics, examining the undersides of tables and chairs, far more thorough about it than I'd ever have been. One definitely needed a woman's touch on an exercise like this. I was glad I'd asked her. She couldn't have been more enthusiastic if she'd been choosing it all for herself. In one afternoon, I looked at more furniture than in my entire life, and before long, found I'd purchased a sofa and two chairs, a bed, a pair of stools for the kitchen, and a huge "entertainment center" for the stereo and TV. After flashing the credit card around, I felt a definite sense of achievement, as though dropping a whole heap of money is an accomplishment.

When the buying frenzy was done, or as much as I could take, we wandered up First Avenue to a touristy restaurant near the market, one of those fern-decorated places with no particular personality. I'd have suggested somewhere smaller, more upscale, if it hadn't been for the baby, but Sarah didn't seem to mind. She was thrilled, she said, to be out among people. Lots of people. We sat at a table by the window, overlooking the sound and the ferryboats, and Sarah put the backpack and baby on the seat beside her. He kept right on sleeping. The waiter admired the baby and brought a bottle of cold white wine, we ordered pasta, and Sarah took off the huge jacket, revealing a slender-ribbed sweater that showed off her breasts. She gazed round the crowded restaurant, eyes shining, not at all waiflike, clinked her glass to mine, sipped the wine in silence for a moment, then said, suddenly and melodramatically, "I'm dying out there in Edward's Bay, Noah. Dying."

For a moment, I couldn't think of anything to say. I fumbled for words. "Then why stay there? I just moved from somewhere that didn't please me anymore. You could do it."

Her dark eyes glistened, a flash of angry resentment in them. "I can't move, don't you understand? I'm locked in this ridiculous battle with my husband. I can't afford to move out of that damned house."

I wanted to repay her for the help with the shopping and was prepared to listen to what would surely be a tale of woe. It seemed to me that Sarah McKenzie needed to be relating her tale of woe to someone, not to me, necessarily, but I was the only one available at that precise moment . . . "Tell me about it," I said, and she took a breath and told me.

"My husband bought that house before it was even built. I didn't want to live out there; I wanted to stay in Seattle but when he took off for the mountain, it was too expensive to keep two places, so he said to live in the house at Edward's Bay until he got back and we'd discuss everything then."

Already I was confused. "Mountain? What mountain?"

"Everest." She tossed the name off as though it were some insignificant place just around the corner. "Didn't I tell you he was climbing Everest?"

"Everest?" I was astonished. "That's his profession—mountain climbing?"

Sarah laughed a little, shook her silky head. "You think I'd be stupid enough to marry anyone quite that crazy? No. He's an engineer. He's a Scot, actually. Not really American. McKenzie, you know. Mountains are his passion. His only passion I'm beginning to think."

Her husband, I noticed, hadn't yet been given a first name, as if she didn't want to acknowledge his existence. The pasta arrived, and Sarah dug into it, hungrily, as though she hadn't eaten for days, and kept talking, hardly missing a beat. "He'll risk everything for the chance to climb, it seems. He made me so angry, going off to the Himalayas so soon after Christopher was born. He'll be gone for three months on unpaid leave. I said, 'You go off to that mountain, and I might not be here when you get back.' So he slapped the restraining order on me. Is that fair? He can go risking his life at twenty-nine thousand feet, but I'm not allowed to take Christopher home to New Zealand to see my family."

It *didn't* seem quite fair. I started to say so, but Sarah was listening to what she was saying, not to me.

"I hate Edward's Bay, Noah. It isn't a real place, just a bunch of houses with nice views. I need more than a view, more than shiny floors. I need shops and pubs and churches. People in the street. People anywhere."

"But why did he buy a house out there if you were so opposed to it?"

She lifted her shoulders helplessly, the motives of males beyond comprehension. Under the sweater, the nice rounded breasts rose and fell.

"He bought it before we married. Probably because it was a good deal. The builder was trying to unload the houses at the time. You know how it is with these spec builders. And being a Scot, my husband can't resist a bargain."

"How long ago was that?"

"Well, we'll have been married two years in May. Sometime before that."

Two years? Bigs and Ralph have been trying to unload those houses for more than two years?

The baby stirred in his warm nest, blue eyes opening and closing, and Sarah pushed her plate aside, unzipped the carrier, and sat him on her lap. He yawned and stretched plump baby arms.

"He's very well behaved." I was impressed. "You'd think he'd be crabby after last night."

She gazed down at Christopher intently, as if she'd only just noticed how well behaved he was. "He's been asleep ever since," she said, forked more pasta into her mouth, took a sip of wine. "But you know, Noah, I just never knew how it would be, all day long without an adult to talk to. All night. I feel as though I'm going mad sometimes."

Sarah McKenzie didn't have to explain to me about the destructive disease of loneliness. "It'll be all right when your husband comes home."

She seemed to think about it for a moment. "*If* he comes home," she said. "You think I don't know that's a possibility? If he comes home, we have to settle the rest of it. I'm not sure about any of it, to tell you the truth. Will it be another mountain, more months of waiting and dreariness? Will we ever have a normal life? Does he really care? Do I really care?"

Of course, I had no answer to her questions. I'd no answer to my own life, let alone anyone else's. I poured more wine. "If he's in the Himalayas, I suppose you haven't been able to tell him about Christopher's problem."

"Even if I could, what's the point? What can he do about it?"

"But couldn't he come down from the mountain anytime he needed to? These days there are helicopters and two-way radios, even cell phones on the top of Everest. If it were me, I'd want to know."

"Yes, but then you wouldn't leave your baby in the first place, would you?"

I fudged the question, pictured instead the daunting ordeal of high altitudes, rock and ice and thin blue air. "Mountains aren't my thing. I'm no hero."

"Heroes aren't easy to live with," she said and jiggled the baby on her lap. "So how did you end up in Edward's Bay, Noah?"

I said, simply, "I needed a new place to live," but it wasn't as simple as that, of course. The whole story was more complicated, and as Sarah seemed to want to hear the whole story, I told her some of it. About the malpractice suit that turned to murder, about the Ambroses and their broken hearts, how the office and house in Springwell had been trashed, how Charlie Forsyth had offered to help with Angel Ambrose's defense. How I didn't want to stay in my father's practice after he died, how I'd never wanted to go into his practice in the first place. "So you see," I said finally, "I needed to start afresh. To move somewhere without the memories. Edward's Bay seemed the perfect place."

Sighing, Sarah fiddled with the stem of her wineglass. "Starting afresh. It sounds so easy."

"It's never easy, of course. We collect a lot of baggage en route."

"Like children? At least you don't have any of those." She smoothed Christopher's soft sparse hair and gazed at me over the top of his head. "Aren't you just a bit lonely, Noah?"

I wanted to say, lonely as hell, but I recognized a leading question when I heard one. I had to admit there was a lot about Sarah McKenzie that appealed to me. Her funny accent and her brown eyes and friendly smile. Her obvious loneliness that struck a sympathetic chord in me. But I didn't need, or want, to be involved with someone else's wife.

"Children," I said. "They're a big commitment."

She sighed again. "You're so right. A very big commitment."

But all in all, we'd had a pleasant afternoon, I thought. The restaurant turned out to be better than I'd expected, the pasta good and the wine very drinkable. And I'd made all those momentous purchases. Sarah smiled at me and said she'd had a wonderful time, thank you, and eventually we made our way back to the ferry. The Olympic Mountains on the western horizon were sharp against the setting sun, and the new condos along the waterfront added an extra buzz of activity, a lift to the scene, a hint of big city to the air.

I said, "Don't you feel a little bit lucky to live in this part of the world?"

Sarah turned her head to look at the mountains and the setting sun as though she'd seen a million similar sunsets before, then turned away. "You think it's lucky to be marooned out here in a far corner of America? That's not luck in my book, Noah. It's damnation."

I had to laugh. If anywhere was far away from everywhere, it surely had to be New Zealand. "You're wrong about Edward's Bay, Sarah. You'll feel better about it soon. One day you'll wake up and find you love it there."

On the ferry, I asked her what she knew about the title to the land her house was built on, but she wasn't interested. "How the hell do I know? Or care? I just live in that house. It's Harry's."

Harry. So was that his name. Harry McKenzie. It rang a faint bell with me. Even though I wasn't into mountain climbing, it was a name I'd heard before. Something to do with heroics and peaks, danger and death. I'd ask Charlie tomorrow. Charlie knew everyone.

On the way back to Edward's Bay, Sarah said, "I'd like to make dinner for you one evening, Noah. Because you've been so kind. Maybe I'll ask a few neighbors. So we can both meet some of them. I don't know them either."

"That'd be nice," I said vaguely, stopping outside her house, helping her out, waiting while she opened the front door. "Come on in," she said, and once again I was tempted. But I was too aware of the consequences, too lonely and vulnerable. "I think you and Christopher should get an early night," I said, as though it was their welfare I was considering, not my own.

She gazed at me for a moment in that cool appraising way. I thought she could see right through me and my fear of involvement. "I had a good time, Noah. Anytime you want to spend more money, let me know."

But when I unlocked the door to my house, it felt even more lonely than the house in Springwell had ever been. And so it was that before going to bed, to escape the echoes of yet another empty house, another night alone, I went for a walk on the beach.

NINE

THE EVENING WAS BRILLIANT WITH STARS AND THE AIR WAS sweet, the sound of the surf gently insistent. I scrunched across the shingle, assuring myself that Edward's Bay *was* a wonderful place, that Sarah McKenzie was the one who'd got it wrong, and then it was that I came upon the shape on the beach. The seal that wasn't a seal, the log that wasn't a log, the arms spread wide, the drenched clothes clinging around the heavy limbs, the seaweed draped over the face. It was a terrible shock to recognize the face that such a short time ago had been so alive and full of assurance. The handsome coppery skin was gray now, the wide mouth carved into a perpetual stony silence. I stood transfixed for minutes, unable to move or react, then I kneeled down, took one of the cold hands in mine, and spoke to him as though he might answer.

"Jay! For God's sake, what the hell happened?"

Of course, there was no reply. I stayed on my knees beside him for a long while, the icy inert hand in mine. It was such a lonely place to die, on a beach in the dark, and I hated to leave him there, but at last I rose to my feet to go for help. Except he was quite beyond help. Stumbling along the sand, legs not working well, I climbed back over the driftwood and called 911.

The minutes dragged into what seemed like hours before help finally arrived. Eventually, two vehicles came screeching down the silent road, an ambulance followed by a police car, both with lights flashing, sirens blaring unnecessarily. In the quiet of the night, the red-and-blue lights whirled and dazzled and the radios crackled, and all along the street, doors opened and faces appeared at the windows, the neighbors finally in evidence.

A pair of paramedics jumped down from the ambulance as though they might be in time to save a life, and two uniformed officers climbed out of the police car, slowly and laboriously, hitching at their belts. The policemen stood shoulder to shoulder, eyed me with suspicion. "Officer Roberts. Officer Jameson. You say you found a body? Where's it at?"

"On the beach. We can get there through my house."

I wanted the spectacle off the street, but they wouldn't move until I identified myself with a driver's license and a business card. They peered at the card. "An attorney?" they said and sounded incredulous. As though attorneys had no business with policemen and dead bodies. "What were you doing on the beach in the dark?"

"Just out for a breath of air. I know who it is. His name is Jay Bishop."

Speaking his name out loud made the whole wretched business seem more real, affirming something I didn't want to believe.

The cops hitched once more at their belts. "Okay. Show us."

The four of them clattered noisily across the bare wood of the floors and down off the deck, climbed awkwardly over the driftwood, and trailed after me along the beach. Jay Bishop was in the same place, of course. Shining their flashlights, they stooped down, felt for a pulse at the wrist of an outstretched arm, directed beams of light into the blank face.

Roberts said, "He's dead all right. Looks Indian."

"Yes," I said. "He has an uncle in the village. Wayne Daniels."

"Wayne Daniels? Son of a gun. I know him. Quanda Indian, isn't he? Well, this guy drowned, by the look of it."

One of the medics said, "He hasn't been in the water long. Can I turn him over?"

"Why not? We can't leave him here. What's the tide doing?"

"Coming in," I said, and the four of them turned their eyes on me as though it was none of my business.

Roberts said, "Probably been out in a boat and drinking. Some damn fool is always drinking too much and falling out of a boat."

But I couldn't quite believe that. Jay Bishop was no fool, and when I last saw him, he was as sober as a judge. One of the paramedics took hold of Jay's shoulders and flipped him over onto his back, like a rag doll, legs and arms flopping and flaccid, and I had to look away. Whatever it was that made Jay Bishop human had vanished, leaving behind an empty, inert shell, the essence of a human being gone, flown away somewhere. How quickly the dead become mere bodies instead of living, breathing, sensate flesh. I caught myself glancing up at the sky, as though Jay Bishop's soul might linger there, on the end of a silken thread, and when I looked down again, his soulless face was pointing toward the stars, unseeing, unknowing. I was the only one there who mourned him. To these men, he was nothing but a dead body. They stood and stared at his body some more, and along the shore, insubstantial shapes gathered and watched, at last drawn out of their houses and down to the beach.

The medic on his knees turned to look up at us. "This guy didn't drown," he said and spread his right hand out; in the glow of the flashlights, the stuff on the palm of his hand looked like tar, black and sticky, but even I knew it was blood. I gasped in disbelief. The medic tugged the wet shirt out of the belt at Jay's waist and exposed the broad pale convexity of his chest. Right in the center was a jagged hole, an irregular dark and torn blotchiness that had absolutely nothing to do with drowning.

Roberts said, "Son of a bitch," and they turned Jay over again, dragged the shirt away from his back. Below the left shoulder blade was a small neat round hole. The entry hole of a bullet.

The casual acceptance of accidental death disappeared in a flash. The medics reared away from the body, and the cops grew grim-faced, hands flying instinctively to the leather holsters at their hips. They glanced at each other, passing some signal. Roberts pulled out his radio and spoke urgently.

"Looks like we got a homicide. We'll need a photographer and a doctor. And soon. We're on the beach at Edward's Bay, and the tide's coming in."

The radios crackled back and forth. I stepped away, trying to fade into the darkness. A drowning accident was bad enough, God knows; that a young man like Jay Bishop was dead was shocking enough, but that someone had shot him in the back? It had to be deliberate. No way could a shot like that have been an accident.

In that instant, all my good feelings about Edward's Bay vanished.

I wondered what they thought they were going to photograph. The wavering flashlights revealed the wet sand scuffed into the meaningless footprints of five different people—the police, the medics, myself. The footprints were disappearing fast like the sign Jay had made with his finger that morning. His body had already been disturbed. How would they tell where he'd been shot from? If he'd washed up from somewhere else? Or been shot right here on this beach? And how could that have happened, in front of all these houses? Without anyone noticing?

"Nothing more for us to do here," the medic said. "We'll get on back to base."

Roberts's voice was strained, as though he didn't want to be abandoned on the dark beach. "You get an emergency call, then you can go. How long do you think he's been dead?"

"We don't have too much experience with dead bodies, Al. We aim to get to them before they die."

The second policeman, Jameson, was kneeling beside Jay, searching the sodden clothing. He pulled a wallet from inside the jacket, shone his flashlight on it, handed it to Roberts. The sand felt as though it were clutching at me, dragging me down, and it made a small sucking sound as my weight shifted from one foot to the other. Drew their attention back to me.

Roberts said, "Why don't you tell me again how you happened to be on this beach?"

"No reason. Does there have to be one? I live right here. Surely I can walk on the beach anytime?"

I couldn't see his face clearly. All their faces were lost in the darkness. Roberts held something between his fingers, turned it over.

"This card in his wallet. Look like yours?"

I'd totally forgotten about the card.

"I gave it to him. At the Eagle's Nest last night. He came to see me this morning, as a matter of fact. Around ten o'clock. Then he left. I didn't see him after that." I thought of Jay Bishop walking away from me, his figure disappearing into the mist.

"What did he come to see you about?"

"He's a law student. At St. Benedict's. He wanted to tell me about the tribal claim to this land. Look, I met him for the first time last evening. We had a relatively brief chat this morning. I don't know anything more about him. Except he was a bright smart guy and he has an uncle here."

"Uncle, cousin, whatever. They all claim to be related. Doesn't mean a damn thing usually."

The shadowy scene was like an ill-lit set of a Greek tragedy, the group of men standing around on the wet sand, the bright narrow beams of the flashlights, the sound of the waves lapping at the shore, the watching figures beyond the driftwood, the silent dark shape on the ground. I wanted to leave now. I didn't want to stand around any longer staring at Jay Bishop's body.

"I'll go back and wait at the house for the doctor," I said. "He won't know how to get down to the beach."

Roberts said, "You and me'll go back to the house together. The rest of you stay here and watch the body."

The medics said, "You don't need us." He gestured to Jay. "He don't need us."

"Someone's got to cart the remains away."

"Coroner's office takes the body."

"Not if the tide gets here first. And it probably will. You can bet your life it'll take that crew hours to get here."

The medics sighed, resigned, as though they'd expected to lose the argument.

I didn't care to hear Jay Bishop referred to as the "remains." He should be picked up and taken from this dark, wet place with some sort of dignity. He was more than just another statistic. But how could they deal with their unpleasant tasks if they had to think of every dead body they came across as a real person?

Roberts trudged beside me back to the house, and along the way he seemed to shed some of his suspicions about me, enough to talk, at any rate. "The damnedest thing," he said. "We don't get many homicides out this way. Domestics, yes. You know the sort of thing, husbands and boyfriends beating up on their womenfolk. Sometimes the women take a gun to the men, though not too often. Gunshot wounds, accidents, yes. We get a few of those. We'd a real nasty incident a couple of weeks ago, couple of kids playing with firearms. Now that's what I call tragic, people not keeping their guns under lock and key." Once he'd started talking, it didn't seem he was going to stop. "Drownings, too. Get quite a few drownings round about. But someone shot on a beach? No, that's not typical. At home or in a tavern, yes. But on a beach? In the back, too. Nasty that. If you're going to shoot a man, you should at least do it decently, face-to-face."

He sounded perfectly sincere. We negotiated the driftwood. "Hell of a good spot this," Roberts said, breathing heavily. "Nothing like waterfront property. If you don't get too many bodies on your beach, of course. That can ruin property values."

Everything boiled down to property values.

In the kitchen, cold and saddened, I ground fresh coffee beans, thankful to be doing something positive, however trivial. Roberts lounged against the countertop, stared around with suspicion at the barren house. He had a long heavy jaw, small deep-set eyes that probably regarded all the world, not only me, with suspicion.

"Just moved in?"

"A few days ago."

"Where from?"

"Up north," I said, vaguely.

He chewed on his lower lip, as if he were a smoker longing for a cigarette. "So, what sort of lawyer are you?"

"Defense law," I said, but I wanted to say, maybe I shouldn't be a lawyer at all because obviously I don't have the correct convictions. I should care about property values and whose land this is, who signed what treaty and when and how and who's going to lose money on the deal, and all I could think about was the water-sodden shape that used to be Jay Bishop. What the hell did anything matter, apart from being alive? Property and money and cases won or lost, what the hell did any of it matter? In the bright white brand-new kitchen, in the brand new bright white house that belonged to someone else, I clutched the coffeepot in my hand and felt as if I were Jay Bishop, drowning, struggling for air.

I took a long steadying breath. Jay Bishop hadn't drowned. Someone shot him. In the back. I sucked in more air, placed the pot carefully on the countertop.

"A scotch might be a better idea," I said.

Roberts accepted a scotch. Claimed he had cold wet feet, too. "Defense law, huh? So tell me, counselor, what did you do after you talked to the dead guy this morning?"

"I went to a neighborhood meeting. Then I went shopping. In Seattle. With a friend."

Somewhere was the flyer for the meeting, the receipts for all that stuff I'd bought for my new life. I found them in the pocket of my parka, handed them to Roberts. He read the flyer with pursed lips. "Indians on the warpath, eh? Well, someone was on the warpath, all right. And your Indian friend on the beach got in the way, didn't he?"

There is no new life. There's only the same old one, same old, same old, until it's over and done with. One life. And someone took Jay Bishop's life away from him, before it had time to get old.

TEN

THE PURVEYORS OF DEATH TRAMPED BACKWARD AND FORward through the house and finally departed, a black and sagging body bag between them. I shut the door behind them but couldn't shut away the thoughts, went out to the deck, took deep breaths of the cool night air. Lights still burned in the houses along the spit, and the moon struck a path of light on the water, but I couldn't get rid of the picture of Jay's body rolling and floating in that path, heading homeward to the shore.

Suddenly, inside the house, the phone rang; suddenly, of course, because that's the only way a phone can ring, but the abrupt noise startled me, a fierce jangling clangor that echoed around the bare walls. I went to answer it, compulsively, then decided I didn't have to answer a telephone at past eleven o'clock at night. Whoever it was could wait until the next day. And then I thought, God! Suppose it's the baby again, and snatched the receiver off the hook.

"Noah? It's Sarah." My heart flipped, but all she said was, "What's going on? I saw all those cars and the ambulance . . . ," and I was merely irritated.

"There was a . . . a body on the beach."

"Oh, my God! No! Whose?"

"Look, Sarah, I don't feel like talking about it now I'll tell you another time, okay?"

She said, "I only rang to make sure you were all right."

"I'm fine," I said, put down the phone, poured another scotch, and returned to the deck. On the deck I didn't get the feeling of being watched.

The next morning, in the bright light of day, Edward's Bay seemed as innocent and clean as ever, ducks bobbing, herons brooding, the snowy peaks of the Cascades glowing in the early morning sunrise. As beautiful and entrancing as ever. If one didn't think of dead bodies.

There was nothing in the morning paper about Jay Bishop, found too late, of course, to make the deadline. In the office, I told the others what had happened.

Sibby put a hand to her metal mouth. "Oh, Noah. How terrible."

"I still can't believe it. Just the fact that he's dead, let alone shot in the back like that."

"You met him in the tavern?" Charlie said. "Already hanging out in taverns over there, Noah?"

Which had absolutely nothing to do with Jay Bishop, but it reminded me of Wayne Daniels and the conceit in his laughter when he'd said, "Radical. That's a tribe, you know." I hated to think how Jay's death would affect Wayne.

We settled down to work eventually, and I did my best to forget Jay Bishop, Edward's Bay, Sarah McKenzie, her sick baby. We had a case coming to trial in two days, the shoplifting teenager, hardly an earth-shattering crime, a mere tempest in a teapot that should have gone away quietly without ever coming to court. But it had blown up into exactly the type of high-profile circus act that Charlie enjoyed. The girl's father, a big wheel in town, wasn't about to let a department store get away with accusing his little girl, and it had become one of those cases that are good for attorneys and not much else. God knows what my straitlaced attorney father, who disapproved of judges, courts, and publicity, would have thought of us. Halfway through the day, in the middle of a perfectly serious meeting about a personal injury case, Charlie said suddenly, "You seeing anyone these days, Noah?"

I was taken aback. Charlie and I weren't in the habit of discussing personal matters. "Seeing anyone? As in dating, you mean?"

"That's exactly what I mean. You seem rather low. I wondered if there was a problem in your life."

"The problem is, Charlie, that I thought I'd found a perfectly nice place to live, and now I don't think it's so nice anymore. You don't discover someone dead on your doorstep and be in love with the neighborhood after that."

Leaning back in his chair, Charlie twiddled a pencil between his thin fingers, peered down the length of it at me. "I thought you had something going with a nurse up in Springwell."

"Lauren? How do you know about her?"

He grinned. "I have my sources. You don't think I'd have taken you on without checking all aspects of your life, do you?"

I guessed his source was Sibby. "Lauren went to stay with her mother in Minneapolis."

"And isn't coming back?"

"I don't know. She nearly died, you know, Charlie. It's going to take her a while to get over an experience like that."

"And in the meantime . . . ?"

I couldn't see why Charlie was so concerned about my well-being all of a sudden. Did he feel I'd been slacking on the job? But all in all, I considered it decent of him to show some interest in my life outside the office, and just so he'd know I didn't resent his interest, I volunteered, "There's this woman who lives in Edward's Bay. Attractive. Divorced. Or thinking about it. Ready for a fling, I'd say. If she didn't have a baby . . . If she didn't live just a few doors away . . ."

Charlie chucked the pencil down on the desk. It clattered and rolled to the floor, and he bent down to pick it up, jabbed the point at me. "Oh, for heaven's sake! Where are your juices, man? Either you want the woman or you don't. She has a baby, you say? You're not sure she's getting divorced? I say, don't touch it with a barge pole. You don't need entanglements like that, for God's sake. Find yourself a healthy single woman. That's what you need, Noah. Something straightforward and uncomplicated. Life's quite complicated enough."

He was right. That's what I needed. A straightforward, uncomplicated relationship. And what I needed was a warm body in bed with me at night. I hated going to sleep without the sound of another human voice, hated getting up in the morning with more silence. I'd had too much practice at being alone.

"Tell you what," Charlie said and flashed the dazzling smile at me "I'll broadcast your name to my society friends. You'd be a godsend to them. They're always looking for single males, if only to make up a table at fundraisers. Lots of nice women at things like that. Rich, too."

"Rich wouldn't hurt."

"Anything to cheer you up," he said. I resolved to appear more cheerful.

As the days went by, there was surprisingly little fallout from Jay Bishop's death. I don't know exactly what I expected. Teams of detectives combing the beach? Door-to-door questioning? Some degree of interest from the authorities at the very least. After all, this was murder, wasn't it? Shooting someone in the back is definitely murder. But nothing of significance seemed to happen. I did get a request from the Seawards police to make a formal statement about finding the body, and that was about it.

I called my friend Chauncey Carlsson in Springwell to talk to him about the matter. Chauncey is not only my oldest friend, but a doctor as well, and like most people, I persist in the belief that doctors are wiser than ordinary mortals.

"You seem to have developed an instinct for trouble," Chauncey observed. "I thought you moved there for peace and quiet."

"Trouble, trouble," I said. "The world's full of it."

"I can't see why you feel responsible, Noah. Apart from an unfortunate belief that you're responsible for everything. Seems to me you were just an innocent bystander."

"I talked to him that very morning. I may have been the last person to see him alive. And there's no such thing as an innocent bystander, Chauncey. By our very presence we alter reality."

There was a moment's pause while he digested that point of view. "What sort of philosophy is that? You spend too much time alone, Noah. Some idiot was probably just popping off a rifle somewhere. An unfortunate accident. A logical outcome of too many guns."

"Shot in the middle of his back? Someone had to have taken deliberate aim."

There was another pause. I could tell Chauncey was losing patience with this conversation. He changed the subject abruptly. "Why don't you come up and see us? It isn't the same without you being along the road."

"No," I said, diverted. "You and Daphne come down and see me. I'm forever driving up to Springwell, trying to sort out the office and the house. There just hasn't been enough spare time to stop in to say hello. I'd like you to see Edward's Bay. It's a lovely spot, Chauncey. Or it was, until this happened."

"Okay," he said, without further prompting. "Next weekend, maybe. I'll check with Daphne. I don't believe I'm on call."

The thought of Chauncey and Daphne paying a visit to Edward's Bay brightened me up no end.

The rest of the week was too full of legal scut work for social niceties. In the office, Beth and Grace and Sibby churned out masses of papers that flew around in distressing amounts, whole forests laid to waste for one small legal operation. Every evening I was late back to Edward's Bay, usually past ten o'clock. I'd hoped for a quiet day so the furniture could be delivered; setting up house was proving far more trouble than I'd ever envisaged. By Thursday, I was sick of sleeping in a sleeping bag. If the bed wasn't delivered by Friday, I'd have to spend another weekend on the floor. So after I got back to Edward's Bay that evening, I called the only person I knew to ask for help. Sarah.

First I remembered to inquire about Christopher. "How is he?"

"Seems fine," she said coolly. "Thanks for asking."

I recognized the coolness and apologized. "I've been so busy this week. And now I'm calling to ask a favor, Sarah. Could you, would you, let the deliverymen into my house tomorrow? For that furniture we ordered last week?"

She was immediately forgiving, which was nice of her since I'd ignored her and the baby for a whole week. "Oh, sure, Noah. No sweat. I'm always here."

"I'll bring you a key," I said. "I'll come down with it now, if that's okay."

When Sarah opened the door, she was holding the baby on her shoulder and she smiled at me. This evening, she was wearing a long clinging skirt and pale pink lipstick and looked cheerful and pretty. Another change of personality. I thought it a pity she had a husband because we could be . . . friends. I was in need of a friend.

She said, "The whole of Edward's Bay is agog with what happened, you know. At least it's got people talking to one another. Come in and tell me all about it."

But Jay Bishop's death was exactly what I didn't want to talk about. I remembered Charlie's admonishment about babies and entanglements and brushed her invitation away again. "I'm really beat, Sarah. It's been a hell of a week," I said, handed over the key, and went home.

The phone rang as soon as I got into the house, and I expected, hoped, it would be Sarah, offering me another chance. A glass of wine, maybe. This time I'd take it. I'd get her to tell me more about New Zealand. We'd talk together like two human beings. Chauncey and Charlie were right. I spent too much time alone.

But it wasn't Sarah McKenzie. It was Bigs Harrison, and once again Bigs sounded as though he'd been drinking.

"Just wanted to know how the house is going, Noah. Liking it there in Edward's Bay?"

I found myself talking about the very thing I hadn't wanted to talk about. "I liked it fine," I said, "until I found a dead man on the beach."

"Hell of a thing about that Indian, Noah. Got any word who might have done it? You found him. You're a lawyer. The police must have told you something."

I sighed impatiently. "They wanted to know where I was the rest of that day. Lucky for me, I wasn't here."

"They're going around asking everyone those same damn fool questions. Silly devil shouldn't have been hanging around Edward's Bay in the first place. Stirring up trouble. Shit, Noah, you know they've been asking for trouble. People get mad about these things. And desperate. Their property is everything, their life savings, their kids' futures. Them Indians are trying to take back something they've no right to."

I held the phone away from my ear for a moment. "What are you trying to tell me, Bigs? That you know something about his death? Because if you do, you'd better talk to the police, not to me."

"Talk to the police?" He laughed, but I didn't see it as any laughing matter. "I don't know anything. I thought maybe you did. My guess is it was an accident, some damn fool taking a potshot at a seal or something. Probably some kid or other. You know they've all got guns. All I'm saying is, everyone should cool down about it and get back to normal."

They've all got guns? What a depressing thought. "Too late for Jay Bishop to get back to normal, isn't it? Aren't you the least bit sorry about what happened, Bigs?"

"Sorry as hell, Noah." But he didn't sound sorry. "I just hope it'll be a lesson, that's all. To everyone. About keeping their noses out of other people's business. That's all I'm saying."

"When it comes to murder, it's everyone's business."

"Murder? I bet you they'll decide it was an accident."

Bigs was giving me some sort of bullshit, and I couldn't see why he was calling me, except to pump me for information I didn't have. I said bitterly, "An accident? I just bet that's exactly what some people will decide. But it's not what I've decided."

"Keep out of it, Noah. Just giving you a friendly word of advice."

I tried not to be angry. Tried not to curse him. Didn't succeed. "Go to hell, Bigs. I'll not keep out of it. Don't tell me not to mind something that's very much my business."

"Oh, well," he said, as though he were doing me a favor, "don't say I didn't warn you." I slammed down the phone, then thought, Where was Bigs that day? Wished I wasn't thinking it. I'd known Bigs forever. He was a good old boy, really. But he wasn't at that meeting. Out crabbing, someone had said. I thought of all those angry, upset people at that meeting. Where were any of them for the rest of the day? When had it happened, the taking of Jay Bishop's life? And why exactly? What had it possibly accomplished? Except, as Bigs said, to be a warning.

ELEVEN

THE SHOPLIFTING CASE DIDN'T GO WELL. THE GIRL WAS A POOR witness in her own defense and came over as a spoiled, petulant brat who always got what she wanted. Which was absolutely true. But her father, adamant she'd been railroaded because of his politics, insisted on appealing, an utter waste of our time and his money. To my amazement, Charlie was willing to have another go. "It's his money," he told me, wagging a finger, and it seemed obvious to me that I didn't have the right stuff for cases like this. Shoplifting wasn't life or death, except, as the girl's father said, "How'd you feel if your kid had to go through life with something like this on her record? How'd you think the other kids at school are going to treat her? How's she going to get into a decent college?"

Guilt or innocence wasn't the issue, as they so often aren't.

Defense lawyers have to believe in their clients and their rights to a fair trial, be on their side, do their utmost to get them off. I couldn't work myself up for this girl. Such lack of enthusiasm didn't auger well for a long-term future with Charlie Forsyth.

Not that I participated in the trial. I remained in the office with Sibby, who always lifted my spirits with her inordinately good nature, her silly short skirts and metallic smile. Sibby organized everything with a light hand, juggling appointments, clients, Charlie, and me, with tact and dexterity, and zipped through an amazing amount of paperwork each and every day, word-processing at the speed of light. Charlie and I were lucky.

By Friday afternoon, though, we were all weary, and when Charlie suggested quitting at a reasonable hour to go get a drink at the Celebrity Bar on First Avenue, I was more than ready. Beth and Grace stayed to lock up the office, while Charlie, Sibby, and I hightailed it to the Celebrity with its pressed tin ceiling and sepia-colored photographs of celebrities on the walls and arguably the best martinis in town. But even over the drinks, we couldn't resist talking shop, until the bar filled up with a Friday evening crowd that made any sort of conversation impossible. It was as if every unattached male and female from every office around Pioneer Square had gravitated there, young women with blonde hair and tailored suits, fresh-faced young men in striped shirts and ties, all laughing and shouting at each other, knocking back drinks, bending close in easy intimacy. I envied the intimacy.

Bars have distinct personalities. The Celebrity was quite different from Joe's up in Springwell, quite different from the Eagle's Nest at Edward's Bay. Which reminded me not only about Jay Bishop but also about Sarah and the furniture.

I shouted to make myself heard. "Got to make a phone call."

Charlie, already on his third martini, leered at me. "Not enough good-looking women here for you, Noah? You don't really have to call anyone else." He was eyeing the women himself. "Thought this was the sort of thing you had in mind." He definitely should steer clear of martinis.

The telephone was in a booth at the back of the room, but even when I closed the door, the frenzied roar of the crowd wasn't drowned out. I dialed Sarah's number, and she answered at once.

"It's Noah," I said, pressing the receiver close to my ear. "I'm still in Seattle Did the furniture get there all right?"

"Yes," she said. "Yes." Then she gasped, rushing over her words, "Noah, it happened again. Christopher stopped breathing. I'm on my way to the hospital. Now."

"Again? My God! Did you call 911 this time?"

"I can't talk. I have to go."

The phone went down with a clatter, and echoed, as though she hadn't replaced the receiver on the hook. I shouted into it, "Sarah? Sarah?" and dialed the number again But there was only a busy signal. I hung up and returned to Charlie and Sibby. A fresh beer sat at my place.

"Something wrong?" Sibby asked.

"It's my neighbor at Edward's Bay. Her baby keeps having this problem with his breathing. She's had to take him to the hospital again."

"You have a hospital over there?"

"Yes," I said, irritated. "Of course, we have a hospital over there. It's hardly the end of the earth, you know."

"If her baby has a problem," Sibby said, "she should take it to a specialist in Seattle. Everyone knows there are better doctors in Seattle. If it were my baby, that's what I'd do. I wouldn't mess around with those hospitals out in the sticks."

Awful memories of the Springwell malpractice case filled my mind. "You're right, Sibby. She should bring him to Seattle," and I jumped up from the table and rushed back to the phone. But now someone else was ensconced inside the glass doors. When the booth was finally clear, I called Sarah's number again, and this time the phone rang without answer.

I returned to Charlie and Sibby. "She's already left."

Charlie said, "That the woman you were telling me about? The neighbor with the baby?"

"Yes."

"Like I said, Noah. Don't touch it with a barge pole. A sick baby? Does she have insurance?"

"Insurance?" I stared at him blankly. "I don't know. What's that got to do with it?"

"Medical treatment is expensive. Just make sure you don't get stuck with the bills."

There's something so uncivilized about equating medical care with money. Like having to pay the local firefighter to put out your house fire. *Did* Sarah McKenzie have insurance? God knows, it's awful enough to have to cope with a frightening medical problem, let alone have to worry about paying for it.

"Why would Noah have to pay?" Sibby asked with interest.

"He's such a soft touch," Charlie said. "I could see him offering to help out."

"I hardly know her," I said. "But I might, if push came to shove. What would you do? Leave the child without a doctor?"

"See?" Charlie said with drunken triumph. "See what I mean, Sibby? Soft as mush."

Sibby regarded me with something suspiciously like affection. "I think that would be wonderful of you, Noah. Noble, in fact."

Both of them had had too many martinis. The buzz and roar of the bar was beginning to make my head ache, and it was time to get out of there, back to the peace and quiet of Edward's Bay. Except the peace and quiet of Edward's Bay had been disrupted by dead bodies and sick babies. Shouting good night to Charlie and Sibby, who didn't appear to care whether I stayed or not, I left them to their Friday night celebrations, walked to the ferry, and left the city behind.

But I couldn't leave my concerns behind, and when I reached

the other side and slid the Saab out of the park-and-ride lot at Seawards, I felt compelled to drive to the hospital to find out what was happening. If the other evening was anything to judge by, Sarah and Christopher would be there for hours yet. I went reluctantly. If I never set foot in a hospital again, it would be too soon.

There was the same rigmarole to get into the emergency room. A nurse whose blond hair reminded me of Lauren's told me Christopher McKenzie had been admitted and directed me to the main part of the hospital. I found Sarah in a room sitting beside a crib, turning the pages of a magazine, her body language signaling that the latest crisis had passed.

She looked up as I came into the room, dropped the magazine. "Why, Noah! How nice of you."

Tiptoeing forward, I peered into the crib, exactly like an anxious parent. The baby lay on his back, pink and soft, arms flung out, sleeping peacefully, breathing normally, long eyelashes fluttering on his smooth cheeks. I stood gazing at him for a long while, and Sarah came and stood by me, her elbows on the rails. She said, "They want to keep him in for observation. They still can't find anything wrong."

Baffled and unhappy, I stared at the sleeping child. He looked perfectly normal and healthy. "Was it like the last time?"

"Just like the last time. I gave him mouth-to-mouth, and he started breathing again. The doctor says it's perhaps like SIDS—you know, when babies seem to stop breathing for no reason."

"SIDS?" I echoed "My God, Sarah, isn't that deadly serious? Aren't you worried?" I was astonished at her serenity, the absence of panic in the face of such alarming symptoms. If he were my child, I'd be a basket case, running around, asking too many questions, stirring up some sort of action. Not sitting by the bed reading a magazine.

Sarah pointed to the oxygen outlet on the wall, the tiny mask hanging over it, the electrodes fastened to the baby's chest, the machine bleeping beside the crib. "I don't have to worry at the moment, do I? Not now he's in the hospital."

The beer I'd had at the Celebrity Bar sat sourly in my stomach. I felt queasy and slightly ill. "Are you staying the night?"

"You don't think I'd go away and leave him, do you?"

At that moment, a heavyset woman in a white dress, ankles bulging over thick-soled white lace-up shoes, backed into the room, dragging a foldaway cot heaped with blankets and pillows. I leapt to hold the doors for her, to help unfold the awkward contraption. She whipped the sheets and blankets onto the thin mattress, fluffed up the pillows.

"There we are." She smiled happily at the two of us as though we were in some kind of motel. "You'll be quite comfortable on this, Sarah. Now you're not to worry too much. Your baby's hooked up to the monitor, we can hear it at the nurses' station, and we'll be in to check at least every half hour. Just make sure you're here for him when he wakes, poor little thing, or he might be frightened by his strange surroundings." The nurse smiled at me in turn. "Isn't she being wonderful? Just what we like, a nice calm mother. You'd be amazed how some mothers go frantic, no use to anyone, especially their children. Are you his father?"

"No, just a friend."

"Well, lucky for this lovely little baby his mother knew what to do. Everyone should know mouth-to-mouth resuscitation. And have the presence of mind to use it."

Warm and motherly and reassuring, she patted the pillows invitingly. "There now, Sarah. Make yourself right at home. Don't forget to ring the bell if you need anything," she said, and she backed out of the room, still smiling.

The room was silent for a moment, only the beep of the monitor filling it.

Sarah sat on the edge of the cot, gingerly. "Thank you for coming, Noah. I can't tell you how much better it makes me feel.

To know someone cares. Where were you when you called? In a restaurant? It was awfully noisy."

"In a bar. Having a drink with the people from the office."

She gazed up from the cot. "Tonight's Friday night, isn't it? I'd sometimes go out for a drink on a Friday, in Auckland. That's how I met Harry, you know. He was on his way to climb the Southern Alps. I should have known better, shouldn't I?"

I sat on the chair she'd just vacated. The warmth of her body lingered in the curved plastic seat. "Sarah," I said, earnestly, trying to convince her. "You'll have to tell him now. And you must take Christopher to a specialist. No more running off to emergency rooms. Did you call your pediatrician?"

"I called the doctor here. You remember, Dr. Hayward? He thinks I'm just a panicky mother."

Testing the pillows on the roll-away, Sarah swung her legs off the floor, ready to settle down for the night. I said, "There's got to be someone who knows about this sort of problem." I hesitated for another second. "If you want, I have a friend, a doctor, who'd know the best person for you to go to." She made no response to the suggestion. "Sarah, do you have medical insurance?"

She frowned. "Oh, yes, that's no problem. I hope. Through Harry's job. But I get a bit confused about it. It's all so complicated. We have nationalized medicine in New Zealand, so we don't have to worry about that sort of thing there."

"This isn't New Zealand," I reminded her, and as if we were rehearsing an old conversation, she said, "Yes, Noah, I do know that."

On my way out, the nurse who fixed the cot was at the nurses' station, filling charts. I stopped at the counter, leaned over. "What do they think is wrong with Christopher McKenzie?"

She smiled the fixed smile, frowned at the same time. "Well, now, I can hardly discuss his medical problems with you, can I? You're not a relative. You'll have to ask the doctor." She rattled a couple of charts into their slots. "To tell the truth, I don't think they know what's wrong. They're going to do more tests tomorrow. They'll have a better idea then."

I supposed I had to be content with that. But I was definitely going to ask Chauncey for a referral. He'd know the right person. Maybe it wasn't my business, but it was nonsense to let this frightening scenario drag on.

When I arrived back at the house in Edward's Bay, a brand new bed was in place in the bedroom. Thanks to Sarah. The sectional sofa, covered in plastic, sat in the living room, and a huge packing case that contained the entertainment center filled the middle. I was able to eat sitting down, because of the new stools she'd seen into the house. I whipped up an omelet and didn't enjoy it, spread the sleeping bag on the mattress, and rolled onto the bed. It was soft and comfortable and soothing to my aching body, and I spared a thought for Sarah on the thin mattress of the foldaway.

The sound of the surf that had washed the body of Jay Bishop onto the beach finally lulled me to sleep.

TWELVE

THE NEXT DAY, WAYNE DANIELS CAME KNOCKING AT MY front door. When I opened the door, I was startled to find him standing outside, startled to see how diminished he'd become since the night we'd met at the Eagle's Nest. There was a slump to his large frame, and his face was carved into silent gravity, all that exuberant confidence seeped out of him. Even the long hair lying about his shoulders seemed to have a thinner, grayer texture.

"Wayne!" I threw the door open wider. "Come on in."

At first he hesitated, as though intending to refuse; then he sighed and stepped into the hallway, heavily, filling it with his grief.

"Just made fresh coffee," I said, and he shuffled after me into the kitchen, hovered in the middle of the room, clasping and unclasping the big calloused hands as if unsure what to do next, as if he couldn't quite remember why he'd come. He accepted a mug of coffee, still without speaking, as if the power of speech had quite deserted him. He was wearing the same jeans and jacket he'd worn in the tavern, but otherwise he bore little resemblance to the cheerful personality who'd so dominated the gathering at the Eagle's Nest. Just a week ago. He avoided my eyes, and the sound of his breathing echoed in the room.

"I'm sorry as hell about Jay," I said, inadequately. "You know I found him? I wish to God it had never happened."

Wayne's feet seemed anchored to the center of the room. I pulled out one of the new stools, the price tag still attached, and offered it to him, but still he didn't move. The silent unspeaking presence began to unnerve me. "Have you heard any news?" I asked. "Have they found out how it happened?"

He cleared his throat with a harsh scraping sound, and when he finally spoke, his voice was husky, as if he hadn't used it for a while. "You talked to Jay that day?"

"Yes. He came in the house, just like you, had a cup of coffee; then we sat on the beach for a while and talked about the problem of the tidelands. After that, he walked off along the beach." It was hard to know what else to say. "I didn't see him again. Not until much later. When I found him."

Wayne stared down at his hands. His chest heaved, and there was another silence. Then he said, "His project wasn't just the tidelands, you know. He was doing the whole thing about the Quanda and its tribal status. The treaty's no good to us unless we get recognized as a tribe. Jay did a bunch of work on it. He's got documents and all. Pictures and letters and interviews. He's got all that stuff. Somewhere. The tidelands round here belong to the Quanda, and the developers are selling them off with the houses. But they got no right. These are our tidelands. We got a treaty. But I guess we got to prove we're a tribe for the treaty to be any good. And without Jay, how are we going to do that?"

The morning sun, light and bright with the promise of a new day, flooded into the kitchen. I wanted to like this beautiful place, but sunny days and new houses were one thing, rights and treaties and a dead man another. Wayne gazed out the window at the same view, but I could tell he was seeing none of it. "Jay didn't die in no accident. It's not like he fell out of his boat and drowned. Someone drilled him right through the back. With a gun." His eyes came back to me. "After he talked to you."

The words unsettled me. "You can't really believe his death had anything to do with his talking to me? I never said anything about him to anyone. In any case, what we talked about, the tidelands, the appeal, is already well known around here."

Wayne shrugged his shoulders and didn't meet my eyes. "I just know he came to see you and then he ended up dead."

There was another long silence. Wayne seemed to be waiting for me to say something more, but what more could I tell him? Jay Bishop and I talked, and then he walked away, out of my life. Out of his own. I'd no idea how anyone could stare down the sights of a rifle and deliberately shoot someone in the back, for any reason. People kept telling me it could have been an accident. Chauncey. Bigs. I almost wanted to believe it myself.

"There are too many people out there with too many guns, Wayne. They get an urge to use them sooner or later. On something, someone, somewhere." I was echoing Chauncey. Even Bigs. "A potshot at a seal, for instance, that went astray."

Wayne shook his head. "An Indian fishing in his own waters? I don't believe it was some damn fool mistake."

I didn't believe it either.

I emptied the cold coffee out of his mug, refilled it, took the skillet out of the cupboard, eggs and bacon from the fridge. Soon the seductive smell of frying bacon filled the kitchen. "Tell me about Jay," I said. "He's your nephew, you say? Your brother or your sister's son? Fill me in on his life. He wasn't Quanda, was he? I thought he looked as if he was from east of the mountains."

Wayne subsided suddenly onto the stool, big hands dangling between his knees, lank hair drooping around his thick neck. "Jay's father was Nez Percé, and he married a girl from our village, so we always thought of Jay as one of our own. We loved him like a son, you know. He came to the village not just because of his relatives and the history stuff, but because he liked to fish and mess around on the sound. It's not the same fishing over in eastern Washington, not out on the salt water trolling for salmon, setting crab pots. Jay's always been bright, real good at schoolwork. He had a high-school teacher encouraged him to go to college. They give good scholarships for minorities over in Spokane. That's what we need, Mr. Richards. Educated Indians. To stand up for our rights. Who know how to get things done. How to operate in the white man's world And that's what was good about Jay. Not just because we loved him like a son but because we could be proud of him. And because he was someone who'd help us get our dues."

I flipped the bacon out of the pan, broke a couple of eggs into it.

He said, "Some people think we're nothing but drunk and hopeless. But it's changing, Mr. Richards, it's changing. We sure as hell ain't going to be that way any longer. We're going to have lawyers and doctors and businessmen of our own."

I slid the eggs and bacon onto two plates, poured two glasses of orange juice, sat on the stool beside Wayne. He picked up a fork and started to eat automatically, not thinking about it.

"I want you to find out what happened," he said. "You're a lawyer. You can find out these things."

"I'm only a lawyer, Wayne. Not a detective."

"They don't tell us anything, the cops. They won't answer our questions or give any updates. Just say inquiries are proceeding. If you ask me, they're not doing much. Because Jay was Indian."

I knew enough Native American history to understand how he felt. I'd have liked to be more confident about the Seawards police pursuing Jay's death to the utmost, but their performance that night had hardly impressed me. "I guess it's standard police procedure, Wayne. They're not going to tell you what's happening from day to day, especially if they don't have a suspect. You might not hear anything until they charge someone."

"If they charge someone. A big if."

We ate in silence for a few more moments. Wayne finished the last of the egg and stared down at his plate as though surprised to find it empty. "That was real tasty, Mr. Richards. Thanks. Sharing food is companionable." He pushed the plate away, leaned against the back of the stool, and sighed again. "So you'll look into it for us?"

"The police aren't going to tell me any more than they've told you. I've no more right to know what's going on than you do. Less, in fact."

"I don't just mean about Jay's death. I mean about the tribal issue. There's got to be papers somewhere. He spent years collecting stories and photographs, letters, and diaries. It was his project. He's gone through old documents and papers, at libraries and historical societies and places. But where is it all now? Maybe at the law school. That's somewhere you'd know your way round, isn't it?"

The suggestion caught me off guard. I hadn't seen it coming. People imagine any lawyer can handle any legal matter, which isn't true, and Wayne couldn't know how little expertise I possessed about Indian treaties and sovereignty claims and tribal agreements.

"Wayne, honestly, I'd like to help, but it's not my field."

Not my field. Exactly what I'd said before committing to the malpractice case that ended so messily, only a few months ago. It would be very foolish to get in over my head again.

Folding his arms, Wayne stared around the kitchen, at the cupboards and counters and appliances as though they held some great fascination for him, and then settled his eyes back on me. "I thought you seemed like a sympathetic kind of guy. I thought maybe you'd be the sort who'd help us out." He looked away again. "We'd pay. Don't think we want anything for free. We just want you to find out where all those records are. The documents and stuff."

"Any documents would belong to his family. It's the family who should claim them."

"Jay didn't have no family except us. But if we was to ask you to find them, that'd be the same thing, wouldn't it?"

I admired the way he led me into that little trap, like a fish he'd hooked and was playing with. Of course, I should have continued to say no, for his sake more than mine, because no one needs attorneys without expertise messing around with their legal affairs; treaties and agreements, sovereignty rights, and tribal status are a complicated minefield, mired in the mists of time, in slipping memories and inadequately written documents. But a foolhardy little bubble of interest rose in my chest at the idea of uncovering such evidence, as if it could undo some of the harm of Jay's death. I'd witnessed Wayne's decline from confident bluster to sorrowful grief, and now, as the expression on his face changed from blank despair to a faint flicker of hope, I couldn't bring myself to say no to him. I supposed the least I could do was make an attempt to locate any paperwork. If it existed. It wasn't much to ask, and it shouldn't be too difficult. One didn't need legal expertise for that. And if I did find anything, an expert could take it from there.

"Have you looked in the place where Jay lived?" I asked finally. "His apartment? Wherever?"

Wayne's face screwed into an expression of distress. "Hell, Mr. Richards, I couldn't bear to go to his place. I couldn't bear the thought of looking through his things. That's what I want you to do."

I thought about it for a little longer. "Okay," I said at last. "I'll do my best. I can't promise anything, but I'll try."

Didn't I have enough to occupy my time? Hadn't I already burned my fingers, and much more, getting involved with matters I knew little about? I shouldn't go off on any more wild-goose chases. I definitely should have known better.

THIRTEEN

WAYNE DROVE OFF IN A BATTERED PICKUP TRUCK, SWINGING round the curve of the cul-de-sac, back up the street past Sarah's house. I watched his truck disappearing up the hill toward the village and thought that if I had to worry about anyone, it should be Sarah McKenzie, alone in that house with her sick baby. I *was* worried about her. And about little Christopher. If he were my child, I'd be running around to everyone in the world seeking advice and help, not waiting to bolt to an emergency room at the last moment. That seemed to be fraught with nothing but danger.

Sarah McKenzie needed good medical hands for her child. I wanted to ask Chauncey, whose judgment I trusted, to take a look at the baby, but of course I couldn't do that without Sarah's permission. Except there was no reason not to pick up the phone and speak to Chauncey. About something. Anything. We'd lived in each other's pockets for so long, so close to each other up in Springwell for so much of our lives, that I was beginning to feel deprived of that closeness, of the warmth of his home. Of Daphne's smile. We'd made a tentative date for them to come and see me in Edward's Bay. If Chauncey came here, surely he could cast a professional eye over Christopher and be able to tell me what was wrong with him. Where Sarah could go for a proper diagnosis and treatment.

I dialed the familiar number in Springwell, and Daphne answered, as I half expected and hoped she might. Her smiling English voice wafted down the phone line.

"Noah, darling! How on earth are you? God, we miss you, you know that? I can hardly bear to walk past your old house. It looks so sad and empty. Are you loving it down there? We'll have to come and check on you one of these days. Soon."

The truth was that I adored Daphne Carlsson. My foolish longings weren't entirely hidden from Daphne, who was wise and perceptive, but I had to hope they were hidden from Chauncey. My oldest friend. The sin of desiring my best friend's wife was one more reason to get out of Springwell.

Daphne said, "Noah? Are you still there?"

"Yes. Yes, you must come and see Edward's Bay. I talked to Chauncey about it. He said this weekend, perhaps, if he wasn't on call. The house isn't straight yet but . . ."

"Who cares? How about tomorrow? Are you going to be home? We could drive down with the boys, look the place over, have lunch. Chauncey's not on call. What do you think?"

It was exactly like Daphne to make plans on the spur of the moment. I was slower, needed time to mull things over. My latest empty nest wasn't really ready to be shown off, but why wait? I said, "There's nowhere decent round here to have lunch, but we could picnic on the beach."

"Lovely," she said.

The prospect of visitors the very next day galvanized me into action. Even if they were old friends who'd take me as they found me. I set about arranging the new furniture, removing the price tags, spreading the Oriental rugs in different places. If I worked at it, the house was going to appear quite respectable. But there was also the oversized, unassembled cabinet-cum-bookcase "home entertainment center," upright in its unopened carton in the middle of the living room, and as I circled the box, I decided I must have had delusions of grandeur to choose such an enormous thing. It was for books, of course, for the stereo and CDs and a TV set, but it was so large it was going to dwarf the rest of the room. And it still had to be put together.

"Some assembly required" are dangerous words. Tearing the carton apart, I unwrapped endless lengths of shelving, dozens of little plastic bags of screws and dowels, found the vital instruction booklet with black-and-white drawings of screwdrivers aimed at numbered holes. Carpentry for idiots, just about my standard. I read the instructions carefully, as my father always lectured, and started piecing the jigsaw together. The wood was a pale maple, pleasing to the eye and hand; the smooth feel of it under my fingers inspired me to keep at the task, to complete the monster in all its glory, and anyway, there was no choice now. The room was soon strewn with deconstructed cabinetry, as though a small hurricane had struck. But sunshine was streaming in through the windows, the Saturday opera was on the radio, and the whole house was peaceful and serene and filled with music.

I hadn't turned on the radio early enough to know which opera was playing, but as I listened idly, the melodies reminded me of *Rosenkavalier.* I wasn't tutored in opera, coming to it late, and then only because Janet loved it so, but now I was a convert and fantasized about visiting the opera houses of the world, Covent Garden or Glyndebourne, Salzburg or Sante Fe. Someday.

The opera, it turned out, was *Daphne* by Strauss, who composed *Rosenkavalier. Daphne!* I was delighted by the coincidence of title name and by my musical acumen; then the announcer said,

"In the end, the nymph Daphne transforms herself into a laurel tree in order to escape the pursuing Apollo." Daphne? Laurel? *Lauren?* The odd juxtaposition of names made me wonder about Lauren Watson, so far away in Minnesota.

It took most of the afternoon to assemble the cabinet/bookcase/entertainment center, and in the end, it occupied the whole of one long wall with only inches to spare. The results were gratifying, but the damn thing was so large I reckoned I'd have to buy the house now. To buy this house, I'd first have to sell the one in Springwell, and before I did any of that, I had to find out more about Edward's Bay. I'd been so absorbed in the construction task and the plot of the opera that Edward's Bay and its problems had quite slipped from my mind. I'd almost forgotten there was a beach right outside my back door. Perhaps that was why the neighbors weren't outside all day. Perhaps, unlike me, they were busy with projects that kept them inside.

The idea of getting Chauncey to look at Christopher McKenzie had also escaped my mind. If Sarah was home from the hospital, I'd invite her round at the same time as Chauncey. An informal meeting, a fortuitously chance encounter. I set off down the beach.

The sun was lowering now, sinking below the headland to the west, but there was still plenty of light. I scuffed along the shingle, prodding at rocks with my feet, unearthing tiny crabs, and it would have been enjoyable, messing around like this, if not for the ever-present thought of Jay Bishop. The stretch of beach was not nearly as inviting as it had seemed at first. At least today there were other people, live ones, out and about. None of them appeared the slightest bit threatening. A middle-aged man wielded a spade at the edge of his property, beyond the piled driftwood, and he lifted a hand in greeting as I passed; further along, a couple of kids shot baskets behind a house, jumping and aiming in silent concentration, the familiar *thud, thud, thud* of the ball on the concrete pad evocative of my own adolescence. God knows how many hours I'd spent aiming at the hoop fastened high above the garage at my parents' house, driving my mother crazy with the constant, repetitive sound.

I passed by Ralph Harrison's house, glanced sideways at the wide windows with the wonderful view down the sound. Around the end of the spit, where there was less driftwood, I made a casual diversion across the sandy grass behind Sarah's house, but before I was halfway across, Sarah appeared on her deck as though she'd been expecting me. She waited at the top of the steps, the circles below her eyes dark and distinct, bruised by another night at the hospital. But otherwise she seemed perfectly calm and collected, just as she had at the hospital. I admired her fortitude.

"I've only been home a couple of hours," she said. "Was everything okay? The furniture and everything?"

"Oh, yes. Of course. Thanks for seeing it in for me, Sarah. I got a decent night's sleep for once. How's Christopher?"

Sarah leaned on the railings of the deck, looking down at me, the shiny hair falling about her neck. "They still can't find anything to put their finger on. They did all these tests to see if he was allergic to something, but they didn't find anything specific. They gave me all this equipment to keep at home, just in case. But they said the problem might never happen again."

"Poor little tyke. Stuck with needles at his tender age."

She brushed the hair away from her face. "He won't remember, will he? Children recover perfectly well from that sort of thing, don't you think? When I was little, I was in hospital for weeks with pneumonia, but I don't remember a thing about it. Would you like a cup of tea?"

"Sure." I went up the steps of the deck, into the gleaming spotless kitchen. "So where is he now?"

"Asleep. Worn out. Like me. There's a monitor on him, so if anything happens, I'll know at once."

She filled an electric kettle at the sink and plugged it into the socket and paused, her hand still on the plug, as though the electricity might surge through her and give her energy. I thought she must be bowed down by the weight of her responsibility, by a fear of the unknown, a dread of the next moment. What a terrible way to have to live, on tenterhooks all the time.

"Sarah, you've *got* to get a proper diagnosis." I spoke with authority, as though I knew what I was talking about. "Can I go look at him? I won't wake him."

She shrugged, as though I was making a fuss about nothing, and I followed her across the hallway, up a short flight of stairs into a room where the windows faced the inland bay and the hillside beyond. As soon as I was through the door, I knew it must be her bedroom. A big double bed took up most of the space, and like the rest of the house, the room was obsessively neat, not a wrinkle on the bedcovers, not a stray garment lying around or a discarded pair of shoes on the floor, not a picture on the walls. The baby's crib was pushed into a corner, a green oxygen cylinder alongside in a wheeled carrier, plastic tubing and mask looped around the tank valve; on a low table beside the crib, a small black box beeped with regular ticking sounds. In the crib, the baby was flat on his back, exactly as he had been at the hospital, arms flung out, eyes closed, face pink and healthy, his breathing easy. It occurred to me that I'd hardly ever seen Christopher awake.

Sarah rested her forearms on the rails, lowered her chin on her hands, and gazed down at the baby with an almost detached interest. Then she sighed and sank onto the bed as though her legs wouldn't hold her up anymore. "I don't know, Noah. I really don't know," she said, and she covered her face with her hands.

Reaching out, I touched her on the shoulder. "It's going to be all right, Sarah, I'm sure it is." What the hell did I know?

She looked up at me. The dark hair fell away from her white neck, the delicate flesh under her chin stretched taut. Her skin was a rich creamy consistency that made me think of ice cream, thick and lickable, sweet and satisfying. I could almost taste it. She smiled, very slightly, a mere upcurving of her moist mouth, and I had a sudden irresistible desire to throw myself at her. I could feel the heat rising in me, a marvelous surge of sexual energy, and I'd have done it, because we both wanted it, needed it, and there was no real reason to resist, was there? Was there? Except, at that precise moment, the baby hiccuped and stirred in his crib in the corner, and the black box on the table beside the crib beeped loudly and unevenly. I was across the room in a flash. Immediately, it was obvious that nothing was amiss; Christopher merely sighed and made little blowing movements with his mouth and tongue, slipped back into his sleeping mode again. The machine resumed its steady beat. But the moment of passion and desire had passed, definitely and irrevocably, and I suppose I was relieved. And disappointed.

I turned to look at Sarah, and she, too, recognized that whatever might have been, wasn't going to happen. She sat up straighter on the bed and made a small strangled sound in her throat. "Still want that cup of tea, Noah?"

Back in the kitchen, we were awkwardly silent. Sarah's face and the whole of her body exuded frustration and weariness, her forehead creased, her lips pressed together in a tight line. I thought we both wanted out of there, and didn't quite know how to make a graceful retreat. She unplugged the kettle, poured water into a teapot to warm it, and made the tea with loose tea leaves, like Daphne, in the English fashion. When she handed me a mug of tea with milk and sugar, the way Daphne made it, I remembered why I'd come in the first place.

"Sarah, if you're not busy tomorrow, come and meet some old friends of mine. From Springwell. They're dropping in for lunch, to look over my new place. Just casual. Nothing fancy."

Her face cleared quite suddenly, frown disappearing, dark eyes lightening. "How nice, Noah! I'd love to do that. I don't get to see anyone anymore, you know."

"And you'll bring Christopher, of course?"

"Of course."

"You'll like them," I said. "Daphne's English. Practically a fellow countrywoman."

"That'll be nice," Sarah said again.

We sat and drank the tea in companionable silence. I didn't explain that Daphne was a nurse, that Chauncey was a doctor. That maybe they could give us an answer to the problem. Stop all this worrying.

FOURTEEN

THE CARLSSON CLAN DESCENDED ON EDWARD'S BAY LIKE A whirlwind, kids and dogs and adults filling the spaces of the house, driving the emptiness out of it. They rushed from room to room, exclaiming over the house in general and the view from the deck. I hugged them all in turn, as though we'd been separated for months instead of a few weeks.

Daphne's gray eyes shone, and delight bubbled out of her like fresh springwater. "So beautiful and peaceful!" she exclaimed. "Just look at those mountains! The water, the beach! You're so lucky, Noah. A beach of your very own. See how well the houses are laid out, Chauncey, so you're not staring into any else's windows. You'd hardly know any others were here."

Chauncey stared around with surprised approval. "I have to

admit Bigs Harrison seems to have done a pretty good job," he said. He'd never particularly cared for Bigs.

I smiled proprietarily and lapped up the praise as though personally responsible for discovering Edward's Bay, for being smart enough to build such houses there, and almost forgot about Jay Bishop. Neither Chauncey nor Daphne mentioned anything about him, and I wondered if Chauncey had told her.

We climbed over the logs to the beach. The day was mild and gray, no wind, the water still and quiet, the tide way out so there was plenty of beach for exploring. The boys whooped with excitement and ran off, skinny arms and legs windmilling, thin high voices quickly lost in the space between sea and land. The dogs barked at their heels and sent two blue herons rising majestically from the shallows. Out on the sound, a couple of boats flapped useless sails in the nonexistent breeze, barely making headway.

The boys disappeared around the end of the spit, and the adults followed in their wake, making slow progress. Daphne stooped to search for agates, picking up rocks and discarding them, examining shells and the pink bodies of tiny dried crabs. She held up a butter clam shell. "Obviously there are clams here."

Obviously. The problem was who was laying claim to them.

"I never see anyone digging on this beach," I commented. "There's not much activity of any kind, in fact. People seem to stay inside their houses. I can't imagine why they choose to live in a place like this and not be outside all the time."

"Is this the right season for clams?" Daphne wanted to know.

None of us could remember. Nowadays there are so many rules and restrictions and it was so long since any of us had gone clamming that we were out of touch with current regulations. When Chauncey and I were kids, we'd dig for clams anytime, fish for salmon whenever we wanted, never had to worry about limits or red tide or any other of the signs of rampant human growth. In those days, there were more than enough clams and salmon for everyone.

Chauncey picked up a flat rock, skipped it across the water. We watched it bounce on the surface, the circles spreading and fading. "You should bring the dinghy down from the old house, Noah. Get in a little fishing. There must be salmon out there beyond the point."

"There must be," I agreed. "But I need a better boat for the sound. I'll sell the dinghy with the house."

They both stopped and stared at me. Chauncey said, "You're selling the house?"

"Even if I don't buy this one, I can't live in that house again."

Chauncey kicked at the sand with one toe. "You're probably right," he said. "It's time you moved on."

A twinge of disappointment surprised me. Perhaps I wanted them to talk me out of moving on and leaving them behind.

At the end of the spit, where the water eddied and swirled round the corner, the tide on the turn, Daphne clapped her hands as if she'd never seen a tide rip before. "Chauncey, why don't we have a house on the sound? The lake is terribly dull in comparison."

Edward's Bay was a different world from the mountains and rather claustrophobic lake and conifer trees of Springwell. No tides around back doors there, no smell of salt water, no ships passing on open seas. The Carlssons lived in the house inherited from Chauncey's parents, just as mine was inherited from my parents. His was a big old-fashioned barn of a place, comfortable and worn, with a long porch to catch the westerly sun, a river-rock fireplace, a dock on the lake, and he'd filled it with a family and with dogs. Now he appeared quite horrified by Daphne's frivolous suggestion. "My dear woman, I have no intention of ever moving anywhere. I like it just fine where I am."

"Well, how about a place in the islands?" Daphne suggested. "A cabin for the weekends. I miss the smell of salt water. I've been deprived of it. After all, I *am* English. The English are an island race. They have an affinity to salt water."

Chauncey laughed. "This is the first I've heard of saltwater deprivation. I thought it was Harrods you'd been deprived of."

Daphne sighed melodramatically. "And double-decker buses. And decent sidewalks. And pubs. And policemen who don't carry guns." She shrugged, walked a few yards away from us. "Oh, well, we can't have everything, can we?"

There was an unexpected whiff of homesickness in her voice, like the longing in Sarah McKenzie's voice. They'll get on well together, I thought. But Daphne didn't usually sound homesick. She usually sounded contented and happy, at least to my ears, someone who'd made her choices and had no regrets. I suppose we all have regrets about something. There'll always be something we have to leave behind.

Daphne said, "Go after the boys, Chauncey. Make sure they don't drown. I'll go back with Noah and help fix lunch."

It was months since I'd had a chance to be alone with Daphne, but when we turned back together toward the house, I remembered my mission about the baby. "Wait there a minute, Daffy," I said and sprinted after Chauncey, already out of sight round the end of the spit.

I called to him, and he stopped in his tracks, bright hair gleaming in the gray day. I didn't often come upon Chauncey from a distance like this, and it was as though I was seeing him anew, tall and spare, light blond hair, sharp angles to the bones of his face, as if he'd just walked off the boat from Scandinavia. The same heritage as most of the people who lived at Edward's Bay. Chauncey and I might be a contrast of genetic materials, but I'd always looked upon him as a brother.

I caught up to him. "I have a favor to ask," I said. "I've invited a neighbor to have lunch with us. With her baby. Can you cast an eye over him and tell me what might be wrong with him? Without mentioning you're a doctor?"

He frowned. "Now what are you up to, Noah?"

"Nothing. Swear to God. Just hoping to get a confidential professional assessment."

"So why not come right out with it? Why keep it a secret?"

Why did I need to keep it a secret? I wasn't at all certain. "Maybe I don't want to be seen as interfering. Or, frankly, to be seen showing too great an interest. Something about the scenario makes me uneasy, Chauncey. I don't know what. You know how one gets those odd feelings?"

"What's wrong with the kid?"

"Some sort of breathing problem. That's up your alley, isn't it?"

Chauncey stuck his hands deep into his pockets and regarded me with suspicion. "It sounds harmless enough. Except that you're an attorney. Nothing attorneys do is ever harmless, especially where the medical profession is involved. What's your interest in this, Noah? Who is this woman?"

"Just a neighbor."

"You concern yourself with the medical problems of all your neighbors?"

"She's had to go to the hospital twice because the child stopped breathing. I went with her the first time, late at night. The docs couldn't find anything wrong with him." I held Chauncey's arm, trying to convince him. "She's all alone. And he's such a beautiful kid."

He stared at me with the penetrating blue eyes. "And the mother? Is she beautiful, too?"

"Oh, come on! Can't I just be concerned about the baby?"

He grinned. "Quite neutral, are you? Ah, well . . . You say the child stopped breathing? Really stopped?"

"Really stopped."

I hoped he'd agree if I appealed to him as a friend, and eventually, reluctantly, he did. "All right. But only because you're a friend. No one can just glance at a patient and know what's wrong, not without examining them first. Or shouldn't anyway. Don't test me too far on this, okay?"

I thanked him, genuinely grateful, and hurried back to Daphne. She hadn't gone far. She was squatting down like a little girl, examining the life-forms under the rocks, absorbed in her self-imposed task, and she didn't ask what I'd wanted with Chauncey, though the curiosity was evident in her eyes. But she wanted to know everything else that had happened lately, how the partnership with Charlie Forsyth was going, if the new office arrangement suited me, about the Ambrose case, how Angel Ambrose was, if Lauren Watson was ever coming back. Daphne always took a proprietary interest in the minutiae of my life and it was comforting to have her inquire into the details of my daily existence, to feel she cared.

Daphne also wanted to know whether I'd found another lady friend. That's exactly how she put it. "Found yourself another lady friend yet, Noah?"

It was one of Daphne's perennial questions. She was forever trying to fix me up with available females. "I'll let you know the minute I have. However, I have invited someone to come and have lunch with us today."

Her eyebrows shot up. "A woman?"

It was satisfying to tease Daphne, all the quick reactions showing, surprise and delight and disappointment chasing through her clear gray eyes.

"Don't go jumping to conclusions. She's just a neighbor. And she's bringing her baby with her. Her name's Sarah, and she's from New Zealand so she talks the same language as you. I'll give her a call to remind her."

But Sarah didn't need reminding. Daphne and I were messing with orange juice and muffins and bowls of beaten eggs when Sarah called from the front door. "Hey, there, Noah. We're coming in, okay?"

She came into the kitchen, Christopher on one arm, baby seat and bag on the other and for once, Christopher was awake. His round blue eyes gazed intently from Daphne to me and back to his mother, light head swiveling on the tiny neck, his expression solemn and deadpan, unsure whether to cry or to smile.

Daphne put down the eggs to shake Sarah's hand, but all her attention was focused on Christopher. "What a lovely, lovely baby," she cooed, the goofy expression on her face that women get when they lay eyes on a baby. He reacted perfectly to Daphne's voice, his face alight with joy, his mouth gaping, two white teeth glistening wetly, small hands flapping. Daphne threw her arms wide. "Oh, please. Can I hold him?"

Clutching him to her breast, she gazed into his eyes and then held him at arm's length. "He's much too beautiful. He reminds me of mine at that age. You'd better take him back before I carry him off."

When Sarah placed the baby seat on the counter so Christopher was at eye level with us, I had a sudden urge to put my hand on the small downy head, as though by touching him I'd somehow understand what was wrong with him. My hand was huge and masculine on the soft head, and I could feel all the delicate bones of his skull, the pulsating opening of the fontanelle. A frightening, protective emotion rose in me, bubbling in my chest and I snatched my hand away, as if it were burning, and saw the two women watching me, the expression on Daphne's face maternal and sympathetic, Sarah's harder to assess.

"He's so small," I said, apologetically. "I can't imagine I was ever that small myself."

They smiled at me, at each other, in a knowing female understanding that excluded a mere male like me. Today, Sarah wore narrow blue jeans, sweatshirt, and sneakers, just like Daphne, but otherwise they didn't resemble each other at all. Daphne's face was so clear and open, her eyes gray, her hair short and wispy, while Sarah had those dark eyes and shiny sleek hair, that enigmatic quality to her. But they launched into an immediate and friendly conversation and in a matter of seconds were exchanging breathtaking intimacies. As Sarah toasted the muffins, she described the rigors of Christopher's birth, and she and Daphne laughed together about ways of American obstetrics. I was saved from further hair-raising revelations when the boys rushed into the kitchen and emptied their pockets of shells and rocks and dead crab bodies, spreading them out on the counter for us to admire.

Robbie was my godson, a skinny ten-year-old version of his father. He looked exactly as Chauncey had at that age, all angles and bright blond hair, while Jeff, his younger brother, reminded me of myself, dark-haired, more solemn and cautious.

Robbie said, "You're so lucky to live on a beach, Noah. Can we come again? Soon?"

"You can come anytime," I said. "You and Jeff. It'll be even better here in the summer."

"Can we go in the hot tub then?" Jeff wanted to know.

"Great idea. I'll get it fired up, and we can all lie out there at night and stare at the stars."

"Cool," they said.

I opened a bottle of champagne to toast my new digs, and we ate in the kitchen, too much trouble, after all, to carry the food down to the beach. Robbie and Jeff sat on the floor, Daphne and Sarah on the stools, Chauncey and I leaning against the counter; the baby shrieked with delight at the panting yellow dogs, and everyone was in very good humor. But I noticed Chauncey watching Sarah and the baby, his eyes narrowed.

After brunch, the boys headed for the beach again, and Daphne and Sarah went after them, and Chauncey and I were left with Christopher, asleep in his baby seat. We both stood over him, stared at him. Chauncey put one finger out, touched one dangling hand. "This baby looks just fine, Noah. Quite normal. As you said, a beautiful child."

"But don't you think that's strange, one minute perfectly fine, the next not breathing?"

"Perhaps not so strange. He could have had an allergic reaction to his food or to his blankets or to grass or something. He needs testing."

Daphne and Sarah came back to inspect the house in greater detail, and I trailed after them as they admired the new cabinet, tried out the sectional, moved the rugs, and generally tossed out so many suggestions for furniture arrangements that I stopped listening and imagined Daphne transformed into a laurel tree. The baby slept in his chair, blond head tilted to one side, eyelashes fluttering, and we seemed to be having a good time.

Then it was time for another walk on the beach.

"It's a shame to wake the baby," I said. "And we can't leave him here."

Daphne said, "Oh, Noah, don't fuss! He won't come to any harm strapped in that seat. Just for a few minutes."

"What about his monitor?" I said, and Sarah replied, "I didn't think I'd need it."

I looked from Christopher to Sarah, to Daphne and Chauncey, already putting on their jackets. "He's had this problem with his breathing," I said. "It keeps stopping for no reason Sarah's had to take him to the hospital twice already."

Daphne stared at the baby. At Sarah.

"He stopped breathing? Whatever is wrong with him?"

Sarah said abruptly, "They don't know. They thought it might be an allergy or something. He has to have more tests."

Allergies were Chauncey's specialty, and despite my careful groundwork, I instantly blew his cover. "Chauncey's a doctor. Maybe he could have a look at him for you."

Chauncey's blue eyes cooled into an ominous slate-gray, and I understood I'd overstepped the bounds of medical etiquette. He said, deliberately, "If that's what Sarah wants. But as he's under the care of a doctor already, it would be preferable to have a professional referral."

Sarah's neck and cheeks flooded with a bright red color, and she stammered a little, running the words into one another. "Oh, I didn't realize you were a doctor. It's very kind of you, but really, I wouldn't want to bother you. Don't you live up north? They're doing tests at the hospital in Seawards."

Everyone stared at me, accusingly, and because it seemed to be expected, I apologized. But I wasn't sorry. "I'm not suggesting you change doctors, Sarah. But why not let Chauncey have a look at Christopher? I worry about him, you know that, don't you? He's so . . . so little."

Sarah's voice rose higher, her accent more pronounced, the vowels flattened and lengthened. "Thank you for worrying, Noah. I think perhaps it's time to take him home now." She started gathering her belongings together, jacket, bag, the seat with the sleeping baby. "I'm sure we'll manage. I'm sure it'll get sorted out. It was nice to meet you, Daphne. Chauncey. Thanks for the lunch, Noah."

I attempted to assist with the baby seat and the bag, but she brushed me aside. "Really, I can manage. Go for your walk." And in an instant she was gone, quickly, through the front door, leaving a silence behind.

Daphne and Chauncey stood in the middle of the living room and waited for me to say something.

"It wasn't right to leave that baby alone, not after what happened."

"I thought you didn't want to interfere, Noah. Wasn't that interfering, Daphne?"

Daphne frowned. "I think it's taking a personal interest. Perhaps Noah cares what happened to the baby. What *did* happen to him?"

I explained the hurried journeys to the hospital, the monitor and the oxygen cylinder in the house. Chauncey listened without comment.

"I don't know what to say, Noah." He zipped up his parka. "Anyway, it's time we were getting on our way. Let's you and I go find the boys."

We negotiated the logs once more, walked in silence for a while. The tide was coming in with a rush now, the sand vanishing fast.

Chauncey said, "What was the name of the doctor who saw the baby at Seawards?"

I could recall the doctor's face, pale and puffy, the bored expression in his eyes, the bright blue stethoscope around his neck, but not his name. I remembered the baby-sitter's name, Gretchen; Sarah's panic and the drive to the hospital; the conversation when we walked home from the tavern that night. I remembered perfectly well the noise of the band at the Eagle's Nest, the men around the table, Wayne Daniels, and Jay Bishop. Jay Bishop's dead face intruded on the face of the doctor I was trying to remember.

"It was about here I found the body," I said.

Chauncey stopped in his tracks, stared at the rocks and the sand, at me. "Jesus, Noah! You come here to get away from that sort of trouble, and you end up with trips to a hospital in the middle of the night and a body on the beach."

"You haven't told Daphne, have you? She'd have said something if she knew."

"You know she worries about you. And to tell the truth, I forgot."

I was shocked. "Forgot?"

"Noah, the dead guy wasn't anyone I knew. You take everything too much to heart."

Did anyone but Wayne Daniels and me care about Jay Bishop's death? I tried to forgive Chauncey. "I suppose I don't see as many dead bodies as you. They make more of an impact on me." I gazed at the encroaching waters. "Tell me, Chauncey, would a body wash out and then in again with the tide?"

"Hell, Noah, I've no idea. Go ask an oceanographer. A forensic expert. Did you actually see that baby stop breathing?"

I dragged my mind away from Jay Bishop, back to Christopher McKenzie. "Yes, the first time. He was white and limp, his lips were purple, you know that awful color? I was terrified for him, poor little bastard." I snapped my fingers. "Hayward," I said. "That's the name of the doctor we saw in the emergency room. Hayward."

"Hayward? I might give him a call."

"What did you think about the baby? What on earth is the matter with him?"

"I don't know," Chauncey said slowly. "I can't tell just from looking."

But, of course, I expected him to be able to tell just by looking. Despite all the evidence to the contrary, I still expected doctors to know everything. To be sympathetic and to understand all.

FIFTEEN

SUDDENLY, AFTER THE CONTROLLED FRENZY OF THE PAST week, the level of activity in the office trailed down to quiet and orderly and dull. The docket was cleared of cases, and nothing else was slated to come up for trial for another couple of weeks. Sibby, Beth, and Grace took to sorting files and sending reminders on overdue accounts.

Charlie was cheerfully philosophical. "It happens," he said, feet up on desk. "Feast or famine. One minute too damn much, the next not a damn thing."

This seemed as good a time as any to go in search of Jay Bishop's evidence about the Quanda's tribal status. I sat down and explained the project to Charlie. "I reckon they could do with a bit of help."

His eyebrows shot up. "What are we talking here? Tribal sovereignty? There'd not be much money in that, I reckon." Charlie wasn't the sort to ride off on wild-goose chases. "Of course, you never know these days. Some of the tribes have gotten rich of late."

"I can't believe that's true of the Quanda. But if they really do have a claim on that land . . . ? If it's okay with you, I could take a day to go see what I can track down in Spokane."

He shrugged and didn't seem very interested. And why should he be? This was entirely outside his sphere of interest. "Well, okay, I guess," he said reluctantly. Then his face brightened. "Maybe we could bring suit for the Indians against the contractors? Or the contractors against the Indians? Where would the money be, do you think?"

"How about a little pro bono?"

He grimaced.

"I've got to show up to sign the statement about finding Jay Bishop," I said. "Maybe I'll do that today and fly to Spokane tomorrow."

"Whatever," Charlie said.

I caught an early afternoon ferry to Seawards. The precinct office was in a building in sore need of repair, one more sign that little of importance in police matters happened in Seawards. I tracked Roberts down in an airless room, behind a desk with antique computers and overflowing in- and out-trays, and when he saw me, he appeared almost pleased to have something to divert him. Under the mustache, his teeth bared in the semblance of a smile.

"Hey there, counselor. Found any more bodies lately?"

I ignored the remark, read through the bald document that stated the time, the place, the conditions of the discovery of Jay Bishop's body, but which contained no flavor of the sort of person he was, or how it felt to stumble on his corpse in the darkness.

"Any news?" I asked.

"We're following leads," Roberts said and then gave the impression there weren't any.

"You haven't found the weapon, I suppose?"

He thought about not telling me, shrugged offhandedly. "No. You think anyone would leave it lying around someplace? But it was most likely a high-powered hunting rifle."

That much was obvious, even to someone like me who didn't handle guns. The bullet had made a small neat entry wound and an explosive exit. "High-powered" merely meant it could have come from a considerable distance. From anywhere on the shore. Or from out on the water.

"Was he shot on the beach? Out in the boat? There must be a clue from the angle of the entry wound. You have a time of death?"

Roberts stared at me. "Defense lawyer, aren't you? Got anyone in mind to defend, counselor?"

"No. Do you? I have a personal interest in this young man. I found his body."

Roberts wasn't impressed. Dead bodies, it seemed, were as common in the daily lives of policemen as in the lives of doctors. He chewed on his mustache, rustled a few papers on his desk. I could tell he was bored and uninterested in the whole subject of Jay Bishop's death. "As far as we know," he said, "he went out fishing after talking to you. No one claims to have seen him any later. Forensics reckon he was most likely shot in the boat. But I'll tell you this. If there's one good place for losing evidence, it's out in a boat."

"And the boat?"

He shrugged again. "One's been reported abandoned on a beach at Vashon. They're checking it out, but as it's been upside down in salt water for days, I don't think they're going to find much, do you?"

Vashon Island was miles away down the sound. The answer to all this seemed miles away too.

I pushed the signed statement across the desk. "So that's it?"

Roberts glanced at the statement briefly, tossed it into the out-tray. "If we need anything more, we'll be in touch, counselor. But I wouldn't hold my breath if I were you. This sort of case is slippery, you understand. No witnesses. No motive. No clues."

And no one making waves.

I thought about Roberts and his attitude as I drove on to Edward's Bay. Was he uninterested merely because there were so few clues and therefore little hope of a solution? There's nothing so dispiriting as a dead-end investigation. At Edward's Bay, I trekked down the beach to the end of the spit, watched the tide rip round the corner, stared at the houses up on the bluff and down on the beach, and knew there were a hundred different places where someone could have taken aim. That someone could have been almost anywhere, inside a house or outside, and still be completely hidden from view. The opposite curve of the bay was thick with Douglas firs, hemlocks and cedar, madronas and wild rhododendrons; only on the beach was everywhere open and exposed. And it was easy to believe no one had heard the shot. Our lives are so full of sound and fury these days—radios and televisions and airplanes, chain saws and leaf blowers, engines racing on the water and on the roads—that a single rifle shot could surely pass unnoticed.

I imagined a boat circling in the water, the figure in it bending and straightening, imagined the distant crack of a rifle, the figure slumping, the rudderless boat drifting out on the tide, spinning and slopping aimlessly. The sound had been calm that day, but somewhere, sometime, perhaps in the surging wake of a passing container ship, Jay Bishop slipped over the gunwales and into the water.

Back at the house, I looked up the tides for that Sunday. On that particular morning, the tide was exceptionally low, minus one at one forty-seven P.M. That was after the meeting, when Sarah and I were on our way to Seattle. If Jay was fishing at that time, whoever shot him surely reckoned the boat would go out on the ebb, far into the sound, but he must have fallen overboard close by, as the tide began to turn; otherwise, he'd have washed up, like the boat, miles away. High tide that same day wasn't until eight forty-four P.M., when darkness had long fallen. By ten P.M., when I stumbled on his body, more than an hour had elapsed since high water.

None of which helped solve anything.

For the trip to Spokane, I needed information from Wayne. His phone number wasn't listed in the local directory. I reckoned the place to track him down would be the Eagle's Nest. I hadn't been back there since the night I'd met him. When they'd all been there—Jay Bishop. Sarah, Bigs Harrison, and Ralph Harrison. The evening was very crowded in my memory. I got back in the Saab and drove up to the Eagle's Nest.

It was almost empty, the smell of old beer and stale cigarette smoke hanging heavy in the dim, unventilated space, and even though there was no band screeching on the raised area at the far end, the Eagle's Nest wasn't silent, as though silence wasn't a desirable quality. Video machines still squawked electronic messages into the thick air, and a rock band thumped on tape like an irregular heartbeat.

I ordered a beer and saw four men in baseball caps sitting at the far end of the bar, staring at me. One of the faces under the caps was vaguely familiar, and after a while, I took a stab. "Aren't you Frank? Weren't you with Wayne Daniels the other night? I'm Noah Richards."

The face under the shadowing cap didn't react for several moments. Eventually, he said, "I'm Albert."

"Albert. Sorry."

I slid down the bar toward them, but if I expected any sort of spontaneous conversation, I was going to be disappointed. They watched me inching closer and they remained silent and unmoving. "I'm looking for Wayne Daniels," I said.

"He ain't here," Albert said.

"You think he might be coming in sometime soon?"

He shrugged.

"Wayne wanted a word with me. You know where I can find him?"

They digested the question for more seconds, collectively shifted their backsides on the stools. "He could be anywhere," one of them said at last. "He could be home."

"It's about Jay," I said, and they grew even more still and silent. "If you know Wayne's phone number, I could call him."

Albert said, "You wanna know where Wayne lives?"

"That'd be good."

Taking a pencil and a scrap of paper out of an inside pocket, he licked the tip of the pencil, wrote something, passed the piece of paper to the others, who looked at it carefully and then pushed it along the counter to me. It was like watching a silent movie in slow motion. I was almost certain they were putting on an act for me, but maybe I was reading them wrong. On the scrap of paper was a string of numbers.

"This is his address? Where is it exactly?"

Albert got off the stool, slowly and deliberately, hitched at his pants. "You wanna go there now? You wanna follow me?" And without waiting for an answer, he headed for the door. Abandoning my drink, I went after him.

Outside, the daylight was almost startling. Albert was already climbing into a beat-up Chevy truck, without a backward glance, and by the time I'd reversed out of the parking lot, the truck was disappearing through the village. I put a heavy foot on the gas to keep up. A mile or so farther on, without signaling, he swung abruptly off the highway into a narrow opening between the trees, and I had to brake hard to make the sudden turn. The road wound up the hillside among the dark oppressive fir trees. The truck made a quick left and then a right, still without signals, as though trying to lose me. There were no road signs at any of the turns, no houses or any other buildings. The paved road became gravel, then dirt, and all of a sudden we emerged into a clearing, a dead end, to a cluster of small houses. I'd never have found it by myself.

The pickup rattled and banged to a stop, and I drew up alongside. Albert leaned out his window. "That one there," he said, inclining his head to one of the houses, and without another word, screeched into reverse and drove off fast, dirt flying. I got out of the Saab, watched the truck vanish among the trees. When it was gone, the peculiar smothering silence of a conifer forest descended—a stillness, a hush, no bird sounds, no leaves rustling, no dogs barking, no children crying. As though nothing were alive in the little community. But from two of the houses, thin columns of smoke rose straight into the still air, and I had the distinct feeling of being watched. It would have been impossible to miss the arrival of two vehicles in that silent place.

If there'd been any sunshine that day, it would have shone down into the clearing, but there were no signs of cultivation, just an assortment of old vehicles lying around and about, none of which looked as if there was the least likelihood of it ever moving again. Overhead, the huge cedar trees that surely had been standing there for hundreds of years reduced the dwellings to an even smaller and more insignificant size, and gave them a huddled defensive quality, as if they were in retreat from the rest of the world. It seemed an odd sort of place to live when there was so much land down below, where one could see open water and open sky.

I approached the house Albert had pointed to, and Wayne Daniels appeared in the doorway. Even from a distance, he seemed to be standing taller, his face less mournful. He didn't greet me in any way, which didn't surprise me anymore. I was growing accustomed to the taciturn habits of the Quanda.

My voice echoed among the trees. "I just came from the police at Seawards. I didn't learn anything new. Except they probably found Jay's boat. Did you know?"

"I heard. Keeping it as evidence they say. Same as they're keeping him. Won't even let us bury him."

There must have been time for an autopsy. "You should question that," I said.

Wayne shrugged, as if it was of no great consequence. I was ignorant about the beliefs of the Quanda and their burial rituals and ceremonies.

"You thought anymore about what I asked?" he said.

"Yes," I said. "I'll go to Spokane to look for those papers. If you still want me to. But you'll have to give me some sort of authority."

"You got it."

"I need it in writing. I have to have permission to root around in someone's personal effects. I'm not the police."

"I know you're not the police. That's why I asked you. Come on in."

Inside the house, it was dark, the tiny windows letting in little of the meager daylight. The house seemed to consist mainly of one large living room; a television set played sotto voce, the volume turned down so low I couldn't hear it clearly, but the picture flashed vividly in the dim room. After a moment, I realized someone was sitting on the sofa in front of the set, a woman, her face turned away from us, concentrating on the program.

"Hi," I said.

She glanced over her shoulder, nodded without smiling or speaking, swiveled her eyes back to the television. On her lap was a sleeping child, face downward. The woman was patting its bottom with one hand, idly, not paying it any other attention, as if she'd forgotten she was holding a child.

"My wife, Cynthia," Wayne said. "It's the soaps. She watches every afternoon. That's my grandson she's got there."

"Hi," I said again.

"We got some paper and a pen?" Wayne asked, and not taking her eyes off the television, Cynthia said, "In the kitchen. On the counter."

The kitchen was at the back of the house, farther into the trees, darker. An old-fashioned potbellied stove, elaborately decorated with brushed steel, the type found in antique stores at vast prices, dominated one corner, a black metal pipe rose through the ceiling, and the whole contraption was pumping out an unbelievable heat. But the house still smelled of moss and decay. Wayne rummaged around on the counter and unearthed a pad of paper and a pen. He held the pen awkwardly. "What do I say?"

"Write your address and today's date. Then say, 'I, Wayne Daniels, uncle of Jay Bishop, request Noah Richards, J.D., to search his personal effects.' Write Jay's address, and then sign it."

It took a while. I peeled off my jacket, sweltering from the heat of the stove, and when he showed me what he'd written, I realized it wouldn't hold up to inspection. Not that I really expected to be put to any test, but if I had to go to the law school, for instance, I'd need something more official than this.

"You're quite sure Jay doesn't have any other relatives with a better claim? He didn't leave a will by any chance?" I didn't ask with any hope. Young men never leave wills.

"Hell, Jay has a thousand relatives. Had a bunch of girls, too. More girls than you could shake a stick at. He was one busy guy. I don't know about any will, but there's a piece of paper from Jay says I'm to take care of his affairs."

"There is? Where?"

"Hey, hon," he yelled to the woman on the sofa. "Where's that paper Jay wrote out? Said to keep safe?"

She called back, "In the second drawer on the left."

Pulling the second drawer on the left out of the cabinet, Wayne tipped plastic bags, rubber bands, balls of string, a tape measure, pieces of paper, into a heap on the counter; then he sorted through the pile with one finger, picked out an unsealed legal-sized envelope, and handed it to me.

The document inside was neatly typed, dated eight years ago, a simple but straightforward in loco parentis agreement authorizing Wayne Daniels to act on behalf of his nephew Jay Bishop in case of his inability to act on his own behalf. Notarized and signed by both of them, it had been re-dated and re-signed three years ago. I was impressed.

Wayne said, proudly, "Jay liked things to be legal even then, even before he went to law school. He wrote that himself and got me to sign it when he first went off to college. In case of an accident, he said. Then when he got to be twenty-one, he signed it again. You never know, he said. Guess he was right, wasn't he? You never know."

I turned the paper over in my hands. "Not many people take care of their affairs like this. What happened to his parents?"

"Well, that was bad news, Mr. Richards." Wayne sighed heavily. "They came to bad ends, both of them. His mom, she got some cancer, and his dad, he was in an auto accident. Out there in eastern Washington."

"I'll make a copy of this and take it with me," I said. "You've got to take better care of it, Wayne. You should keep it in a safe-deposit."

"That's what Jay said. But I don't have no safe-deposit."

I edged my way past the sofa and said good-bye to Cynthia, who showed absolutely no curiosity about the stranger who'd walked into her house. I wondered how many strangers showed up at their house. The daylight outside was bright after the inside. Wayne and I stood on the doorstep for a moment. "Who else lives up here?" I asked.

He pointed with a thick finger. "Over there's my son. Used to be my sister's home. That one there is my daughter's. She and her hubby both work down at the casino near Seawards. It's her baby the wife takes care of. Couple of cousins over there."

"A regular family enclave. Must be nice."

"Yeah. But then we're all family, aren't we? The whole damn lot of us."

When I returned to my own house and contemplated the disorder I still lived in—the unpacked boxes, the sparse furnishings—

I thought it might be better to organize my own life instead of attempting to organize other people's. But there was a tweak of anticipation about the visit to Spokane. Maybe I hoped to find a little place in Indian history, to be included in the whole damn family.

SIXTEEN

ON THE EARLY MORNING FLIGHT TO SPOKANE, I SAW THE CAScades ripple and unfold like frozen waves beneath the wings of the plane; then the mountains and clouds were left behind, and the skies expanded into the unsullied blue of eastern Washington. The arid stretches of land around the Columbia River were brown and sere, the river itself a broad silver streak through the desert. This was a land known only to Indians not so long ago The white men who saw it for the first time considered it totally inhospitable, the bare hills, the stark cliffs of the Columbia, a barren strangeness that didn't fit with the innate nature of those who like water and shade and land for farming.

The desert gave way to rolling wheat fields, not yet green, scored by tractor rows into abstract sculpture. As the plane banked and began its descent, the city of Spokane rose like a Lego model on the horizon, a child's version of a city, unnatural and unreal, straight streets and tall buildings unconvincing in all that emptiness.

I stepped out into the clean sharp air and felt as if I'd arrived in a different country, not just another part of the same state. But eastern Washington *is* a different country, geographically, politically, and socially, a wide and treeless land of strong sunshine and dark defined shadows, not at all like the damp, green, cloudy western side of the state. It's the home of the Yakima, the Spokane, and also the Nez Percé, the other half of Jay Bishop's heritage, all of whom roamed these plains not so long ago.

I caught a cab, intending to go straight to the college up on the hill to the southwest of the city. The law school seemed as logical a place as any to start on this quixotic search, but when I checked to make quite certain Wayne Daniels's letter of authority was safe in my briefcase, I saw Jay's home address and decided to begin there instead.

The cab deposited me in front of a tall, narrow house, in a quietly soporific street of neglected houses, too large for today's families, all with cracking siding and untended yards, the type of neighborhood that clings round many campuses. The shades were pulled at the windows of the house as though it hadn't yet opened its eyes. The air was chill, much colder and drier than in Seattle. I threaded my way between bicycles and barbecues and garden furniture that seemed to be waiting for summer, up wide and uneven steps to a wooden porch. The porch sloped in two different directions, inducing a queasy sensation, as if the whole building was about to tip over and crash on me. Most of the front door was an opaque glass panel etched into an elaborate floral design, and beside the door was a series of buttons with a list of names in faded ink. One of the names was *Bishop,* so I pressed that button.

A faint echo of ringing sounded somewhere deep inside the house. There was, not unexpectedly, no answer. I tried the handle of the door and it didn't open, so I pressed another bell and then another. After a long while, after I'd given up hope of anyone ever answering, a muted shuffling came from the other side of the door and a dark shape loomed through the glass. The door creaked ajar, agonizingly slowly.

Through the gap, a sallow-skinned youth gaped at me, as though astonished to discover a real person standing outside. Lank blond hair flopped around his face, and a thin growth of beard dusted hollow unhealthy cheeks; his jeans had ragged holes at the knees, and his feet were bare and none too clean. From the blank expression in the pale eyes, I guessed he'd only just staggered out of bed. He screwed his eyes against the daylight and blinked foolishly.

"Hey, man. What's up?"

I offered him a card, but he didn't seem to notice. "My name's Noah Richards. I'm a lawyer. I'm looking for Jay Bishop's room."

His jaw dropped. "Hey, Jay's dead, you know that? What a crock of shit, eh?"

"That's why I'm here. Can I come in?"

He hung on the door, as if it were the only thing keeping him upright, and after a while, I leaned against it and eased my way inside. He didn't try to stop me but backed away uneasily into the center of a dark hallway. There were closed doors on all sides, a wide uncarpeted staircase, a pervasive odor of unwashed clothes, cigarettes, old pizza, and pot.

I looked around. "Is there some kind of manager here?"

"Hell, we don't have no manager. We've a landlord, that's about it."

"I need to get into Jay's room. Can you show me the way?"

He yawned and scratched at his chest and was sensible enough to ask, "You say you're a lawyer?" I shoved my card into his unresisting hand, and he peered at it for a full five seconds. I said, "I just want to look in Jay's room."

The boy looked around vaguely, then mumbled, "There might be a key in the kitchen. And some coffee." I followed as he scuffed his bare feet through the hallway into a large untidy room dominated by a huge TV, the floor strewn with newspapers and books and clothes. He seemed confounded by the sight of the room. "Everyone's at school, I guess. I don't have class until one."

"You're a student?" I was surprised. He didn't appear to have enough physical or mental energy to attend classes.

"Computer science," he said, which surprised me more.

Beyond the living room was the kitchen, another scene of disaster, countertops littered with boxes of cereal and mugs and plates, catsup bottles, jars of jam and mayo and peanut butter, a sinkful of dirty dishes, a table in the middle with yet more dishes. The boy fished in the sink, rinsed a couple of mugs, filled them from a coffeepot on the counter, handed me one, and then collapsed into a chair, the effort obviously too great for him. He took a swig of the coffee, groaned, and closed his eyes. "Geez. I was fast asleep when all those bells started ringing."

I took a sip of the coffee. It was very black and bitter, brewed too long. "What's your name?"

He opened his eyes. "Pete. I thought the place must be on fire or something. I got out of bed too quickly, you know how that is? Like the whole world goes round?"

I sat down at the table. "So, Pete, you heard what happened to Jay?"

He brushed the hair from his eyes. "Sure, we heard. It's not every day one of your roommates gets shot, you know. A policeman or something came last week to look in his room and said it was probably some sort of accident." His mouth pulled down in a grimace. "Fucking guns."

So Pete and I had something in common, after all. I, too, hated guns and what they did to people. "Where's the key to Jay's room?"

He stared around vaguely. "It'll be here somewhere. Over there on the bulletin board?"

The bulletin board was covered with scraps of paper, instructions about the garbage, reminders to turn out lights, reminders about cleanup duties. Obviously, nobody ever read the instructions. Half a dozen keys hung on nails, none of them labeled.

"One of these?" I asked.

He shrugged. "Don't ask me. Ask Maria."

"Maria?"

He swallowed more of the unpleasant coffee, savoring it as though it were nectar, opened his eyes wider. I thought I could detect the beginnings of a glimmer of intelligence. "His girlfriend, man. She's pretty cut up. She's up there asleep for all I know. She comes and goes all hours; some waitress job keeps her out till past midnight."

"She isn't a student?"

Pete reached for a box of cereal, filled a bowl with cornflakes and milk, and started shoveling it into his mouth, not looking at me. "Sure, she's a student. At the community college. Same as me. And she works, same as the rest of us. How do you think we're gonna pay for school? You know how much tuition is? You know how much it is to rent a place?" He gestured with the spoon at the flakes in the bowl. "To eat?"

No, I guess I didn't know. Rent and food weren't so expensive when I went to school, and anyway my folks paid the tuition and rent. Sometimes I forgot how fortunate I was.

"Did Jay work?"

Pete's smile was knowing and lopsided. "Hell, man, Jay was Native American. He was on scholarship. Third-year law. He didn't have to do grunt work like the rest of us. I think he did something with some lawyer somewhere." He shrugged again. "Ask Maria. Top of the stairs, first door on the left."

I picked up my briefcase, left the coffee "Sorry I woke you, Pete."

"No sweat. I guess it was time to wake up anyway."

I watched him devouring the cereal as though he hadn't eaten for days. It reminded me how hungry I was at that age, how I'd eaten like that at all hours of the day and night, cereal and pasta and junk food. Pete looked as though he needed something more solid inside him; he was too thin and haggard, too stretched out in the painful process of a boy struggling to become a man. "What do *you* do to keep food on the table, Pete?"

"Me? I got a real fun job, man. Three nights a week, I do data entry at a warehouse store. It's a real blast."

"But then you'll be set for life. Computer science. Can't fail these days."

"Yeah, well. If you hear of a good job, let me know. I can't wait."

I remembered how that felt, too. How those years and years of school spin out to infinity when one is twenty years old, how hard it is to believe it will ever be done, how anxious one is to finish and yet fearful of what lies beyond, worried whether any jobs will be waiting and unsure which job will be the right one. How we're all on some kind of treadmill, school and work and uncertainty, trying to keep body and soul together, waiting and hoping for some bright unknown future.

I put a hand on his shoulder. It felt frail and bony beneath my fingers. "Take care, Pete."

A streak of milk ran down his chin. "It's shit about Jay, isn't it? I used to help him out with his PC sometimes, you know."

"You did?" I placed my briefcase back on the chair, carefully. "You don't happen to know what he was working on, do you?"

"I never looked at what he was working on. Some sort of legal stuff, I guess. Jay was a real geek about the computer at first. I'd sort out the files for him . . . basic stuff, you know."

"It's here? His computer?"

"Yeah, sure. In his room."

"Pete, you might be just the person I'm looking for. I'm not too hot on computers myself. Maybe I'll come to you for some help."

The prospect didn't appear to overexcite him. He remained slumped over the table.

"I'll pay you," I said.

The pale eyebrows raised and hope seeped into the watery eyes, and I patted his shoulder again, went through the communal living room and up the dark wooden stairs. The stairs were uncarpeted and dusty. I wondered if anyone ever cleaned this place. The first door on the left at the top of the stairs was closed, like all the other doors. I knocked, gently at first, then louder. There was no answer. The knob turned under my hand, the door swung open. "Maria? Are you here?"

The room smelled even worse than the rest of the house, like old sour food and unwashed clothes. From the opposite wall, a window let in a faint glow of daylight through the blinds. The room was quite large, a bed against the wall nearest the door, a couple of easy chairs, and under the window a desk with a computer. The bed was unmade, bedclothes heaped haphazardly.

"Maria?" I said again.

A faint moan came from the heap of coverings, a slight upheaving, then the quilt fluttered and subsided into stillness once more. From under the covers, there came a gentle rhythmic snoring. One has to be very young to sleep like that. I thought about leaving her to sleep, but I was here on Wayne's mission, all the way from Edward's Bay.

"Maria," I whispered, not really wanting to waken her. "I've come from Jay's family. I'm going to look around. I'm going to put the light on now. Don't be alarmed." I flicked on the switch by the door. An old-fashioned overhead fixture lit the room, not brightly, the big bed, the worn carpet on the floor, the desk by the window. I could just see a fan of dark hair spread on the pillow. Crossing to the window, I snapped up the shade, a fast rolling sound that clicked and clattered in the silence. "Sorry," I apologized to the bed behind me.

The computer was an elaborate affair with a large monitor and a sound system. I rummaged around on top of the desk, not know ing what I was looking for. There was a pile of law-school textbooks, not too many, and I riffed through their pages, pulled out the desk drawers one by one, some stuffed with papers, some with clothes. The papers were neatly typed treatises on constitutional law, tort and tax law, ordinary law-school material that took me back to my own law-school days. I guess I knew all this stuff once upon a time.

The information that Wayne or anyone else might need was almost certainly stored right here in this computer's little plastic heart. I pressed the power switch, and the machine sang into life, literally, with a merry little tune that fractured the silence of the room. It was fancy hardware and software for a student. The monitor flashed into life, running commands and pulsing, waiting for me to give it the password, and I was already lost.

I kept glancing over my shoulder for signs of movement from the sleeping Maria, but even when the computer broke into its song, the shape under the heaping bedclothes just twitched. When the blind went up so noisily, she'd merely moaned slightly. I thought she'd wake suddenly and start screaming, and was impressed that any female could sleep so peacefully with a stranger in the room. A man, no less. Were there no warning devices built into her system?

Making a cursory search of the closet nearer the bed, I found nothing but a few more clothes and the ordinary belongings of a healthy young male. They seemed infinitely sad now—a football with the air gone out of it, a worn baseball mitt, a well-used baseball bat. I was uncomfortable at playing detective without a warrant, uncomfortable with the sleeping presence in the bed so near to me. Inching closer to the bed, I peered down at the black hair tumbling across the pillow. I wanted Maria to wake up now so that I could at least ask her some questions, was wondering how to waken her without frightening her, when I realized the bad smell in the room was stronger here, as though it was emanating from the bed. A rotting human waste smell.

Sudden alarm shot through me.

"Maria?" I shook the mound under the bedclothes, urgently, roughly. Another slight moan was the only response. "Maria?"

I pulled the quilt back, gently at first, uncovering her face. There was absolutely no reaction. The dark head lay still, eyes closed, head turned sideways, and tiny bubbling noises came from the flaccid mouth. As I drew the quilt back farther, I saw that, beneath her face, a pool of vomit was soaking into the pillow and sheets.

She wasn't sleeping. She was unconscious.

"Dear God!" Yanking the quilt from the bed, wrapping it roughly around her, I plucked her off the mattress. "Pete," I yelled. "Pete, are you still here?" I headed for the stairs, the girl a deadweight in my arms, her head bobbing and flopping against my shoulder, the quilt dragging around my feet. I couldn't see the stairs beneath me, groped for each one with my feet. "Pete!" I yelled again. "For God's sake, where are you?"

He appeared just as I reached the bottom step with my burden, and the expression on his face might have been comical under other circumstances, his mouth drooping open, pale eyes round and astonished, completely awake at last. "What the hell . . . ?"

"Call 911. Quick. She must have taken something. She's totally out of it."

He dithered for a moment, skittering on his bare feet, shot back into the living room. I heard his voice on the phone, high and excited.

Now I had the girl downstairs, I didn't know what on earth to do with her, didn't know the right thing to do for someone who was unconscious, apart from keeping the airway clear. But her breathing was regular enough, if a little labored, and after a moment, the rush of panic subsided, and I sank on the bottom step, cradling her in my arms. I pulled the quilt away from her face and saw how young it was, soft and puffy, like an overripe peach, her mouth slack and open, a spittle of stale vomit sliding sideways along one cheek, the smell of it unpleasant. Her skin was damp and cold to my touch, and her dark-lashed eyes were swollen shut, and when I lifted one eyelid, only the whites were visible, rolling up into her head. The sightlessness made me shudder. God knows how long she'd been lying there in that room. I cursed myself for not having realized sooner that something was terribly wrong. I thanked heaven that chance brought me to the room this morning because how much longer might she have lain there?

Mercifully quickly, a team of medics came screaming up to the house, and as I handed the limp body over to them and watched them work their magic, I couldn't help think how often this same scenario had repeated itself lately, as though everyone who came into contact with me these days ended up dead or near death. An unpleasant, unhappy thought.

SEVENTEEN

THE MEDICS ASKED FOR MARIA'S NAME, AND IT TURNED OUT that Pete didn't know it. I was appalled by this ignorance, but obviously, unidentified victims of trauma and overdoses were everyday normalities to the medics. They searched her arms and legs for needle marks. "Any sign of pills?" one of them wanted to know.

I hadn't thought of looking for pills and started back up the stairs to the room, but before I was halfway up, they were already bundling the girl and the stretcher out the door, together with the drips and the beeping machines. Gone, it seemed, almost as soon as they'd arrived. As though it had been nothing but a bad dream. Except for the all too familiar sound of sirens wailing in the quiet street, lingering in the morning air.

I came slowly back down the stairs. "For God's sake, Pete! How could you possibly not know her name. She lived here, didn't she?"

He hunkered down on the bottom step, legs folded into sharp vees, knees poking through the holes in the jeans, head drooped over his thin neck, his face screwed into a semblance of shame. But he shrugged his shoulders almost carelessly. "She didn't pay rent or anything. She was just Jay's girlfriend. That's what he said. 'This is Maria, my girlfriend.' I never asked questions. Not my business, was it?"

I shook my head in despair. "How long has she been here?"

"Two, three months? They come, they go. Boyfriends, girlfriends. Some stay longer than others." He tried looking hopeful. "One of the others might know something about her."

"How many others are there?"

He had to think about it for a moment. "Eight, maybe? It changes. Sometimes more. Sometimes less." His hands flapped feebly. "Hey, you know how it is. I go to school. I go to my job. I hang out with my friends. Maria, I just saw her now and then. She wasn't my business, was she?"

I wanted to be angry with him, but the way his body collapsed in on itself, arms and legs too thin, face scrawny and dejected, made me understand he was merely inadequate, a child attempting to grow up and cope with life, without strong enough ties to his everyday world. He should still be living at home with his mother and father. Maybe all of us should still be living at home with our mother and fathers. But it depressed me that a young woman could lie unconscious and unnoticed in a room in a house where eight of her peers lived, even her name unknown, as if this were a place of transients, of nobodies, children of no account.

"Someone, somewhere, has to care whether she's alive or dead," I said. "There has to be something in that room to identify her. A purse or something. We'll go look. Someone needs to be told about her. She has to have relatives somewhere."

Pete didn't look happy at the prospect. He mumbled, "I got class at one."

I clutched him firmly by the bony shoulders, pushed him up the dusty stairs. At the bedroom door, he dragged his feet and scuttled in sideways, eyes darting in fearful anticipation, as if we might come across another unconscious body. He avoided looking at the bed. "God, it stinks in here," he said and shuffled quickly to the window, pulled up the sash, and stuck his head out into fresh air, breathing deeply. I looked under the pillow for pills, then under the bed, but found only more dust, and bundled the stained sheet off the bed and dumped it outside the room.

Pete turned to face me. "Hey, listen. I'm sorry if Maria tried to off herself. I'm sorry none of us came up here and checked on her. I'm sorry about Jay. Geez, man, I'm sorry about life, that's the truth." He wiped the back of his hand over his mouth, and his eyes teared up as though he was the one who needed sympathy. Which maybe he did. And maybe he'd take more notice of his roommates from now on.

Maria's abandoned clothes lay in a small pathetic heap on the floor by the bed, where she'd dropped them before crawling under the covers and into oblivion. I picked them up, one by one, a dark skirt and white blouse, a pair of sandals, a cheap vinyl purse. In the purse was a driver's license with her photo, without the swollen shut eyes and slack mouth; in the photo she was smiling at the camera, not confidently, but with open eyes and full curving lips. In the photo she looked about seventeen, but the birth date on the license told me she was twenty years old and that her name was Maria Guadalupe Cruz.

Her home address, as of a year ago, was Omak, Washington, in the central valley. It could be difficult to track down the Cruz family in Omak. A lot of families with names like Cruz worked in the orchards up and down the Yakima valley, through the Okanogan, many of them illegal, whole communities of transient workers, rarely of any fixed abode, temporary addresses here and there, kids sometimes going to school, often not. Maria Cruz was among an unusual minority who got as far as community college, which already labeled her as different. Like Jay Bishop. It was Jay's life I was supposed to be investigating, but now I was diverted by someone else's, someone who'd literally landed in my lap.

"Is she Mexican?" I asked Pete.

"She's American."

"Are you sure? Not an illegal?" But I didn't really expect Pete to know, and it was probably only important for locating her family. I held Maria's driver's license in my hand for a moment. "I'll call this address into the hospital. Hospitals have ways of tracing people."

I folded her clothes into a pile on the bed. The time was already past noon, and not a thing accomplished. Unless saving a life counted. Going over to the desk, I gazed at the fancy computer. "You have any idea how to get into this? You know the password?"

Pete galvanized into action, obviously glad to do something he knew how to do, plonked himself down at the desk, and rattled some letters on the keyboard. The computer responded immediately.

"I helped Jay set this thing up. He didn't know squat about computers when he started. But he had to have a password, of course, so he used this one, something about bird watching, he said." Pete spelled the word out. "k-i-r-o-w-b-i-n-i."

I wrote the word out on a piece of paper, stared at it. I remembered Jay had mentioned bird watching, but I hadn't taken much notice. It seemed such an unlikely pastime for him. "What is it? An Indian word?"

"I don't know. A sort of joke," he said. "More about girls than birds, I think."

Pete's fingers were going faster than his mouth, and now the computer was playing little tunes as he flicked rapidly in and out of the labyrinths as if changing gears on a racing car. In no time, a list of documents appeared on the screen. He stared at the list and frowned. "Not much on the hard drive. Jay hasn't had this PC for long, and see, he's used very little space." He zipped in and out of the texts, the words going by too fast for me to read and understand them. "Looks like law-school crap. Beats me. You better read it." Pete flicked away some more, compulsively. "Hey, this machine might be on-line to another one, though."

The screen display was changing so fast it made me dizzy. I didn't pretend to know what Pete was doing or how he was doing it.

"See," he said, pointing, and of course, I didn't see, "if I go to Map Network Drive, there's this path to another computer. Then I go to Dial-up Networking and get a connection, but it's a dedicated line to another computer. I can't get in without the password. Which I don't know." Pete brushed lank strands of hair away from his eyes and hit a few more keys. "No. Nothing obvious. Not yet. But I could break in for you. Might take a while, though."

"Break in? Like hacking, you mean?"

"Sure," he said and licked his lips. "No sweat. We do that sort of stuff all the time." His pale eyes had lost their faint idiot glaze; now they gleamed with a kind of intelligence. "You'd be amazed what we can get into when we really try."

"I might be amazed, Pete, but I also happen to know it's not legal. Don't do it for me. I'm supposed to practice the law, not break it."

"Aw, hell." He couldn't disguise his disappointment "It'd probably only take an hour or two. And it wouldn't cost a fortune."

"It isn't the money I'm thinking about."

"No? But I am."

His eager expression made me laugh "Unfortunately, by the terms of my license, I'm not permitted to make reimbursements for illegally obtained information."

"Shit. You make life tough for yourself, don't you? Being a lawyer?"

"Life's tough all over, Pete."

"Hey, man!" He pointed to the clock on the computer. "It's nearly one. I gotta go. I'll be late for class," he said, and he jumped to his feet, almost energetically. He stared around the room as if he'd forgotten where he was, and then he must have realized, Maria's room, Jay's room, a room of ill fate, and he headed for the door as though he couldn't wait to get out of there. I caught hold of one scrawny arm.

"Make sure you go to the hospital and check on Maria. Maria Cruz Don't forget. Don't leave her there alone. Promise me that?"

"Okay, okay, I will." He must have recognized the doubt in my eyes, because he repeated earnestly, "I promise."

I still had hold of his arm. "What's *your* last name, Pete?"

He looked alarmed, as if he was about to be accused of a crime. "Why? Going to check up on me, too?"

"I'd like to know, so that if anything ever happens to you, I won't feel ashamed for not having asked."

"Okay, okay, I get the point. But don't go making trouble for me, okay? It's Sherman. Pete Sherman."

"I won't make trouble for you, Pete Sherman. Just don't forget Maria's name. Cruz, remember? And my name's Noah Richards. Here's another card." I folded his limp unwilling fingers over it. "Call me and let me know how Maria is."

He looked at the card and grimaced, stuck it quickly into the pocket of his jeans where I was sure he'd forget it, and slipped out of the room the same way he'd come in, sideways. His bare feet made no sound on the stairs.

I stayed at the computer, examining the list of documents he'd brought up on the screen, punched up the different texts, and scrolled rapidly through, but they seemed to be identical to the papers in the desk, term papers for the most part, nothing pertaining to tidelands or Edward's Bay or the Quanda. Nothing useful to me. If anything else was stored in the computer, I didn't know how or where to look. I messed around with commands, clicking on several different icons, getting nowhere, and then, somehow, inadvertently, I hit the right button, and there on the screen, flickering into life, was exactly the document I'd been hoping for. The beginnings of a treatise on the Quanda, a history of the tribe, family connections, and letters and contemporary accounts of the tribe in the middle of the nineteenth century. Fascinating stuff. But only a work in progress, jottings, notes, no attributions, no references or footnotes. No conclusion.

I hit the print button, and the printer spewed out a half dozen pages. I read them again. At least it was something to show Wayne. If I hadn't stopped Pete connecting to the other computer, maybe I'd have been found who Jay was working with. And somewhere there had to be the original documents he'd used as sources.

I watched the buglike icons flitting around the screen and vaguely wondered what the password meant. If it meant anything at all. Girls, Pete said. And what had Wayne said? "That Jay. Had more girls than you can shake a stick at."

Had Maria known there were others? I pondered the fate of those two unlucky young people, Jay Bishop and Maria Cruz, star-crossed, destined never to fulfill the American dream of upward mobility. I supposed there was hope that Maria Cruz might yet make the American dream, but her chances didn't look so hot. Suicide attempts aren't a happy precursor for one's future.

I hadn't called in her name and address to the hospital. I abandoned the computer to go through her purse once more. The wallet contained a few dollars and a snapshot of two small children who could be relatives, the same black hair and thick lashed eyes. Her student ID card was a year old, like the driver's license, but it did prove she'd been registered as a student. Turning the purse upside down, I shook the contents onto the floor. A lipstick and comb fell out, a roll of mints, a coin purse, a Tampax, a key, five pills in a screw of tissue, and an inhaler, the type that asthmatics use. I examined each object in turn. The key had a bright green plastic label attached to it—Spokane City Savings Bank—and looked like a safe-deposit key. I weighed the inhaler in my hand. It could surely have some significance for her medical care. The pills, too. I knew I was about to make yet another reluctant trip to yet another hospital.

Nothing in the purse connected Maria with Jay Bishop in any way, and pawing through it made me feel intrusive and indecent, prying into a life I'd no business with. Which sounded a lot like Pete. Maria Guadalupe Cruz would be my business now and forever. Save someone's life and you're responsible for them forever. I hoped to God she'd make it so I could worry about her for a long time to come.

I replaced the purse's contents, switched off the computer, closed the door to the bedroom, and went downstairs to call for a cab from the phone in the communal living room. The house was big and echoing around me, its disorder dismal. Even unlively Pete had given it some semblance of life. A small heap of newspapers lay on the table by the phone, and as I waited for the cab company to answer, I read the papers idly, upside down, and realized they were all folded to stories about Jay Bishop. His narrow black eyes stared out of grainy photographs, disdainful and proud. Local Student Found Dead. St. Benedict's Law Student Shot Dead in Western Washington. The reports with the photos were superficial and noninformative, and though it was more than anything I'd seen in the Seattle papers, nowhere was the possibility of murder raised. As if Jay Bishop were shot by an act of God.

At the hospital, I attempted to hand Maria's purse in at the front desk, but no one would take responsibility for it, and so I made yet another visit to yet another emergency room. The rushing and clattering, the stainless steel and the bright lights and the tension in the air, weren't as threatening anymore; I was growing inured to the drama of hospitals. A nurse listened to my explanation about Maria and took the purse from me. I hardly dared ask the question, "How is she?"

The nurse shrugged, casual about matters of life and death. "We pumped her out, but she hasn't responded well. She probably aspirated vomit, which might mean brain damage. The oxygen supply gets cut off to the brain. She's going to the ICU. You want to see her?"

I shook my head. I'd no need for any more bedside vigils. "I don't know her. I just happened to find her. You'll look for her family, won't you?"

I kept the key. It couldn't help the doctors and nurses, but it might help me. There were four different branches of Spokane City Savings Bank in the phone book, and I took another cab to downtown. On the second try, I hit pay dirt. The young woman in charge of safe-deposit boxes said, "Yes, this is one of ours. Registered in the name of Jay Bishop."

I flourished my letters of authority, and she fetched the branch manager, who read the in loco parentis document and the handwritten note from Wayne and handed them back to me. "Sorry, sir. You claim this Jay Bishop is deceased, but we need a death certificate. A power of attorney. We have strict rules."

He was polite but firm, and I wasn't surprised. It shouldn't be easy to get into anyone's safe-deposit. But it's a pity a lawyer is bound by legal rules because I might have fudged my way into it otherwise. I could have forged Jay Bishop's signature. I was almost certain the box would contain at least some of the source materials for the unfinished history of the Quanda. I could see them in my mind's eye, photos and tape recordings, copies of letters and diaries. History in the making.

There was one more visit to make before the flight back to Seattle. It was getting late in the day, and when I reached St. Benedict's, a Victorian stone structure, grim and rather forbidding, the clock on the Gothic tower told me time was running out. The registrar's office was already closed for the day. I wandered the corridors like a new student, the smell of institutional paint and waxed floors familiar, and found no one to answer any questions. The law school was closing down for the day, a sleepy air of business done. I tried to imagine the gleaming young Indian in these echoing corridors, in the empty classrooms, and somehow it was a place he didn't belong. Anymore than he seemed to have belonged in the dusty house where Maria slept. Jay Bishop's spirit had flown.

I took the safe-deposit key back to Seattle with me. Wayne would be able to get into the box. I hoped he'd find Jay's spirit there.

EIGHTEEN

AT THE HOUSE IN EDWARD'S BAY, I TOSSED AND TURNED ALL night long, unable to escape the sound of the surf that once was so soothing. Whenever I closed my eyes, the picture of Jay Bishop's dead eyes, Maria Cruz's bruised-peach face and swollen eyelids, swam before me.

The next day, I related it all to Charlie—the trip to Spokane, about Jay Bishop and Maria Cruz—showed him the unfinished tribal history, heard the explanations coming out of my mouth, and somehow the whole expedition sounded idiotic and without purpose. Maybe it was the way Charlie looked at me, as though I'd lost my mind.

"I don't understand this farting around with this Indian stuff, Noah. You gotta learn to concentrate on what you know, which isn't running around the country playing nursemaid to a bunch of deadbeat Indians. Are we ever going to get paid for the trouble? You think we can live on air?"

"They're no more deadbeat than most of our clients, Charlie. One of them was murdered, remember. That's reason enough to be interested. Anyway, I thought you agreed I should look into it."

Charlie stabbed a threatening finger into the air "Looking into it is one thing; making a living out of it is another. If it was murder, it's a problem for the DA and the police, who, I'd like to remind you, get recompensed for their labors. It's not for attorneys who're supposed to be billing hours and paying their staff."

"And what about the land dispute, the tidelands issue? The tribal sovereignty?"

"Noah, the whole fucking U.S. of A. is disputed land as far as the Indians are concerned. They're claiming territory all over the damn country, tying up courts and developments from here to Connecticut. From California to Maine. Don't ask me to sympathize with them. They signed those treaties way back when, and now they're crying foul. Anyway, most of those tideland issues have already been settled in the courts. If your tribe had a legitimate claim, no one would've dared build on their precious beach."

Charlie was steamed. I hadn't seen him so riled up since I'd come into the practice. He had a point. In a way. But he hadn't listened to Wayne Daniels. Found Jay Bishop on the beach. Plucked an unconscious girl out of her soiled bed. I was personally involved now. I couldn't just walk away.

I said, "I'd like to show this Quanda document to someone who knows about tribal status."

Breathing heavily, Charlie rustled papers around his desk. "The sex harassment deal. We're going to pursue it. I think she's got a good case."

"You think so?" I dragged my mind back to the daily grind. "I haven't spoken to her yet. Some aspects of her story I find pretty hard to believe."

Charlie's eyes narrowed, a nasty shade of blue. "Well, get on and speak to her. What are you waiting for? Christmas?"

I retreated to my own room. I asked Sibby, "What's the matter with Charlie? His temper isn't too sweet this morning."

Sibby shrugged her shoulders in her exaggerated fashion, rolled her eyes upward. "He doesn't have enough work. He always gets upset when cases aren't flooding in."

I couldn't help noticing that Sibby's skirt was shorter than usual today. Which meant very short. The brief material rode up her long narrow thighs, and it was difficult to keep my eyes off the ripple and flow of her muscles. I thought she must be spending a lot of time working out at the gym.

"What you ought to know, Noah," she said, coming closer to the desk, dropping her voice, "is that the divorce settlement isn't going too well. I think we might be in for a bumpy ride." She was practically whispering now. "Better watch out for your stake in the practice. I've a feeling Annie and Joel might be laying a claim on it."

Joel was Charlie's former associate, the one Annie ran off with. Perhaps "ran off" wasn't exactly the right term. One day she'd packed a suitcase and moved a few blocks to his downtown condominium.

I stared into Sibby's face, only inches away from mine. "Is that possible?"

But of course, it was possible. It had just never entered my thick head before. I'd considered Charlie's divorce as purely his own business, but suddenly I saw my new life crumbling into financial disaster, profits disappearing into the maw of a community property settlement. A practice dispute! God knows there were enough of those around. Every legal firm has horror stories about the pitfalls of dissolving partnerships, about fights over financial and client territory. Charlie hadn't told me, and I hadn't asked, what his arrangements were with Joel, but I'd come into the office on a retainer and a percentage of the practice take, which would increase until I reached parity. Parity, I could see, might take a hell of a long time if his ex-wife and ex-partner were going to lay claim to everything.

I said, "What on earth is Charlie going to do?"

Sibby raised her eyebrows. "You're asking me? You're the lawyer."

"Lawyers can't take care of their own lives any better than nonlawyers."

She grinned cheerfully. She didn't seem too worried about impending doom. "Like cobblers and their kid's shoes? Like doctors and their families?"

I kept staring at Sibby, then all of a sudden realized there was something different about her, and was diverted for an instant. "Sibby, you've got your braces off!"

She smiled again, dazzlingly.

"Hey, you look great! Just great."

She did. Without the ugly metal bands that had striated her mouth ever since I'd first known her, and that had made her look like a goofy teenager, she was, all of a sudden, an attractive woman. Almost beautiful. It was quite astounding what a difference the newly radiant smile made.

"I can't believe I didn't notice right away. Congratulations! Is the boyfriend equally impressed?"

"What boyfriend?"

"Charlie said you were getting your teeth straightened for some guy."

Sibby frowned. "I did it for myself."

"Oh! Of course. Who else should you do it for but yourself?"

"Exactly." She smoothed down the silly skirt. "I'll go call that woman in the sex case."

I clutched my head in my hands. "Sibby! You tell me with one breath that the practice might be going down the drain and in the next expect me to deal with a sexual harassment mess."

She spoke soothingly. "You'll handle it just fine, Noah. You're so simpatico to women. Anyway, think about it this way. We need the business. You can get millions in settlements in that type of case these days."

I had to hope we wouldn't need millions. After Sibby left the room, I sat stewing on the perils of the situation. I'd imagined I was moving into some kind of financial security with Charlie Forsyth. What was the joy in dealing with sexual harassment cases, shoplifting, and DWIs if they didn't make one a decent living? I needed to pay the bills, too. Just as well I hadn't made Bigs an offer on the house. I wasn't sure I wanted the house anymore. I'd gone off Edward's Bay. Too bad. I'd imagined I could be settled there for life. But I'd definitely have to hold off doing anything until I knew where Charlie and I stood. I knew I ought to go talk to him immediately and didn't have the stomach for it.

The whole scenario put a damper on my spirits. I couldn't concentrate on the paperwork, shoveled it around the desk, scanned through the sexual harassment notes, and thought longingly of the bottle of scotch I'd kept in my desk in Springwell. Every five minutes or so, I looked at my watch, the day stretching into infinity. It wasn't only the concern about Charlie's problems, which could also be mine. I couldn't erase the memory of yesterday in Spokane. Of Maria Cruz. Of Jay Bishop.

I called the hospital to find out how Maria was doing, reached the charge nurse on the floor. She said crisply, "Maria Cruz's condition is listed as critical."

"What does that mean? Is she conscious?"

The voice was guarded. "No."

Somehow I hadn't expected that. Somehow I expected modern medicine to have taken care of Maria by now, just as it had taken care of Lauren Watson. It wasn't asking a miracle, was it, to wash a few pills out of her system? Surely, in this age of medical miracles, there wasn't any real danger? Was there?

"Is she going to make it? I thought she'd be okay by now."

As though she hadn't heard what I was saying, the nurse said,

"We've been unable to locate her family. Please let us know if you hear from them." And rang off.

I called Wayne Daniels to tell him about the day in Spokane. There was the usual silence while he digested and weighed my words; in the background, I could hear the faint chatter of the TV, pictured the woman in front of the set with the baby on her lap.

Wayne said, "This girl, this Maria, she was in Jay's room?"

"In his bed. You know about her?"

"What did you say her name was?"

"Maria. Maria Guadelupe Cruz."

"Doesn't sound Indian to me."

"Maybe not American Indian. But some other kind of Indian. Does it matter? She was his girl, Wayne. It looks as though she tried to kill herself rather than live without him."

More silence. He breathed heavily into the telephone, repeated what he'd said before. "That Jay was one busy guy."

"Wayne, this one lived with him. Now she's all alone. She's got no one to take care of her. Not those kids in the rooming house. They didn't even know she was up there. God knows where her family is. The hospital hasn't traced them so far."

I told him about the Quanda document on Jay's computer. About the safe-deposit box. "We'll get a death certificate, and you can go to Spokane and find out what's in the box. And you can go to the hospital and see Jay's girl. Will you do that, Wayne?"

Another long silence. At last he sighed and said, "If that's what you want, Mr. Richards, I guess you could say she's sort of family. But don't be surprised if there's more of them out there. Girls, I mean. Let's hope they don't all try to do themselves in, that's all I can say."

I called the coroner's office and arranged for a death certificate to be sent to Wayne. Then I studied Jay's Quanda treatise again, a lot more interesting than anything else on my desk. There had to be someone in town who dealt with Indian affairs, someone who'd tell me if this was of any worth. I wanted to believe it was of worth because maybe that was why Jay Bishop died. I took the yellow pages down from the shelf, opened it to the listing for attorneys, not something I normally needed to do, thumbed through the full-page ads given over to my profession, beaming photos of lawyers and paralegals, adjectives like "aggressive" and "vigorous" on every page. The listing for our office was relatively modest:

> Forsyth, Charles T., Free Consultation, Defense, Civil, and Criminal

No grinning photos of Charlie or the rest of the staff, thank God, but the pages and pages of hype reminded me what the competition was like out there; no wonder Charlie worried about the cases not flooding in. I shoved the yellow pages back onto the shelf in disgust.

I couldn't tolerate the day any longer.

"I'm leaving," I announced to Sibby. She sat at the computer in the outer office, doing her nails.

"Even the phone isn't ringing," she said. "No cases, no phone calls. No phone calls, no cases."

There was nothing to keep either of us chained to the office. "Come for a drink?" I suggested, hopefully. "To celebrate the demise of your braces?"

Sibby regarded me carefully, drew a haphazard line with her ever-present pencil on the ever-present yellow pad. Certain she was about to decline gracefully, I was grateful when she said, "Why not? Charlie's already gone." She reached for her jacket and echoed my own exact thoughts. "God knows, nothing of any value is happening here."

And once out of the office and onto the sidewalks of First Avenue, my spirits began to recover. Even on the darkest Northwest days, there's an air of festivity about Pioneer Square, about its old brick buildings, human-sized and accessible, about the hanging flower baskets and the ever-present tourists, the bookshops and sidewalk cafés, and the seagulls wheeling overhead. Even the characters plying their regular supplicant trade in the streets seemed cheerful. Today, there was the hint of spring in the air, a softening of green on the trees, a waft of salt on the breeze. Beside me, Sibby's stride was jaunty and long-legged. Her hair bounced on her shoulders, and she smiled her new, ravishing smile.

We hovered for a moment on the corner of First and Main, then headed for the restaurant round the corner where the wine is reasonably priced and the pasta arguably the best in town.

Sibby proved to be easy company. It was the first time I'd had her all to myself, and the tightness in my chest loosened as she chatted amiably about the latest play in town, the movie she'd seen the previous week. We ordered martinis instead of wine, and they came in wide satisfying glasses. We discussed the mayor and the destruction of the King Dome, the huge and monstrously ugly concrete stadium that once loomed over Pioneer Square. We agreed it was a shocking waste of taxpayer dollars to have pulled it down, even if it was so unattractive, and inevitably we got onto the perennial Seattle subject, the influence of Microsoft money on the city. "Affluenza," it was known as in Seattle. Affluenza was a disease, Sibby and I decided, that led inexorably to "Newmania."

Which led somehow to the house on Edward's Bay.

"You're really thinking of buying it?" Sibby wanted to know.

"I'm not sure. The magic has rubbed off. Nothing like coming across a body to disenchant you."

Sibby nibbled on the complimentary hors d'oeuvres with her fine new teeth. "Has anything ever come of that?"

"It's almost as though it never happened. As though it's been wished away. Which isn't reasonable, of course. They must want to know who's taking potshots at their neighbors as much as I do."

She polished off her martini. "But he was Indian, wasn't he? You think they care what happens to Indians?"

She'd come right out with it, the very thing I didn't want to admit to myself. "I hate to believe that."

"If you weren't such an idealist, Noah, you'd know it's a perfectly rational conclusion."

"Me an idealist? I'm a realist."

She laughed, not unkindly, shaking her head. "Noah, Noah! A babe unborn in the big harsh world. Why on earth did you take up something as hard-nosed as law in the first place?"

I launched into a speech, martini-driven. "I happen to believe in the rule of law. It's what this country was founded on. We're a people without a shared heritage or a long attachment to the land, strangers bound together only by man-made laws. The strength and the weakness of America. Without those laws we mutually agreed upon, what would we be?"

It was a nice little oration, noble and pretentious. I knew Sibby would be impressed. She looked at me for a moment, reached out, and touched my hand. "Shall we order another martini?"

I laughed. We had another drink. A pleasant alcoholic haze began to settle over me, driving the cares away. I suggested dinner, hoping Sibby didn't have something better to do. She said immediately, "Yes, why not? I have only a cat to go home to, you know."

We chose the food and a bottle of wine and Sibby said, inconsequentially, "I could never live on the other side of a ferry, always anxious about missing it. I like being in the city. I like my condo."

So we discussed her condo on Second Avenue, the merits and demerits of city living versus a beach and a ferry ride. She said, "Whatever happened to that neighbor of yours? The one with the sick baby? Did she ever take it to a doctor here in town?"

In my concerns about Maria Cruz and Jay Bishop, the concerns about Sarah and Christopher McKenzie had escaped my mind. So much seemed to have happened since the Sunday lunch with the Carlssons when I'd upset Sarah. "I tried to make the suggestion, but she thought I was interfering. Which I was, I suppose."

"But why does she live so far off the beaten track? A woman all alone with a baby? That's what you told me, wasn't it? That there's no husband in evidence?"

"Believe it or not, her husband is climbing Everest even as we speak. Apart from that, I don't know much about her." Which wasn't really true, now that I came to think of it. I knew a lot more about Sarah McKenzie than I realized. Knew she was unhappy and knew her loneliness attracted me. Or perhaps it was her baby that attracted me.

Sibby frowned. "Charlie was right, Noah. She's someone you ought to be careful about. I'd have found out all about her by now if I were you."

"Careful about her? Why do you say that?"

"You're awfully mixed up with her, if you ask me. Running off to the hospital every five minutes with her and her baby. Getting her to see your furniture into the house."

Obviously, I'd been talking too much to Sibby about my life outside the office.

"I know it's not my business, Noah, but you are a bit of a target. A nice single fellow, a lawyer, all alone. I'm a woman. I understand the motives of other women. For instance, I know all about you. About your wife. About your problems in Springwell. I made it my business to know. You should make it your business to know about this neighbor of yours."

I shook my head. "She's just a neighbor. One doesn't have to go looking for ulterior motives in everything."

Sibby shrugged and smiled, apologetically. "Just a friendly warning, that's all."

Maybe she was right. Maybe Sarah McKenzie was turning out to be more than just a neighbor. But what else did I need to know about her? She was married, and that was that. What else did I need to know about Sibby, for instance? She'd had her teeth straightened. And she worked in the same office as I did. And perhaps I was getting too friendly with her as well. Which wasn't such a smart idea if I wanted to remain working in the same office. Office relationships are far more of a complication than any sort of relationship with someone down the street.

I drank the last of my wine, taking care not to gaze too intently at the transformed Sibby. Her condo was just down the street from this restaurant. I could walk there with her instead of catching the ferry to Seawards. But even through all the martinis and the wine, I knew it wasn't a wise move.

If Sibby and I didn't work in the same office, I might have suggested we have dinner like this again, go to a movie or a play. And if she didn't work in the office with me, I supposed we'd not be here in the first place.

I paid the bill and said an altogether too abrupt goodnight to Sibby and her new smile and sprinted for the ferry.

NINETEEN

THE NEXT DAY, SIBBY WAS AS CHEERFUL AND FRIENDLY AS usual. she didn't seem to harbor any resentment about the abrupt end to the previous evening, didn't ask why I'd suddenly leapt to my feet and dashed for the ferry. I suppose I expected her to sulk with wounded pride because I hadn't gone home with her. Or at least *asked* to go home with her.

It was I, in fact, who sulked. Closed my door on Sibby, and on Charlie, and brooded. I wanted to tackle Charlie on the matter of the practice but rationalized there was only Sibby's whispered, unconfirmed suggestion about trouble brewing, not exactly hard evidence. But I couldn't put Charlie's problems aside, of course. Too much of my future depended on him. I was bogging down in indecision. Put the house in Springwell on the market? Forget about buying the house on Edward's Bay? Put out feelers for somewhere else to go into practice?

Just about then, Daphne called and rescued me from the doldrums. Not for the first time. "If you're coming up to Springwell anytime soon, Noah," she said, without preamble, "come and have dinner. And if you're not coming up for anything else, come and have dinner anyway."

"Funny," I said, "I was just thinking about putting the old house on the market. What do you think?"

Another thing I liked about Daphne was that she rarely waffled. If one wanted an honest opinion, she'd give it, often without being asked.

"I think it's time you sold it, Noah. You've moved on from Springwell. Time you moved on from that house. Imagine how wonderful it would be for some nice young family."

So it was decided. I called a realtor to make an appointment. The house had never been mine, of course. It had always belonged to my parents. And I *had* moved on, whether to Edward's Bay or somewhere else.

That evening, I went directly from the office to Edward's Bay, carrying the notes of a personal injury suit, as if to prove I really had work to do. No more hanging out with the office staff, I cautioned myself.

The last of the daylight was once again fading from the sky by the time I reached the house. The tide was high this evening, but on the turn, a few feet of bare wet sand were left behind as the waters began running out. I stood at the edge of the water, watched the beach grow imperceptibly larger, fascinated as ever by the movement of the waves and the rhythms of the oceans. Puget sound isn't really ocean, of course, merely a huge sheltered arm of the Pacific, but it was the connection of the sound to the Pacific that lured many of the early explorers hoping to find a way to the mythical Northwest Passage and so back to the Atlantic. But there is no lead to the Atlantic. Puget Sound comes to a dead end in the south. It leads only to places like Vashon Island, where Jay Bishop's boat had washed up.

As dusk gathered on the beach at Edward's Bay, the ghost of Jay Bishop seemed to haunt this portion of Puget Sound. His death and the manner of it were becoming an obsession, and I didn't want to be obsessed. But I couldn't stop thinking about the tide as it had flowed in and out of Edward's Bay that day.

Once upon a time, as a kid, I'd known a great deal about the tides in the sound. I'd been fascinated by the phenomena and collected data of tidal patterns from around the world as other boys collect baseball cards. My parents laughed when I wanted them to take me to the Bay of Fundy, where the rise and fall of the ocean is the greatest on earth, and though I never did get to the Bay of Fundy, I waited hopefully and kept studying other remarkable ebbs and flows. Such as the double high tides at Southampton, England, and those places in the China Sea where the tidal interval is every twenty-four hours instead of twelve. I suppose my interest in that particular useless knowledge faded about the time girls became of more interest, but if I'd realized that there were actually some people—oceanographers—who made a living knowing about such things, I might never have taken up law. Perhaps that's why my father hadn't encouraged my hobby.

On the beach at Edward's Bay, in the failing light, some half-forgotten phrases came back to me: diurnal inequality, harmonic development, dynamic theory. If only that sort of information could be of use in solving the mystery of Jay Bishop: who'd shot him and from where. If we knew from *where* he was shot, we'd surely know *who* shot him.

Who, from wherever, might be staring down the sights of a rifle right now, at me, just as they'd stared at Jay Bishop. Compulsively, I glanced over my shoulder. Along the beach, beyond the driftwood, the lights of a few houses winked in the gathering dusk. But if I were out in the bay in a boat instead of down here on the sand, I'd be in full view of *all* the houses around Edward's Bay, those down on the shore or up on the bluff. Scrunching my neck into my jacket, I moved on quickly.

Lights were glowing at Sarah's house as I passed it, and I was tempted to call on her, but I kept walking. It was ironic that after being so pleased to have neighbors, I was making so little use of them. Maybe, as the evenings grew lighter, I'd see more of them. But would I still be here when the evenings were lighter? And if not, where would I be?

Sarah once offered to cook dinner for me, invite some of the neighbors over; an evening like that would surely help break the ice, make me feel part of the community. The only people I'd met, apart from Sarah and Wayne, were those at the meeting, and then I'd not exactly met them. Merely observed them.

Turning around, impulsively, I went across the strip of sea grass that was Sarah's backyard and knocked on the kitchen door. Through the glass, I could see her engrossed at the kitchen stove, her head bent as she stirred something in a small pan, the bright fluorescent light reflecting on her hair. Christopher was strapped into his baby seat beside the table, and at the sound of my knock, they both looked round at the same moment, heads swiveling, eyes widening.

"It's me, Noah," I called and waved through the glass. Sarah frowned, as though not pleased to see me. And who could blame her? I'd hardly evinced much neighborly concern, either for her or the baby, these past few days.

Wiping her hands on a towel, slowly and deliberately, she cracked the door open a few reluctant inches. "Well, Noah Richards, as I live and breathe. I thought you must have died and gone to heaven."

"I've been busy," I said. "Traveling, too." The day in Spokane could surely be justified as travel. "I never seem to get back until after dark. There are, after all, certain disadvantages about living on the other side of a ferry."

She remained in the doorway for a long moment, unsmiling,

just looking at me, then she pulled the door an inch or two wider, without enthusiasm. "You might as well come in. I'm just giving Christopher his dinner."

I stepped gingerly inside the kitchen and prepared to make my peace with her. She slammed the door behind me, an impatient sound, but Christopher smiled with his two wet teeth. He looked, as always, perfectly well.

"How's he doing?" I asked.

Thumping a chair beside the table, Sarah sat down, and shoveled a spoonful of food into the gaping birdlike mouth. "He's fine." She didn't look at me.

"Did they ever find out what the problem was?"

She heaped another spoonful into his mouth. "I haven't taken him back to the hospital."

"Oh, Sarah!" I sat down on the chair beside her. "After all that worry? Don't you think you should?"

"It's not your damned business," she snapped, and her eyes glistened. "Me and my baby are nothing to do with you."

It felt as though she'd slapped me, a firm rejecting slap. There was another of those awkward silences that we seemed to generate between us, broken by the baby banging noisily on the table. I said, apologetically, "I'm sorry you feel that way, Sarah. Really sorry. I assure you it wasn't my intention to interfere."

"Oh, really? So why did you drag your doctor friend into it?"

"I thought I explained. I was concerned about Christopher. Isn't that natural, a little baby like him?"

"Look at him. Just look at him! Does he look as though I neglect him? Does it seem as though I'm not doing my duty as a mother?"

"I never meant to imply that you weren't."

"Oh no? What other kind of implication is there? That I'm not capable of caring for him in the right way? That I don't take him to the right doctors? That somehow I'm doing something wrong so that he gets these choking fits?"

She averted her face, the line of her jaw sharp-angled.

"I thought Chauncey could help with his problem, that's all. He specializes in allergies."

Turning, Sarah glared at me, her eyes hard and shiny, lips pressed tight. "Oh, why don't you just bugger off and leave us alone?" she said, and she pushed another spoonful at Christopher, blindly.

"Okay. I'll leave. If that's what you'd prefer. But remember, if you need anything well, you know where I live."

She didn't answer. I walked slowly to the door, and when I looked back, I saw tears rolling down her smooth cheeks and into her mouth. She made no sound or any attempt to wipe them away, just wept silently and somehow angrily, as though she didn't want to be weeping. Which was somehow more like the Sarah I hardly knew.

But when she dropped the spoon with a clatter and put her hands over her face, her shoulders hunched, a picture of misery, inevitably I was drawn back across the room to sit beside her. I put an arm around her shoulders. "It's all right," I said. "It's all right, Sarah. Maybe you just need to let it all out."

For a long moment, her body was stiff and unyielding, pulling away from me; then she collapsed against me and began to weep noisily, until her tears were wet on my shirt. She muttered muffled and incomprehensible words, her mouth pressed into my chest. And once she allowed herself to give way, the more out of control she became, more tearful and distraught, clutching at me, twining her hands into my clothes, as though, by being offered release, some dam had broken, letting loose a flood.

"Hush, hush," I tried to comfort her "It'll be all right, Sarah; it'll be all right."

The baby stared at us, his blue eyes round and unblinking, and then he began to cry, too, his sobs matching his mother's, rising in the room. Freeing one arm from Sarah, I plucked him out of his chair and held him as well, so that soon the three of us were locked in an embrace, our bodies warm together, gathering heat.

Quite suddenly, they both stopped crying and were quiet. Sarah pulled her head back, looked into my eyes, and kissed me, a hot moist kiss, her mouth urgent and clinging. And then somehow we were in the bedroom, where the last of the evening light shone dimly through the window; the baby was in his crib, where he sniffled and sighed and fell immediately asleep; and Sarah and I were on the bed together, groaning and kissing and pulling at each other, her body smooth and delicious, those rounded breasts heavy in my hands. I needed her, God, how I needed her, and she seemed to need me just as much, repeating my name, "Noah, Noah," again and again, her hands all over me, pulling me into her, drowning me in soft desirable female flesh. My own body was tumbling and rolling, unable to stop, never wanting to stop, needing more and more of the deep ocean of her body.

At some point, I fell asleep, abruptly, losing consciousness. At one moment I had been wide awake—all my senses, touch and taste and sight and hearing, alert and desperate—the next moment I was gone, as though I'd died. Happily.

But I hadn't died. I awoke, just as suddenly as I'd fallen asleep, my eyes wide open, the faint light of dawn creeping through the uncurtained windows. I could hear the baby breathing, regularly and lightly. I knew instantly where I was and why my body was so light and free. I lifted my head to look at Sarah. Her dark hair was spread on the pillow, and her face was slack and peaceful, mouth slightly parted, her breathing as gentle as the baby's. I watched her for a long time as the morning light grew gradually brighter; then I touched her shoulder and whispered into her ear, "Time for me to go now, Sarah." She reached for me without opening her eyes.

"I must go," I said again and kissed her face, lightly. "Thank you. Thank you, Sarah."

Perhaps I should have felt guilty as I slipped away from the house to walk back along the beach to my own house to shower and change and get ready for the day. Guilty for making love to a woman who was married to someone else, her baby right there in the room beside us. A woman as vulnerable and needy as Sarah seemed to be. But what I felt was only this incredible lightness of the flesh. And gratitude. And warmth.

TWENTY

BUT BY THE TIME I WAS ON THE FERRY AND IN LINE AT THE espresso stand, the warm fuzzy feeling was definitely wearing off. Sarah was married. I couldn't believe I'd let myself forget that so easily. Overstepped that basic canon of ethics. I found myself avoiding the eyes of my fellow passengers. No one was looking at me, of course. The early morning crowd, on their way to work in downtown Seattle, sipped their coffee, gazed at their morning newspapers, books, magazines, laptops, absorbed in their own world. Certainly not in mine.

I took the cup of foaming coffee to a window seat, stared out at the morning mist on the sound, at the clouds low over the mountains. The mountains inevitably reminded me that Sarah's husband, Christopher's father, was somewhere up among the clouds on the highest mountain of the world.

As the ferry nudged into the dock under the downtown towers, I knew I had to talk to Charlie about the practice problems today. I didn't look forward to it. Then I remembered that today was the day the woman in the sex harassment case had an appointment, something else I didn't look forward to. Did I imagine all legal problems could be handled without troubling the conscience in some way? That partners never got into financial difficulties? That men and women didn't ever have extra-marital sex? Was I naive enough to believe everyone behaved, always, in an upright, honorable manner? I guess that's what I'd been brought up to believe.

The sexual harassment woman arrived promptly at ten o'clock. Hardly a woman, just a kid really, twenty years old, soft and squishy with pale soft skin and a nervous giggle. But she wasn't too nervous to sit on the other side of my desk and recount, in a tiny thin voice, the sordid details of unwanted attentions from her boss. The lewd and graphic suggestions of sex didn't appear to embarrass her nearly as much as they did me; the explicit words of a male lusting after a female are not for repetition in the cold light of day. It was difficult stuff to have to listen to. Especially for someone who'd just climbed out of the bed of another man's wife.

I'd hoped to be able to judge whether this young woman could be believed, but at the end of an hour, I was no wiser. A perfectly ordinary young woman, in a perfectly ordinary skirt and sweater, she spoke openly to me, as though to a doctor or a priest, someone who wouldn't doubt her word. But I had to make her understand I wasn't a doctor or a priest. There were questions I had to ask. She acknowledged no one could substantiate her story, agreed she hadn't been threatened with demotion or promised a reward for sexual favors. And no, she hadn't complained to anyone.

"Who could I complain to?" she wanted to know. "He's my boss."

I tried to ask, delicately, if he'd had any reason to believe she'd welcome his advances. She dismissed the suggestion with a derisive shrug. "A married man with a couple of teenage kids? Why would

I be interested in him? I've a boyfriend my own age, thank you very much."

The whole business was distasteful. There was no particular reason to disbelieve her, except for a small uneasy feeling in my gut. The same uneasy feeling I had about Sarah McKenzie. I concentrated on the young woman's story. No one at her place of business had noticed anything, it seemed, but I'd worked in a large office myself, knew the gossip and innuendo that flew around, knew how many suspicious eyes watched every move of the bosses. Especially where nubile young women were concerned.

I said, eventually, "It's going to be difficult to prove, you know, without some kind of material evidence. Or a witness. You tell me he's been with the company for years. You've been there six months. It's going to be your word against his, I'm afraid."

She gazed at me with innocent, indignant eyes. "Well, it's not right. He shouldn't get away with such stuff. I ought to be able to do my job without a slimy old man putting his hands all over me and making filthy suggestions all the time."

"Indeed you should. I sympathize." I *did* sympathize. Even if her idea of old meant someone approximately my own age. Why make up such a story or put oneself through such an unseemly process—except to rake in a large settlement, of course. And if it were true, proving it could be quite another matter.

"I could wear a wire," she suggested. "Then you'd be able to hear for yourself."

She wasn't as innocent as she looked. "Unfortunately," I pointed out, "that's against the law in this state."

My yellow pad was filled with scribbled lurid notes. "I'll talk this over with my partner and let you know what we think."

I had the chance to talk it over with Charlie a little later. We convened in the so-called conference room, a nondescript space with a large table and a half dozen chairs, used mainly for depositions. From one corner window, Puget Sound was barely visible beyond the Alaskan Way viaduct. I loathed that ugly viaduct, the way it cut the city off from the water, the noise and dirt of traffic thundering directly in the line of vision, and I often wished the long-predicted earthquake would bring it down and be done with it.

Charlie didn't look well. There were dark circles under his eyes, and the usual dazzling smile was nowhere in evidence. We sat across the table from each other, and he gazed balefully at me, only half-listening to my estimation of the case, drumming his fingers on the chair arms, his eyes drifting to the window as though he'd prefer to be anywhere else but in this room.

I summed up quickly, giving up hope of engaging his interest. "Perhaps she's telling the truth. I wish I could be sure. But I don't see we have a hope in hell of proving it. Or proving she was injured in any way."

I waited for Charlie to respond. He didn't. There was a long pause. It seemed as good a time as any to bring up the question of the practice.

"Is there something on your mind, Charlie? Other than this case?"

His eyes swiveled to me, his head jerking as though he'd forgotten I was there.

"What?"

"I said, Is there anything you need to tell me?"

He glowered at me. "I don't know what the hell you're talking about."

"I'm talking about Annie and Joel. Particularly about Joel. I hear he's making a claim on the practice. Is it something to be concerned about?"

Charlie's face darkened and shrank in on itself, the muscles of his jaw clenching. The thick black eyebrows drew down in a fierce straight line. "Who the hell have you been talking to?"

"Does that matter? Is it true? Shouldn't you let me know what's going on? After all, I'll be involved if there's a problem."

"No, you won't," he snapped. "What happened between Joel

and me happened before you ever set foot in this office. I don't have to account to you for any of that. It's none of your damned business what Joel or Annie or I have going among us. Our deal, yours and mine, Noah, remains exactly as we agreed."

The tone of his voice was harsh and angry. The whole thing must have been eating him up inside.

I said, "Can't you at least tell me what it is you're arguing about?"

"Damn it, Noah! Don't you think I've enough on my plate without you trying to carve your own piece out of it? Haven't I spent years building up this practice without another vulture trying to tear his piece of flesh out of it? You walk in here with your goddamned noble ideas of right and wrong, trying to change the way I run the practice."

I was taken aback. "I'm not trying to change anything, Charlie. And frankly, I don't care to be termed a vulture."

He sat hunched in the chair, his eyes dark and resentful, and stabbed a finger at the file on the table. "You don't care for this sort of stuff, do you, Noah? Sex harassment. DWI. Shoplifting. Don't think you should soil your hands with it, do you? I can see it on your face. You'd rather be out there fucking around with Indians in another bleeding-heart cause."

I thought I'd kept my feelings better hidden than that. He didn't give me a chance to respond.

"Beggars can't be choosers, Noah. We take what we can get. That's the name of the game, and you should understand that by now. You're not some eager young beaver fresh out of law school. Don't think I don't realize you're only here because of Angel Ambrose. That's the kind of case you want, isn't it? Someone you think of as a victim. Someone who doesn't stand a hope in hell unless you ride in like a white knight on a white horse to save them. But how do you think we're going to pay for that kind of case unless we take all the other dross? Who's going to pay for Sibby and the rest of the gang? Who's going to pay the rent?"

I considered Charlie's accusations unwarranted. Until this moment, I'd assumed our partnership was working well. All this because I'd asked him to explain what might be happening to the practice, something I was entirely entitled to know.

"I'm sorry you feel this way, Charlie. What are you suggesting? That I offer my resignation?"

Charlie squinted across the table at me for another long moment. I stood up, gathered my notes together, prepared to walk out right there and then; but suddenly the anger seemed to seep right out of him. Making an obvious effort to relax, he leaned back in his chair, loosened his neck and shoulders, bared his teeth in a kind of smile. "Hell, Noah, if I wanted you gone, I wouldn't wait for you to resign. I'd fire you."

He reached over and grabbed my wrist tightly, thin fingers digging into my flesh. "Listen, I apologize, okay? I shouldn't have gone off half-cocked like that. I'm a bit stressed out over this business of Annie and Joel. It's bad enough to find out one's partner and one's wife are screwing each other, but then to find out they want to screw me as well . . . Shit, it's enough to make anyone mad."

He let go of my arm, slumped back in the chair and rubbed a hand over his face, and got to his feet, slowly and wearily. "If you think we should drop this sex case, Noah, then we'll drop it. I'm not sure I've the stomach for it either."

Which should have given me a sense of relief, but instead it bothered me that all the fight seemed to have gone out of him. I preferred Charlie feisty and combative, not acting like a beaten dog.

"About that personal injury claim," I said. "I've made some notes . . ."

"Later, Noah. Later." He flashed the unconvincing smile again. "Listen, I'm glad we aired our differences. Good to get things into the open, isn't it?" He stretched his arms above his head and slouched across the room, paused with his hand on the doorknob. "Oh, and by the way, Noah. Don't lead our Sibby down the garden path. It isn't good for office morale. There's already been quite enough trouble in that department."

My jaw dropped. I stood there like a fool and let him leave without a word in my own defense. Get things into the open indeed! He'd vented his spleen on me and then hadn't given me a chance to explain about Sibby. Though, damn it, what was there to explain? What had I done except take her to dinner? Why should he make me feel guilty about that? What I should be feeling guilty about was Sarah.

Sarah! The sudden memory of her smooth skin and silky hair made me dizzy. It doesn't do to allow the mind to linger on the pleasures of female flesh, not at the office. Makes it difficult to focus. I hurried back to my room, shut the door firmly to discourage any more unwanted conferences, saw in the daybook this was also the day I'd arranged to meet with the realtor in Springwell. And have dinner with Daphne and Chauncey. Damn! I considered canceling the appointment with the realtor, but knew I should go through with it. No more messing around.

But I thought I should let Sarah know I wouldn't be at Edward's Bay this evening. The phone at her house went unanswered I tried several times throughout the day. She didn't have an answering machine, and I thought I'd buy one for her. A small gift. Not a very romantic one, but useful. I'd no idea what sort of gift to give her. Sarah appeared to exist without the knickknacks other women liked. She didn't wear jewelry, smelled of soap and water, not perfume. I was already in over my head, already feeling pressure to give gifts, to explain where I'd be and why.

It was past four o'clock before I finally got hold of her. When she answered the phone, there was a lilt to her voice, a softness to her tone.

We spoke in foolish awkward pauses, until the words began to sound much like the words the young woman repeated in the office that morning. It put a definite damper on my end of the conversation.

"Sarah, I have an appointment in Springwell this evening. To meet a realtor and put my old house on the market."

"Oh?" There was suspicion even in the one syllable. "Oh, but showing the house won't take long, will it? You'll come back for dinner afterward?"

"I promised to have dinner with Daphne and Chauncey. They're expecting me. I'm sorry. Another evening, okay?"

There was a chilly little pause, then she said, "But *I* was expecting you for dinner. I've already been to the grocery store. I've made a special effort."

I suppose I was hoping she'd say, "I quite understand, Noah. Of course, you can't let your friends down." Instead she said, "Then I'll see you when I see you. When you can spare the time," and she put the phone down abruptly.

I was doomed to upset Sarah over one matter or another, in one way or another, but at the same moment, I had a sneaking sense of relief, a sense of temporary reprieve. Our next meeting was put off. Until, maybe, I'd have these mixed feelings sorted out.

I still hadn't located anyone who dealt with Indian matters, someone qualified to help the Quanda. I asked Sibby. "Isn't there a department at the University of Washington that deals with Indian affairs? You think you could find out for me?"

She said, "Indian affairs? Charlie probably knows someone."

But I didn't think it would help matters between Charlie and me if the subject of Indians was brought up again. Maybe tomorrow would be better. Tomorrow would be a better day for everything.

I left the office promptly at five, without seeing Charlie again, and set off for Springwell. The drive up the freeway in the evening rush hour was unbearably long and tedious compared to the ferry ride, but even so I arrived too early. There was more than enough time to drop into my old haunt, Joe's Tavern on Main Street. The Saab almost guided itself there.

Joe's, while nothing fancy, was a considerable step up from the Eagle's Nest. It wasn't glitzy or modernized, just comfortable and warm and, above all, quiet. No video games or taped rock music there, thank heavens. I hadn't been in Joe's for what felt like months, but it hadn't changed, of course. It hasn't changed in a hundred years, the dim lights and the long bar, the solid wooden stools, the thick log walls still decorated with the old and dusty tools of the lumber trade. It was good to be back.

"The usual?" the bartender said and slid a Heineken along the counter. "How've you been, Noah? Haven't seen you lately."

"I moved to a place on the other side of the sound. Quite a change from Springwell." An understatement. Springwell was on the wet side of the Cascade Mountains, in thick green conifer forests. Or what was left of the forests. The lumber industry that hacked the old growth down years ago had moved on, leaving Springwell behind, high and dry, you might say, if rain didn't fall on it constantly. Edward's Bay lay in the lee of the other range of mountains, the Olympics, which made for sunnier, almost arid weather, compared to Springwell.

There were never many customers in Joe's, but farther along the bar, I spotted a familiar face. This was, after all, my hometown. I expected to see people I knew. Bigs Harrison was at the far end of the bar, leaning on his elbows, staring into his drink. Lost in thought, it appeared. I walked my beer down to him.

"Hey, Bigs. What's up?"

He turned, startled, grinned halfheartedly. "Usual garbage. Arguing with the powers that be. What are you doing back in town?"

"As a matter of fact, I'm meeting with a realtor. I'm thinking of putting my house on the market."

"No shit? Gonna buy the one in Edward's Bay?"

"If there isn't too much of a problem with the title to the land."

His face changed in a flash, from hopeful grin to dark displeasure. He jabbed a thick angry finger at me. "I know who you've been talking to, Noah, but that issue is just a lot of hot air. We got clear and fair title to that land, and a bunch of troublemakers are just trying to grab it for themselves. It's blackmail, that's what it is."

"Troublemakers? You mean the Quanda?"

He snorted. "Now some other fool lawyer's got his finger in the pie. Always lawyers, isn't it, Noah? God, this would be a great country if there were no goddamn lawyers to fuck it up."

I'd known Bigs long enough to understand that most of the bluster was nothing but hot air. He raged constantly against the strictures the state put on developers like himself. Sometimes I almost sympathized with him. As for his views on lawyers, well, he was hardly alone in those.

"So who exactly is the other fool lawyer?"

He stared at me intently for a long moment. "If you were interested in buying one of those houses, you might be interested in getting him off our back."

"Haven't you got a lawyer of your own yet? Anyway, I get the impression that Ralph doesn't trust me."

"I trust you, Noah."

"Thanks. But you haven't told me who this other lawyer is. I might know him."

"You won't believe this, Noah but it's some outfit in Washington, D.C. Some environmentalist crowd or Native American lobbyists or rubbish like that. Some no-good do-gooders. Some East Coast arseholes who think they know what's best for us out here in the Northwest." He tipped his beer down morosely. "I wish to God I'd never heard of Edward's Bay. I wish to God I'd never heard of Quanda Indians. Or any other damned Indians, come to that. Nothing but trouble for everyone."

"As far as I can see, Bigs, most of the trouble's been *for* the Indians, wouldn't you say?"

He frowned, his eyes baleful. "If I hadn't known you for so long, Noah, I might agree with Ralph. That you're a sniveling liberal bleeding heart. Don't know which side your bread's buttered on. You should go off and join the ACLU. Or the Sierra Club. Greenpeace. One of those. You know who they are, all those bleeding bleeding hearts."

"Thanks, Bigs. I appreciate a frank opinion. Well, gotta go now. Meet the realtor. But who knows? Perhaps I won't be selling my house after all."

The Sierra Club? Not such a bad idea. But then I might have to learn to love Douglas firs, and I didn't think I was capable of going that far.

TWENTY-ONE

THE REALTOR'S CAR WAS PARKED IN THE DRIVEWAY. AS I DREW up in the Saab, she climbed out of the driver's seat and handed me her card, smiling radiantly. "Mr. Richards? I'm Lonny Davies." She was dressed in a smart wool suit, and when she shook my hand, she jangled, one of those bracelets on her wrist with dozens of small objects dangling from it.

I hadn't lived in the old house since the night it was trashed. The night Lauren Watson almost died there. Now it had been cleaned and repainted and the floors refinished, and it was more cheerful and attractive than it had been for years. I looked at it with fresh eyes and regretted how I'd let it fade away around me. Lonny Davies waxed enthusiastic over the large rooms with the high ceilings, the straight-grained fir trim, the old-fashioned light fixtures. "A wonderful old house, Mr. Richards."

It *was* a wonderful old house, solid and sturdy. It would last another hundred years, barring earthquakes and fire, built of the best materials, clear cedar siding and thick cedar shakes. But even as we walked through the rooms and admired the views of the lake from the wide windows, I thought I wanted to be rid of it and the memories that went with it. Not the memories of my childhood and the days when my parents lived here, but the later, sadder ones. The realtor knew the history of the house, of course. My history. Realtors know everything about every house in their selling area, about the people who live in them, their marriages and divorces and deaths. Lonny Davies didn't think the recent happenings in the house would affect the sale. "It isn't as though anyone actually died here, is it?" Her smile was overpowering.

"My grandparents and my mother," I pointed out. "As a matter of fact, I'm rather proud of them for managing to die in their own home."

Lonny Davies laughed, the brittle unamused laugh of someone interested only in a sale, not in the vagaries of human existence. "I meant a death like murder or suicide. That's the kind of thing that really puts people off."

Do houses absorb the unhappiness of those who live within their walls? Does unhappiness soak into the plaster and the Sheetrock? Is that why people are put off by murder or suicide, the tragedy locked into the very fabric of a house? It was easy for me to imagine a lingering scent of grief in the old house.

In the house at Edward's Bay, there was no memory of grief. Except for Jay Bishop. I couldn't forget Jay Bishop.

Lonny Davies and I discussed prices. When she named a figure, I couldn't resist upping it, just to watch her expression. She protested, halfheartedly. "That's a bit on the high side. This isn't Seattle, you know."

She was right. People around Springwell expected to buy houses for a lot less than in Seattle, where software millionaires have jacked property prices into the stratosphere. Springwell was too far away to commute to the big city. But the truth was, I'd taken a dislike to Lonny Davies. Every time she waved her hands, which was often, the irritating bracelet jangled my nerves, and I just didn't want to agree with her too quickly. I shrugged, feigning a lack of interest. "I don't care if it doesn't sell. I can always keep it, rent it out, wait for the prices to go up."

Which wasn't, of course, what a realtor wants to hear. It wasn't particularly what I wanted to hear myself. It would be better to erase the whole Springwell episode out of my life, especially the recent part of it, but suddenly it didn't seem so simple to rid myself of all that history. Perhaps, after all, it isn't a matter of shutting the door and walking away and being done with it. I'd spent too many years in this town, in this house, a boy growing into a man, to be able to shuck it off quite so easily. But I'd come this far, and I finally agreed on an outrageous price, not about to allow all those days of my life, the good and the bad, to go cheap. It would be an insult to my parents, who loved this house. To my grandfather, who'd built it with his own hands. Part of me hoped no one would be foolish enough to pay the price.

I left Lonny Davies hammering her sign into the ground and went off to the Carlssons, before there was a chance to change my mind.

The evening was mellow, the rhododendrons just coming into bud, the azaleas already in bloom. There was a faint greening of alders, and the lake reflected the mountains heaping at its north end. It was less than half a mile around the lake to the Carlsson house, and I could have walked, as I'd walked so many times before, especially in the years before Chauncey and I had both married, when these houses belonged to our parents; but it was already growing dark and late, and I drove so that I'd reach the warmth and comfort of their house more quickly.

When Chauncey opened his door, I announced, "Well, I've done it. The house is now officially on the market."

Clasping me round the shoulders, he drew me into the warmth, handed me a scotch without asking. Daphne planted a kiss on the side of my face, and the dogs threw themselves at my feet. It was just like old times. Daphne had cooked a rack of lamb, followed by a delicious creamy Charlotte Russe, and I scoffed it all up. Yet at the same time, it made me a little melancholy, as if this were some sort of last supper. There was absolutely no reason to feel that way, of course, no reason we couldn't go on having dinner together all the years of our lives, but the occasion had a definite sense of closure to one part of my life.

Inevitably, we talked of those people who'd occupied so much of our lives in Springwell the last few months, and the hour grew late. We moved from the table to sit by the fire with our coffee, and Chauncey said, almost casually, "I talked to Hayward at Seawards Hospital."

It didn't register for a moment, the names not connected with the ones we'd just been discussing. "Hayward? Seawards?"

"You know. The emergency room doc who saw your neighbor's baby."

"Oh, yes! What did you find out?"

Chauncey poured cream into his coffee, fiddled with the spoon, looked away from me. "Noah, what do you know about that woman?"

"That woman? You mean Sarah?" For a half-second, I was tempted to say, I slept with her last night, Chauncey. It was fantastic, wonderful, to have a woman like Sarah in my arms, not just in my fantasies. But I kept my head down and my mouth shut for once and shrugged as if I could hardly remember who Sarah McKenzie was. "You met her. You know what she's like."

Chauncey looked at Daphne and she looked back at him and they both looked at me. "The doctor at the hospital," Chauncey began, "Ed Hayward . . . Well . . ." He seemed to be having trouble getting the words out. "Well, Hayward has seen her child several times now. Three times to be precise." Chauncey paused, his eyes troubled. "I'm not entirely sure I should be telling you this, Noah, but . . ." He cleared his throat. "Well, Hayward doesn't believe there's anything wrong with the child."

I couldn't imagine why he was having so much trouble telling me this. "Hey, that's great news. Sarah will be delighted. I'm delighted. And relieved."

Chauncey made circles on the table with his coffee spoon. "Perhaps I'm not making myself completely clear. It's not just that there's nothing wrong with him . . ." He peered across the room at me from under his eyebrows. "Hayward believes the mother might be deliberately causing the problem."

I didn't think I'd heard right. I looked to Daphne for help. She was staring at me intently, a small crease between her eyebrows.

"How do you mean, *deliberately?*"

"Noah, have you ever heard the term 'Munchausen syndrome'?"

"No. What the hell is it? Some disease?" Both of them knew how ignorant I was about medicine; they knew I didn't understand esoteric medical terms. But even as I disclaimed knowledge, a small disturbing seed of recognition of the word "Munchausen" raised uneasy alarm in me. I'd heard it before, somewhere, about something . . .

Rearranging himself in the chair, Chauncey pressed the tips of his fingers together. "It's named after Baron Münchausen, who lived in the eighteenth century and was known for his lies and exaggerations. It's used to describe a condition where people fabricate illness."

I heard myself make an impulsive, impatient sound. Chauncey ploughed on.

"Nowadays, Munchausen's is quite well recognized. Emergency-room docs especially have learned to suspect it if someone walks into the emergency room and seems to expect an operation. To want one. These are people who demand attention, and they can masquerade all sorts of symptoms. They get very proficient at deceiving the medical profession, and sometimes deceive surgeons enough so they get operated on."

He paused for another moment, looked at me meaningfully. I wasn't sure where all this was leading, but the gravity of his expression disturbed me.

"More to the point, Noah, to your point, there's a further refinement of the condition, known as Munchausen syndrome by proxy. The patients in those cases are children, and typically it's the mother who invents an illness for her child."

He seemed to expect me to say something, but I had nothing to say. I stared at him, fearful of what he might say next, a sinking sensation in the pit of my stomach.

"These mothers make up diseases for their children instead of for themselves. Hence, 'Munchausen by proxy.' And what I'm trying to tell you is that Hayward believes Sarah McKenzie invented her baby's breathing problem. To get attention. For herself."

My first reaction was profound disbelief. "You're telling me he believes Sarah *invented* Christopher's problem? But I saw it for myself, that first time. He was definitely not breathing. It wasn't invented at all."

Chauncey looked at me with something akin to pity. "He believes she did more than invent it. He thinks she *caused* it. Stopped him breathing in some fashion or other."

My own breath was taken away. "For God's sake, Chauncey! That's outrageous! You've met her. She's not a nutcase. No mother would do anything like that to her own child. Daphne! You can't believe this rubbish."

But Daphne looked worried and uncomfortable, and her eyes slid away from mine. "I think you should listen to the evidence, Noah."

"Oh? There's evidence? Or is there just unfounded speculation?"

Chauncey said gently, altogether too kindly, "The trouble is that it's difficult to gather evidence in cases like this, Noah. Like trying to prove a negative. The whole point is that there's nothing to put one's finger on, no clinical proof, and that's because there's nothing really wrong with the child. And too often, no one suspects anything until it's too late. Sometimes not even then." Clasping and unclasping his hands, Chauncey seemed to be as distressed to tell me all this as I was to hear it. "It's been suggested that some crib deaths attributed to SIDS are really examples of Munchausen by proxy."

I could hardly believe what Chauncey was saying. It sounded like outrageous nonsense to me, yet he appeared reasonable enough, convincing almost, until I tried to accept that this words might apply to the woman I'd slept with last night.

"Noah, I want you to listen carefully. They've found absolutely nothing wrong with Christopher McKenzie. Blood tests, X rays, EKGs, and EEGs. Nothing is abnormal. And when the baby is monitored, nothing untoward occurs. There's only his mother's word for it that these apneic episodes have taken place. Otherwise, he's a perfectly normal healthy child. Just as you thought yourself."

The room filled with a chilling silence. The meal I'd just enjoyed lay heavy, nauseatingly, on my stomach. But I still had to protest. For my own sake, as much as for Sarah's.

"Just because they've found nothing wrong doesn't mean there's nothing wrong. Doctors make mistakes all the time. You know that. I know it. Doctors aren't perfect. That's what you've always told me. You're the one who's always telling me how imperfect a science medicine is."

Chauncey sighed unhappily, got out of his chair slowly and heavily, went to the desk in the corner, and produced a sheaf of photocopied papers. "I want you to look at these reprints, Noah. Some are from the medical library at St. Mary's; some I downloaded from the Internet. Take them away with you, read them more thoroughly at your leisure, but I want you to look at one or two now, because there are some issues we should discuss while you're here."

He held the papers out to me. I accepted them reluctantly, with dread, shuffled through them. They were medical reports, with reams of small print, and there was no way to absorb this type of information in a short amount of time. My hands shook, and several of the papers fell to the floor. Chauncey bent to pick them up.

"This one," he said. "Read it. Tell me if it sounds familiar."

The heading at the top of the page read: Profile of Munchausen by Proxy: Parent and Child. I skimmed through it, fast, and my heart sank even further. A lot further. It was as if someone had taken the facts as I knew them and written a medical history of Christopher McKenzie. And Sarah McKenzie.

TWENTY-TWO

THE CHILD IN THE CASE HISTORY WAS EXACTLY THE SAME AGE as Christopher McKenzie. Seven months old. His mother reported that he'd stopped breathing on several different occasions and had taken him repeatedly to the emergency room. He was tested for all sorts of conditions, without result, but later, when the baby was admitted to hospital and placed under secret video surveillance, his mother was actually seen pinching off his nose and mouth to prevent him from breathing. Until that moment, the medical and nursing staff had completely believed her story—believed, until that moment, that she was a caring, competent, and concerned mother.

The medical history, the breathing problem, the timing and description of the attacks, the mother's reactions, bore a striking resemblance to the story of Sarah and Christopher as I knew it.

An awful doubt crept over me. But it couldn't possibly be true about Sarah. Couldn't be. I continued to protest.

"I need more than someone else's case history to convince me that Sarah McKenzie is capable of anything as outrageous as this. She'd have to be quite crazy. Why on earth would any mother do that to her own child?" I glared at Chauncey and Daphne, challenging them. "Explain that to me."

Chauncey sighed again. "We don't know why, Noah. A cry for help? Another form of child abuse? Take a look at some of the other histories."

The other histories were a litany of repeated patterns of illnesses of children, all with final and incontrovertible proof the child's mother invented them in some way or other. A few of the illnesses were real enough—poisonings of various kinds or "accidents" that the mother had caused—but most were completely false, completely fictional reports of kidney stones, for instance, or bleeding that never happened. Some story, any sort of story, that brought the child to a hospital to be treated over and over again. It made for totally bizarre reading, mothers behaving in ways I never could have imagined, but the reports came from Britain as well as the United States, and were altogether a damning and convincing body of evidence. But the most damning of all of them, as far as I was concerned, was the very first one, almost word-for-word the same pattern I'd witnessed myself: a baby who stopped breathing for no apparent reason, hurried trips to the hospital, no evidence of illness, a mother who insisted on tests and X rays and emergency measures.

That particular report also included a psychological evaluation of the mother: "She revealed no signs of psychosis or psychopathic tendencies . . . someone trying hard to deny any upset or distress . . . It was concluded that she was a woman who feels empty inside and must rely on external environment to give her life substance."

I shoved the papers aside, unable to bear looking at them anymore. Chauncey went to the cupboard in the corner, poured me a straight scotch, stood with his back to the fireplace, and waited for me to say something. I took a hefty swig of the scotch.

"Supposing," I began cautiously, feeling my way, "just supposing Sarah McKenzie did something like this—though God knows I find that incredibly difficult to believe—why on earth would she? What's the point?"

There was another ominous silence. Daphne and Chauncey looked at each other again, then at me, as if they had already discussed that very question. Chauncey rocked nervously on his heels, distaste written all over his face. "You know, I'd really rather not be talking about this, but I have to tell you, Noah. For your sake."

"*My* sake?"

"She gained *your* sympathy, didn't she? She got *you* to take notice of her."

His words appalled me. Never in my worst nightmares could I have imagined what he was suggesting: a woman putting her child in harm's way to get *me* to pay attention to her. But now the suggestion was planted in my mind, I couldn't help adding it all up: how Christopher's first spell happened when I turned down Sarah's invitation after the Eagle's Nest, the second after I called from the noisy bar in town. As though she did indeed want me to pay attention. How I had. How the baby appeared so well and healthy otherwise. And it explained the odd feeling about Sarah, right from the start, that something didn't add up properly. A feeling I'd managed to forget all about last night.

A hundred little pieces of the enigma of Sarah McKenzie fell into place. Too easily, too patly. I didn't trust pat solutions. But the mere suspicion made me sick to my stomach, and I was only a little comforted when Daphne said briskly, matter-of-factly, "What about the husband? Climbing Everest, you say? Maybe it's his attention she's trying to attract."

"Whoever, whatever . . . if it's true, that baby's in real danger."

Chauncey picked up the papers again and sorted through them. "Somewhere here, the authors speculate on the number of deaths that result from this behavior."

"Deaths?" I echoed, horrified.

"This particular children's hospital reckons the true mortality rate from Munchausen's among their patients might be as high as twenty-two percent. And that's probably on the low side because so many cases aren't ever diagnosed. Not even suspected."

That statistic reduced us all to silence.

"But what if you and Hayward are wrong, Chauncey? What if Christopher really is a sick child? What if Sarah's being accused of something she didn't do? You can't accuse a mother of something like this without proof."

"What's the alternative, Noah? Wait until the baby dies? Hospitals have proved their case by separating the mother from the child and monitoring it very closely. The trouble with Sarah is that she resists taking the child back to the hospital. If you can persuade her to take him in and leave him there, Noah, we'll be able to put it to rest, won't we?" He paused again. "Unless, of course, you catch her in the act."

"Catch her in the act? How could I do that? Watch her twenty-four hours a day? And what if she *is* responsible?"

But I already knew the answer to that question. If Sarah McKenzie, my erstwhile lover, were guilty of such a thing, they'd put her away.

The day that started out so well, rising from Sarah's bed, satiated and refreshed, then the early morning stroll along the beach between her house and mine, had sunk to awful depths. I could never go back to her bed. Even if she was completely innocent, the fact that for one moment I'd considered her guilty made it unthinkable. I remembered the sound of Christopher's breathing, soft and regular, when I'd wakened in the morning. My heart constricted at the thought of what could be happening at this very moment,

Sarah getting at me or her husband or whoever, shutting off her baby's airway and then calling for help.

Jesus! I leapt to my feet. "I must get back to Edward's Bay."

Chauncey said, "You can't drive now. You've had altogether too much to drink."

Daphne put a hand on my arm. "You and Chauncey must work out a plan of action."

But my heart was thudding in my chest with a terrible foreboding. "I have to talk to Sarah. We mustn't let this happen again."

I certainly wasn't capable of driving to Edward's Bay tonight. I thought I never wanted to see Edward's Bay again. But now I imagined Sarah inventing another emergency to keep me running to her side. As she'd kept me running for the past few weeks. It was difficult to keep a sense of balance. Nothing was proven, all was speculation, but if I erred, it had to be on the side of Christopher.

"When you speak to her," Chauncey warned, "don't let her think you suspect anything. Be careful, or the child could be in greater danger. Persuade her to take him to the hospital. The doctors can take it from there."

I escaped to the den at the back of the house, away from Chauncey's and Daphne's worried expressions, and dialed Sarah's number. *Please let her answer, please,* I prayed, and after five or six rings, she did.

"Noah! Where are you?"

My mouth was dry, and I didn't know how to continue the conversation. "Still in Springwell. I . . . uh . . . I just wanted to check with you that everything's all right."

"Why shouldn't it be?" Her voice was totally normal, a touch amused. "What time will you be back?"

Be careful, Chauncey had said. "The thing is, Sarah, we've been celebrating the house going on the market, you know how it is, starting afresh and all that, and it's gotten to be rather late . . . a bottle of wine, a couple of scotches, you know how it is."

I was babbling. "How's Christopher?"

"He's fine. Ask me how I am."

I could almost feel the warm treacherous skin under my hands. I gripped the receiver too tightly. "I'll be back tomorrow. Will you wait until I get there and take care of everything? Because I will, I promise I will, Sarah."

"Oh, Noah." There was a convincing crack of sincerity in her voice. "You don't know how I've needed someone to say that to me."

"Don't let anything happen to Christopher."

"Of course not," she said and sounded genuinely puzzled. As though she had no idea what I was talking about. "Of course not."

"I'll be thinking about both of you until I get back to Edward's Bay."

What else could I say? It was the truth. I've always had the hardest trouble saying anything other than the absolute truth.

I locked myself in the downstairs bathroom, about to throw up. I hung over the basin for several minutes, my gut heaving. In the mirror, my face was a ghastly color, haggard around the eyes and mouth, as though I was the one who was ill. I stayed in the bathroom for a long time, trying to regain some sense of reality, some equilibrium; then I splashed cold water over my hands and face, took a few deep breaths, and returned to the living room and the safety of Daphne and Chauncey. But they wanted to discuss Christopher and Sarah again, and I had to beg off. I couldn't take any more.

"I've got to go to bed. And before I say anything more, I've got to read those damn papers again. Thoroughly."

Daphne planted one of her feathery kisses on the side of my face, attempting to reassure me all was normal, and Chauncey said, "Try not to worry too much, Noah. I'm sure it can be worked out."

Try not to worry too much? What a hope! In the spare room,

thankful to be alone, I lay on top of the covers, the bedside light a small bright patch in the darkness, stared up at the ceiling as though there might be an answer there. But I didn't begin to know what questions I needed to ask. My head ached infernally. I read the case histories through again. And again. Some so alarming I didn't think I'd ever be able to sleep, but I did, finally, uneasily.

When I woke in the morning, I was no wiser.

TWENTY-THREE

I'D HOPED TO SLIP AWAY BEFORE ANYONE WAS UP AND ABOUT, but at six-thirty A.M. the Carlsson family was already gathered around the breakfast table, eating cereal, drinking coffee, reading the paper, exactly the normal uncomplicated family scene I once fantasized for myself. I didn't even have the heart to sit down and drink a cup of coffee with them, so I just leaned against the door and watched them for a moment.

"Well, gotta be on my way," I said, and four heads turned in unison. "Thanks for the bed. And the advice. I'll call later."

"Nothing to eat?" Daphne asked, anxiously.

I pecked her on the cheek and didn't bother to pretend cheerfulness. Chauncey threw aside the newspaper and said, "I'll see you to the car," as though I didn't know the way. Outside, the sun was barely risen, a damp cool smell coming off the trees, a light rain starting. Chauncey held my arm and peered into my face with an old familiar concern.

"Go talk to Ed Hayward," he said. "The doc at Seawards Hospital. I think that'd be a good idea."

Nothing seemed like a good idea this morning.

"I'll call you," Chauncey said. "Or I'll get Hayward to call you." He tightened the grip on my arm. "We could be wrong about this, Noah, but if we're not, think of the grief we'll be saving that baby."

I backed the Saab out of the driveway and drove along the lake for half a mile, turned where I'd turned for so many years, at the intersection down the road from my old house, and in a few minutes, was heading south on the freeway. I felt lousy. The thick mess of commuter traffic did nothing to make me feel any better. By seven-thirty, the rain was heavier, the traffic stop-and-go, a slow stop-and-go crawl all the way to downtown Seattle, bad for the car's engine and for my nerves. If I'd had any sense, I'd have stayed and had breakfast with Daphne and Chauncey. I thought about driving straight on the ferry to Seawards and Edward's Bay, but Chauncey had said I should make everything seem normal. It would hardly seem normal if I turned up at Sarah's house at nine o'clock in the morning.

In the office, everyone was in better spirits than I was. Not difficult. Charlie's good humor was quite restored, the firm having just been presented, Sibby informed me, with a hit-and-run accident involving an expensive Mercedes and a couple of profootballers. He was positively licking his chops over the case, and he smiled at me with the old dazzling smile, yesterday's invective forgotten.

A message was waiting from the day before. "Pete in Spokane. Has info."

Glad to do something straightaway, I dialed the number immediately, before remembering that Pete in Spokane was most likely still in bed at this hour of the morning. The phone rang and rang, and by the time he finally answered, I'd almost forgotten who and where I was calling.

"Noah Richards. You called yesterday."

"Oh, yeah. Mr. Richards!"

I waited a moment. "So, what did you call about, Pete?"

An audible groan came over the wires. "Oh, man, what *was* it I called you about?"

How old was he? Nineteen, twenty? It was going to take him a long while to grow up. "Go get a cup of that awful coffee you keep in the kitchen," I said. "I'll hang on. Believe me, I've nothing better to do with my time."

He dropped the phone. It banged and clattered in my ear, and I imagined it swinging against the wall of the untidy living room, pictured the house, the chaos in the kitchen, the dark and dusty stairs. I wondered how Maria Cruz was doing. I hadn't heard another thing about her, but Wayne said he'd take care of her, and I trusted Wayne's word. The banging of the phone ceased, and I could hear the crashing of dishes in the kitchen, the sound of a girl's voice near at hand. I'd just given up hope of Pete ever returning when he came back to the phone.

"Okay," he said, a little more coherently. "Got some coffee. Now I'm with it."

"How's Maria?"

"Maria? I guess she's still in the hospital."

"You promised you'd keep an eye on her."

"Hey, man, we went to see her. The other day. Me and a couple of the girls from here. But they wouldn't let us see her. Said she was too sick."

"So you don't know how she is now?"

"Am I supposed to know?"

It was too much to expect. "Have you remembered what you called about?"

"Oh, yeah! Yeah, I fiddled around with Jay's computer some

more. I know you don't want me to get into the other line, but I thought you'd be interested to know it's a 202 area code. That's Washington, D.C."

Washington, D.C.? So maybe Bigs hadn't been talking out of the back of his head when he talked of an East Coast lawyer. "That's all you know, the area code?"

A hint of impatience crept into Pete's voice. "All I get is the dedicated computer line. And like I said, I can't do anything more without the password. But I can still find it if you want."

"Sure, that's what I want, Pete. But not illegally." I thought about it for a moment. "Could you leave a message on that line? My name and phone number? Telling someone at the other end to contact me?"

"Sure. No sweat." He sounded pleased. "Though they might want to know how you found it and all."

"I'll deny all knowledge," I said. "And then I'll send you a check."

As soon as I hung up, the phone buzzed again at my desk. Sibby announced, "A Dr. Hayward to speak to you."

My stomach lurched.

Hayward said, without preamble, "Chauncey Carlsson explained your role in this problem with the McKenzie baby. If you want to help, come and discuss it with me. Confidentially, of course. I'll talk to you as a friend of the family. Not as an attorney."

"Anything to help."

"Can you stop by today? I'm on duty at two o'clock. Or tomorrow? Just don't leave it too long."

The whole thing hung over my head like a sword of Damocles. A nightmare. The sooner the better for me, as well as for Christopher. "This afternoon," I said.

I forced myself to call Sarah, because I was afraid not to. I'd already convinced myself of her guilt, yet when she answered the phone, she sounded perfectly normal and rational. Just as she always did. Just like those mothers in the reports. I tried to sound as normal as she did, told her about the commute from Springwell, how I preferred the ferry ride, how I'd see her later.

"Dinner tonight, Noah. Don't forget."

How could I possibly forget?

At one o'clock, I left for the hospital. I didn't have to explain to Charlie where I was or what I was doing from hour to hour, but a small concern about all the billable hours I was skipping crept into my consciousness. I had to be productive, or we'd all go down the tube, Charlie and Sibby and the rest of the gang. And me too, I supposed.

The day had grown wilder and wetter, whitecaps on the sound, swells banging the flat bottom of the ferryboat. Rain streamed against the windows, obscuring all signs of the outside world, as if the ferry were traveling in a tunnel, in a time warp, like the Flying Dutchman. The huge cavern of the car deck was deserted and echoing, and upstairs in the passenger section, the long unoccupied rows of vinyl seats were melancholy and lonely. The evening ferry was never as empty as this. I pored over the Munchausen-syndrome papers again, wanting to be prepared before talking to Hayward, but I learned nothing new, gleaned no crumb of comfort.

Seawards Hospital, too, had a melancholic air at this dead time of day, in the rain. I'd come to it at night before, when lights glowed in the doors and windows, beacons in the darkness, offering succor to the sick, help to the desperate. The night I rushed there with Sarah and Christopher, I'd been desperate—so thankful to see the neon sign at the entrance, the arrow pointing to the emergency room—and I couldn't tolerate the idea that all the panic and fear might have been totally unnecessary. If Christopher McKenzie and I were pawns in some weird psychological game, at least I was old enough to defend myself.

I tracked Hayward down to a tiny shoe box of an office with barely enough space for a desk and a couple of chairs. He squeezed me inside and closed the door, folded his hands together on the desk, regarded me with caution. "Dr. Carlsson assures me you'll be discreet. You understand it's a ticklish problem, don't you?"

I'd only seen Hayward in the middle of the night before. Then he'd seemed bored and distant, his eyes puffy and lackluster; now his eyes were interested and involved, fixed intently on me. This was, after all, the middle of the day, not the middle of the night. I never knew how doctors managed to stay awake, let alone make crucial decisions, in those hours when the rest of the world is asleep.

I passed the papers over the desk. "I hadn't heard of this Munchausen syndrome before. I'm not a doctor. I think I can grasp the situation, but I can't say I understand the motivations."

"Join the clan." Hayward flicked through the reprints. "To tell you the truth, it's something I haven't ever run across before. At least as far as I know. But that's the tragedy of these cases. They can slip by so easily. Physicians are equally as gullible as any one else, at times. We want to believe what our patients tell us. But when we couldn't find any clinical cause for Christopher McKenzie's symptoms, we began to look for other reasons."

I was untutored in the world of medical and psychiatric problems. Humble. "Just tell me what it is you want me to do."

"Persuade the mother to bring him back here. She doesn't seem to have any family around, and her husband is out of the country. Is that correct?"

How much of anything that Sarah had told me was correct?

"I understand he's climbing in the Himalayas." I clutched at straws. "She's very far from home. Home is New Zealand, you know. She's homesick."

Hayward was impatient, unsympathetic. "Homesickness is no excuse to make your child stop breathing, Mr. Richards. If it's true and she does it once too often, we'll have a dead child on our hands. Don't frighten her off, and don't let her think we suspect anything. It could lead to a desperate act on her part just to try to prove to us that the child truly has something seriously wrong with him."

I groaned. "How can anything be more desperate than what's happened already? Can't you just take the baby away from her?"

"You know we can't do that, don't you? Not unless we can prove she's harming him."

Between the devil and the deep blue sea. If I'd known all this before, could I have done something to prevent it? I was floundering, out of my depth. What was I going to say to Sarah? What could I do to save this situation?

"I'm not sure I'm the right person to handle this," I said, and Hayward commented, "If she doesn't have anyone else, you might be the *only* person."

These were definitely deeper waters than I had thought.

TWENTY-FOUR

AT EDWARD'S BAY, THE STREET BETWEEN THE HOUSES WAS quiet and deserted. As usual. It wasn't too difficult to understand how Sarah might feel, alone here all the day with her child, without adult company to while away the hours; I could even feel some sneaking empathy for her. But there was no way to carry off the pretense that everything was the same as before, and though I tried to remind myself that everyone is innocent until proven guilty, the sick sensation in my gut told me different.

Sarah wasn't home.

At first it was a relief. Then a worry. Where was she? Shopping? At the hospital again? Running away with the baby? I peered through the glass door into the kitchen, as tidy and bare of clues as to Sarah's whereabouts and her personality as the rest of the house. I knew that whatever my future relationship might be with

Sarah and Christopher McKenzie, it would forever teeter between relief and worry. Worry that something terrible was about to happen, relief when it didn't. No way was this going to have any sort of happy ending.

I was about to put the key in my own front door when a car stopped in the street, an old sixties Lincoln, lovingly preserved, all the chrome gleaming, the paint immaculate. A collector's item. A man wearing a narrow-brimmed hat with an old-fashioned plastic cover on it climbed out of the driver's seat, a sheaf of brightly colored papers in his hand, and closed the door with a satisfying solid thump. There was something vaguely familiar about him. When he saw me, he called from the other side of the street. "Hi, there," and then I recognized him from the meeting at Ralph Harrison's house. The speaker who had such trouble making himself heard.

He came across the road, waving the papers. "Walter Drummond," he said. "You're the lawyer guy, aren't you? Just putting out a few more flyers." Then he pushed one into my hand. "Time for another meeting, you know. Got to keep people on their toes. Too easy to let things slip-slide away. A decision's coming down any day now."

"Decision?"

"About the damn shellfish rights. Got to be ready."

The flyer was orange this time, with the same heavy black print: Prepare for Battle!! Fight Your Government!! Your Property Is Your Property!! Remember the Alamo!!

"The Alamo?" I said. "Wasn't that a rather different issue?"

"A rallying cry. It's the principle."

I examined the flyer more closely, the cheap paper, the exclamation marks. "You print these yourself?"

"Sure. Got to do something now. I'm retired. Can't just sit and look through the telescope all day, can I?"

I stared at him, up at the headlands on the other side of Edward's Bay. "You live up there, don't you?" I said, pointing.

"Yeah, that's right. Saddlers Way. Great spot. You can see for miles. Better than down here."

"Does everyone up there have a telescope?"

"Sure thing," he said enthusiastically. "It's a sort of hobby with the people up there. Mine's a Bausch and Lomb. Magnificent instrument. Paid a fortune for it. Not much goes on around here that I don't see."

No wonder I felt watched. Maybe, after all, it wasn't Sarah who'd been watching me. I imagined all those retired people up on the headland with nothing better to do all day than to sit peering through telescopes and binoculars. At the sound. At the houses below. At the beach. At fishing boats.

"You coming to the meeting?" he said. "Nice to have a lawyer on our side."

"But I'm not entirely sure I'm on your side, Mr. Drummond."

He stared at me in outrage, and his face went beet red. The same color it had been at the meeting. "Listen up, young man. If you were in the same position as people like me, like most of the people round here, just your home and nothing else to call your own, and someone's threatening the value of your property, you'd know which side you'd be on." He was off on a tear. "I gave the best years of my life to this country. I was in the armed services, young man. The army. Fought in Korea. Bet you've never fought for your country, have you? You'd think different if you had."

"You're right," I agreed. "I was lucky enough never to have to fight in a war."

He snatched the flyer out of my hand. "Bet you were the sort who weaseled out of Vietnam, weren't you?"

"Mr. Drummond, I was only a student at the time."

"Student!" He sounded disgusted. "That's what they all said, those draft dodgers."

"Sorry," I muttered.

But Walter Drummond wasn't going to stand around and listen to any of my apologies. Wheeling away from me, he stomped off to the next house and pushed the flyer into the mailbox. He didn't look back at me.

I changed my mind about going in the house, got back in the Saab instead, and went to visit Wayne Daniels.

The afternoon sky was still leaden with clouds, but the rain and wind had died down, no longer lashing at the trees. On the hillside up to Wayne's place, the branches of the evergreens drooped wet and heavy, arching low over the dirt road; the black trees, the narrow dirt road between them, were straight out of an Emily Carr painting, gloomy and foreboding. Even though I was a native northwesterner, Douglas firs depressed me, sucked my spirit, just as they did the light from the sky. The tall dark firs, the end product of one of nature's cycles, blanket the earth and prevent anything else from growing in their shade; perhaps one needs generations of ancestors, like the Quanda, to exist beneath them, to live with their weight and oppressiveness and regard them as guardians of the earth. I had the white man's instinct to clear the land so the sun could come in and crops could be raised. Heresy in the Northwest today.

At the end of the road, the small group of houses looked exactly the same as before, huddled beneath the cedars and firs, smoke rising in thin columns from tin chimneys, everything still and quiet all around. The Saab scrunched to a stop on the gravel, and nothing stirred into curiosity; there was no one at the windows or in the doorways, no signs of life. The tiny community seemed not so much peaceful as dead.

I rapped loudly on Wayne's door. The knocking echoed around the clearing. After a long while, Cynthia Daniels came to open the door. The time before, only her back had been visible as she sat watching television with the baby on her lap. I wasn't even sure it was the same woman. But she carried a baby on her shoulder, so I assumed she was. Short and round and overweight, her braided hair was streaked with white, her face smooth and unwrinkled.

"Mrs. Daniels? I'm Noah Richards. I came here once before."

She stared at me without speaking, her eyes as unrevealing as those of the men at the tavern, kept one hand on the door, as though she was about to shut it in my face at any second.

"I was hoping to find Wayne at home."

"He went fishing," she said, at last.

"I have something for him." I'd put the safe-deposit key in an envelope, and now I handed it to her. She accepted the envelope without curiosity. "Wayne will know what to do with it." I hesitated for a moment. "Did he get the death certificate? I spoke to the coroner's office. They were going to send it."

"He didn't say nothing about no certificate."

"When will he be back?"

She bounced the baby on her shoulder. "Maybe tonight. Maybe sooner."

"Ask him to call me when he comes home, will you?" I scribbled my number on one of my cards, handed it to her, and she accepted it as she had the envelope, reluctantly, without interest; but when she looked down at the card, she went quite still, like a statue.

"Jay had one of these cards," she said. "You're the one he went to see that day?"

"Yes, that's right."

"If he hadn't gone to see you, I expect he'd still be alive. He'd have set his pots for the crab and come back here, and then he'd have gone back to school and still be alive."

There was little need to argue such a small point. "When Jay left me," I said, "he told me he was going to get salmon."

"That's it," she said, stubbornly. "If he hadn't spent time talking to you, the tide wouldn't have turned, and he wouldn't have gone out in that boat for the salmon." She shrugged her thick shoulders, patted the back of the sleeping baby. "I guess it don't make no difference now."

The door began to close on me, and I put my hand on it. "I'm very sorry about what happened to Jay, Mrs. Daniels. I hope they find out who shot him."

"Nobody cares who shot him."

She didn't say it bitterly or even resentfully. Just stated it as a fact. Baldly.

"I care. That girl in Spokane, Maria Cruz, cared. There's got to be other girls who cared. Wayne said he was a devil with the girls."

Cynthia Daniels looked at me with the curiously expressionless eyes. "He'd have done better to stick to his own kind. Not go messing with no white girls."

"Maria Cruz is Mexican," I said.

"That Robin wasn't."

"Robin?"

"The one down in Edward's Bay. I'll tell Wayne you called," she said, and then she did close the door, firmly.

Robin? Who was Robin? I hovered in front of the door for another moment or so, turned away and drove back down the hill through the brooding trees. At Edward's Bay, I sat in the car for a while, outside the house, looking at the street. There was nothing hidden about the fronts of these houses. From the beach side, they crouched behind the piles of driftwood and the slope of the shore, but from the street side most of the front doors were perfectly visible because the plantings weren't mature enough to hide them. Just a few struggling shrubs. When Jay Bishop, the young Indian, the natural enemy at Edward's Bay, distinctive in his Stetson hat and long hair, had rung my front-door bell, he'd been standing right here in full view of the rest of the houses. In full view of anyone with a telescope.

When I eventually got out of the car and unlocked the front door, there was a creeping sensation right in the middle of my back. Right at the spot where the bullet hit Jay. As though someone was watching me, as they must have watched Jay. I tried not to whirl around in a paranoid, foolish fashion, and I closed the door quickly behind me, with a small feeling of relief.

The thing was, someone *had* shot Jay Bishop. A fact, not paranoia. Someone had taken a rifle and drilled him through the back. He could have been shot from anywhere, but anyone could have seen him standing at my front door. From anywhere. Not just down here on the spit but from up there on the headland. Anyone with a telescope. Or a pair of binoculars.

From the security of the kitchen, I stared out at the other houses, neat and tidy and impersonal. The neatness and the lack of privacy, the very things that first attracted me to Edward's Bay, now seemed claustrophobic. I'd never choose to live in a cul-de-sac again, where all the comings and goings could be seen, where there was no escape except past those same prying eyes.

I didn't know enough about my neighbors, not who they were or what their motivations were, to guess whether any one of them was capable of murder. The only neighbors I'd met were Ralph Harrison and Sarah McKenzie. And now Walter Drummond. Even though I suspected Sarah of harming her own child, I couldn't imagine, her taking a rifle and shooting anyone in the back—at least not from a distance. Women are perfectly capable of shooting someone, but they don't do it from a distance. Women are up close and intimate in their crimes, hands-on. Not cold and calculating and distant. And Sarah had nothing to do with Jay Bishop.

As I watched, I saw Sarah's little car come along the street, no doubt on the way home to make the dinner I so dreaded. She got out of the car, reached into the trunk for a couple of grocery bags, disappeared into the house, returned to lift Christopher out of his seat. His downy head bobbed on her shoulder. She walked with a long purposeful stride, a sureness in the way she carried herself. Not like a stupid, neurotic woman acting out her own problems on her child. Not at all.

A moment later, the phone rang. It was Sarah.

"I saw your car, Noah. You're home early."

"Yes." I couldn't think of anything else to say.

"I thought we'd eat about seven," she said. "Is that all right with you? I'd like to have Christopher in bed first."

"Sure. Fine. I'll bring a bottle of wine."

"Great. See you later then."

She sounded happy and pleased. I managed not to groan into the phone.

Holding the receiver for a long time, contemplating the evening ahead, I punched in Lauren Watson's number in Minneapolis, a sudden need to hear her voice. I understood Lauren. There were no hidden agendas with her.

She answered, thank God. Her voice was no longer cracked and hoarse, but almost normal, stronger than before, the fear gone out of it. I told her about putting the house in Springwell on the market, and she said nothing. What should she say? I told her about Edward's Bay, the herons on the beach and the ducks and the sunrise over the Cascades, and she sighed and said, "It sounded lovely, Noah. Maybe I'll get to see it someday."

"You will. When you come back. When *are* you coming back, Lauren?"

A small silence stretched to an ominous length.

Her voice was whispery, floating over the miles. "I'd forgotten how blue the sky is in Minnesota in the winter. How cold and crisp and dry it is. Not like the Northwest, rain always dripping out of those gray clouds. When I think about it, Noah, I remember it was always gray."

"It'll soon be summer, Lauren. You know how lovely it is in the summer. We could take a boat up to the San Juans. Go hiking in the mountains. Give it another chance, Lauren."

Give me another chance, I wanted to say, but I didn't. I'd promised never to put pressure on her. I'd wait until May. She had to come back then, for Angel Ambrose's trial. Lauren was an important witness in the case. But a trial was hardly the most auspicious time to resume any sort of relationship, and as I said good-bye to her and put down the phone, it felt as though we were breaking an emotional connection to each other as well as a telephone link.

I had to think about Sarah McKenzie. I thought about what I was going to say to Sarah, as if rehearsing for a cross-examination, which questions to ask, how to pose them, but it wasn't the same as rehearsing for a trial. It was worse than a trial. If I got it wrong, there'd be no appeal.

I chose two bottles of wine from the small collection in the basement, one white, one red, because I didn't even know which Sarah preferred. Then I put a corkscrew in my pocket in case she didn't have one, and at a few minutes before seven, gritted my teeth and walked down the street once more. It was dark by now, and I stared into the other houses as I passed, to see who lived inside, what manner of people they might be. Most windows were lit from within, not hidden by drapes or blinds, as if the inhabitants had nothing to hide: in one house, a man and woman laughed together, glasses in hand; in another, the television flickered in a darkened room, further down, a woman stood alone in a brightly lit kitchen. They all looked like perfectly ordinary people. Not a killer among them.

At the end of the street, somebody climbed into a Ford Explorer and circled around the cul-de-sac, accelerating past me. The driver and passenger lifted their hands in greeting, and I waved back, though I couldn't see who they were.

When Sarah opened her door and smiled at me, it was difficult not to stare into her eyes. What was behind the friendly smile? A devious, dangerously unstable woman? A mother accused unjustly? Her eyes were wide and brown and innocent enough. This evening, she wore a long skirt that clung to her thighs, and her hair was shining and sleek. If it hadn't been for Chauncey and Hayward, I'd have kissed her. Instead I put the wine on the counter and kept my distance.

"How's Christopher?" I asked the question casually, fished the corkscrew out of my pocket. "White or red?"

The smile faded. "White," she said and frowned, blinked and turned away, opened a cupboard, and handed me two glasses. "Christopher's fine."

"A Ford Explorer passed me, and someone waved. Who's got a Ford Explorer?"

She shrugged, looked puzzled. "How should I know?"

I poured the wine, handed her a glass. "You know anyone round here called Robin?"

"No. Why the sudden interest in the neighbors?"

"Because I believe one of them shot Jay Bishop."

"Jay Bishop?" She seemed confused. "Oh, you mean that Indian you found on the beach? I'd quite forgotten about him." She touched her glass to mine. "Cheers, Noah."

"Forgotten? How could you forget, Sarah? How many people get shot around here?"

She shrugged again. "Why do you assume it was someone in Edward's Bay who shot him?"

"Don't you suppose it might be one of our neighbors? I thought you could tell me about them. Then we can pick the most likely suspect."

Sarah had to recognize I was deliberately sidestepping any intimacies. She wasn't stupid. "Well, if that's what you want to talk about," she said, put down her glass, and turned the heat up in the oven. "Dinner will be in about half an hour. Shall we go into the other room?"

I followed her into the room with both bottles of wine, determined not to run out of something to drink, sat opposite her in a pale chair in the pale room. The windows were bare, like those of the neighbors, the walls stark and unadorned, the room, the house, so incredibly tidy and absent of character. I wanted to ask why she lived in such unnatural orderliness, and didn't know which question to ask or where it might lead. And though I'd tried to rehearse the conversation we'd have, now I felt paralyzed by indecision. One of the questions might lead to disaster. Which question would be the right one? Which the wrong one?

The evening stretched long in front of me.

TWENTY-FIVE

SARAH WAS RESTLESS IN THE CHAIR OPPOSITE, CROSSING AND uncrossing her legs, twining her fingers round the stem of the wineglass. The silence was awkward for a few moments, as though we were both trying to think of something to say, and though I didn't mean to bring up the subject weighing so heavily on my mind quite so soon, the words fell out of my mouth, almost unbidden.

"Sarah, about Christopher. I wish you'd take him to the hospital again. So that he could be thoroughly checked out."

A hot red flush ran up her neck and into her face. "But I have," she protested. "You know I have. They can't find anything wrong with him. And I can't bear him to have to go through those tests again without any results. It's as though I'm torturing him."

Her reaction wasn't at all what Chauncey or Dr. Hayward or

those medical treatises had led me to expect. Munchausen-by-proxy mothers *wanted* tests done on their children. Tests and procedures, those medical papers insisted, satisfied some strange psychological need on the part of the mothers. I was confused by it all, sinking in a trough of psychiatry, out of my depth, in unknown murky waters. I should run into Christopher's bedroom right now, sweep him out of his crib, carry him off to the hospital to get it all sorted out. Cut-and-dried. Verdict of guilty or not guilty. Instead I crept around the edges, playing games. I wanted to be able to say to her, one adult to another, "Listen, Sarah, as a lover, you were great. Fantastic. I'm extraordinarily grateful you allowed me in your bed. But we're not meant for each other. You know how it is. Sex is one thing, love is another. Too bad, but that's the way it is. We can't love everyone, can we? Now, about your baby . . ."

Perhaps there weren't any circumstances when I could have been as forthright. Certainly not now, convinced the baby's fate might be in the balance. But how to make sure he didn't come to any harm?

Suddenly, as though she couldn't bear to sit still for another moment, Sarah jumped out of the chair and fled into the kitchen. I sat with the glass of wine for a moment, started to follow, then veered off to the bedroom where Christopher was asleep in his crib. Perfectly normal, as usual. I watched him for a few minutes, puzzled and unhappy, went out to the kitchen where Sarah was clattering pans. "Can I help?"

She didn't look at me. "Nearly ready. Sorry it's taking so long."

There were candles on the table by the window, flowers and mats, plates on the mats. The flickering flame of the candles reflected in the windows, windows that were like mine before there were shades to cover them, black holes bringing the night inside. The dining table was another deep hole, dark and glistening, doubling the two of us back upon ourselves. I said the polite things—"How nice everything looks"—but I was thinking, how do I get through this? how do I sort it out without a scene, a storm, another terrifying episode for Christopher?

I poured more wine—white for her, red for me—sat where my place was laid, our two images reflected upside down in the tabletop, in the empty rectangle of the window. When I looked at Sarah, blotches of pink were flaring high on her cheeks, and her eyes glistened in the candlelight. She took a sip of wine, stared into the glass, picked up her knife and fork, put them down.

"Noah, is anything the matter? Have I done something wrong? I thought you'd enjoy a home-cooked meal. But you seem so . . . so distant. And cool. From the moment you came in. As though I've done something to offend you."

I started to protest. Nothing was wrong, absolutely nothing. I was merely preoccupied, that was all, thinking about that young Indian, Jay Bishop, the dead man you didn't remember. It was the perfect moment to bring up the matter of Christopher again, but even as I opened my mouth, another thought dropped into my head, unbidden, unsummoned, one of those strange twists the brain makes. There was a girl in the Ford Explorer that passed me on the way here. The car had come from Ralph Harrison's house. There'd been a girl at his house at that meeting, a pretty dark-haired girl. His daughter. The name of the girl whom Jay was seeing was Robin. Jay's hobby was bird watching. Jay was a bird. So was Robin.

For a moment I almost forgot about Munchausen syndrome by proxy.

I looked down at my plate and realized that somehow I'd eaten everything. "Are you sure you don't know anyone called Robin?" I asked.

Sarah shook her head and took the plates away and brought out a dessert, and her dark hair swirled in the candlelight and her skin glowed and it was difficult to keep my mind on anything when she smiled at me, those brown eyes shining, leaned that silky head closer. I was in danger of getting lost again in the smell of her flesh and the touch of her hands. As though no one had warned me.

Almost lost. Not quite. I took a deep breath.

"Sarah, we have to talk about all this." My voice came out harsher and louder than I meant it to be. "I don't quite know how to say it. The truth is that I don't want to have an affair with someone else's wife."

Her eyebrows arched upward, and the color in her cheeks deepened. She shook her head again, as if to shake off the sound of my voice. An illicit affair wasn't the problem, of course. I was fudging the truth, leading Sarah astray, leading her on. It confounded me that, despite everything, she still roused my senses. I ought to be repulsed, not drawn to her, not so aware of her body and her skin. That awareness made everything much more difficult, more convoluted. But the first item on the agenda had to be her child's illness, real or imagined. And I had to keep her trust. If it meant being duplicitous, so be it. For Christopher's sake.

I reached for her hand across the table, clutched it too tightly. "Sarah, we're both lonely people. I took advantage of your loneliness. It's not something I'm proud of. But now I'm involved with you, and that means I'm involved with Christopher, too. I worry about him. I can't go any further until we find out what's wrong with him. The two of us, you and I together, must take him to the hospital so we get a proper diagnosis."

She gazed at me with that long, steady assessing gaze, the flame of the candles flickering in her eyes. "What is this, Noah? Some kind of commitment?"

"It's a commitment to Christopher. Is it a deal, Sarah?"

"You're asking me to put him through more tests?"

"If that's what it takes."

Suddenly she pushed her chair away from the table, rattling the glasses and dishes. "I don't see why you keep insisting on this, Noah. You're not Christopher's father; it's got nothing to do with you. Just because we slept together, once, doesn't give you the right to have any say in his medical care. That's like some sort of blackmail."

Which it was, of course. I was trying to blackmail her into cooperating. And if she refused, what should I do then? Abduct the baby?

"Please, Sarah. Let's find out what his problem is, and then we can go on from there. With a fresh slate. Wouldn't that be better for all of us?"

She kept staring at me, as though trying to read me, then she leapt away from the table, retreating across the room. She grabbed a cushion out of the chair, thumped it, threw it back down. "You're scared of taking on a sick kid, that's it, isn't it? Afraid you'll be saddled with the bills. That's what it means to be ill in this damned country, mountains of debt, mortgaging your house to pay the bills. This country can't be like the rest of the world and take care of its sick people in a decent civilized manner. Why don't you do something useful? Get that idiotic restraining order lifted so I can go home where they have a proper health care system."

I wasn't handling this at all well, allowing her to change the subject. "I thought your husband's insurance took care of the bills."

She glared at me. "You see! That's what you're worried about, isn't it?"

"No, Sarah, that isn't what I'm worried about. And there isn't much I can do about the health care system. But if it's the restraining order you care about so much, I suppose I could have a go at that."

She froze into place for a few seconds, picked the cushion up again and hugged it to her breast; then she rushed back across the room and threw her arms around me, almost knocking me sideways in my chair. "Oh, Noah! You mean it? Oh, God! You know what that would mean? I could go home. You can't imagine . . . Everything will be all right, if I could only go home."

Disentangling her arms from around my neck, I looked into

her eyes and thought that was one answer. Not more hospitals and more tests. Just let her go home with her baby. Would that be the right thing to do?

"I don't know, Sarah. Who's your attorney? I'd have to talk to him."

"Attorney? I don't have one. You can be my attorney, can't you?"

I made her sit down quietly, on the other side of the table, putting some distance between us. "When the restraining order was served, you had to have signed something."

Her eyes flicked away from me. "I haven't signed anything."

"You must have. You had to have made an agreement. Nobody can get a restraining order just like that. Not unless you did something you haven't told me about." Pausing, I looked at her carefully. "Did you do something, Sarah?"

"I told Harry to fuck off. Is that illegal?"

"This isn't a joke, Sarah."

"No. It isn't. I don't find it a bit funny either."

It wasn't hard to imagine she'd threatened to take the child away. She'd told me as much. But even then, it would be difficult to convince a judge to issue such an order. Restraining orders are for more serious threats—bodily harm, stalking, that sort of thing. "Are you sure you've got the terminology right? In any case, the order would only be temporary, until your husband gets home again."

She shook her head, the glossy hair slipping and sliding, riverlike, on her neck. "I just know I got a letter from a court telling me I couldn't leave the country."

"Where is it?"

She looked around vaguely. "I'm not sure. I put it somewhere."

But I'd have made a bet Sarah knew exactly where every small scrap of paper was in all that compulsive tidiness. Why did I always get the impression she was telling something less than the truth?

"Okay, then give me the name of your husband's attorney. At least I can go talk to him."

She seemed to think about it for another moment, as though she was about to change her mind; then she crossed to a desk in the corner, wrote something on a piece of paper, and handed it to me. A name, in a neat upright handwriting. Belling Sidworth. The name was vaguely familiar.

I made a pact with her. I'd do my best to get the order lifted so she could go home. Providing Christopher remained well. But if his problem returned, he'd stay in the hospital here until it was worked out. It seemed a reasonable compromise to me. Surely it would ensure the baby's well-being? If Chauncey or Hayward got wind of it, would they consider it interfering in medical matters? I'd face that hurdle when I came to it.

"I'm glad we got it sorted out, Sarah," I said and stood up. "Thanks for the dinner."

She looked shocked and surprised. "Aren't you going to stay? Now we've got it sorted out? There's no need for you to go home, is there?"

I said, firmly, "It's wiser, Sarah. Let's not confuse the issue. Who knows what that order said about you, about your fitness as a mother. You don't need an extramarital affair to mess it up. Things can get rough if it ever comes to a custody battle." There was plenty of truth in that suggestion. "Let's go our own ways for the time being. We can always start afresh when this business is settled."

"I'd hoped . . ." Her voice trailed away. "Oh, well, if you think it's better. Maybe you're right."

She clasped and unclasped her fingers and let me escape without further argument. I thought we were both relieved, somehow. Outside her house, I took steadying breaths of the cool night air and hoped to God I was doing the right thing.

The Ford Explorer was parked in Ralph Harrison's driveway. It was either Ralph or Bigs who'd waved at me from the driver's seat. I was almost certain the passenger was the girl who'd stood beside Ralph at the meeting.

TWENTY-SIX

IT'S JUST AS WELL THE MIND SHIFTS INTO ANOTHER GEAR AT the office; otherwise no one would ever get any work done. The next day, I shunted Sarah McKenzie and her problems into another compartment together with Jay Bishop, and attacked the paperwork accumulating on my desk in alarming quantities. Sibby and I spent most of the day plowing through it.

At the tag end of the day, I said to Sibby, "Don't you sometimes long for a simple straightforward job, so you could see what's been accomplished? Some job like housepainting. Or roofing. Or dentistry."

Sibby laughed. Still unaccustomed to the transformed smile, the glitter and flash of straight white teeth, I caught myself glancing at her now and then, sideways, as if to reassure myself it was the same old Sibby. It was, of course. She hadn't changed, it was only my perception of her that had changed.

It occurred to me that I hadn't seen Charlie all day. I asked where he was.

"He and Annie were going to sign some sort of agreement. He said he wouldn't be fit for work afterward. He's probably in a bar somewhere."

"Our fate is hanging in the balance at this very minute? There may be no job for us tomorrow." Stacking the papers on my desk, folding the files away, I thought about having no job. It might be a relief. "By the way, Sibby, do you know an attorney called Belling Sidworth?"

She looked surprised. "Everyone knows Belling Sidworth. The climber. Everest and K2 and probably every other mountain in the world. He's escaped with his life by the skin of his teeth several times. You want a job with him?"

"You think I'll need one?"

"You'd be lucky."

Mountain climbing wasn't my thing, but the awed respect in Sibby's voice gave me pause. An attorney who risks his life on the great mountains of the world might be a challenge. But it was obvious why he'd represent Sarah's husband, and in a way, it reassured me that at least one part of her story might be true.

"What is he? Some sort of legal guru for all mountaineers?"

Sibby shrugged. "I bet climbers need plenty of legal advice, don't you? What do they do about life insurance, for example? Would you insure someone who planned to climb Everest?"

It turned out that Belling Sidworth's office was just around the corner from us in Pioneer Square. Sibby called and made an appointment for me to see him the very next morning in the matter of Harry and Sarah McKenzie. I began to feel as if something might get accomplished after all. Then, just as I was about to quit for the day, a phone call came from Wayne Daniels. An unexpectedly garrulous Wayne Daniels.

"I'm back from Spokane, Mr. Richards. That girl—you know, Maria—I went to see her in the hospital, like you wanted. They haven't found her people, so far. Seems they move around all the time. I told the doctors she was engaged to my nephew, but that's not strictly true, not as far as I know, anyways. Jay'd have told me if he was planning to marry anyone. But I guess you have to bend the truth a little sometimes, don't you? I made out she was sort of family, because she didn't have no one else. So then they told me she might not ever wake up. She's got some sort of brain damage. Choked, they said, on her own vomit. Cut off the air to her brain. So now they don't know what to do with her. She'll just lie there, forever maybe, with those tubes going in and out of her. That's a terrible thing, isn't it, Mr. Richards? No one to claim you? No one to take you home. They're going to make her a ward of the state or some such thing. So the medical gets took care of."

It was a terrifyingly awful outcome. I was stunned into silence. The Dickensian term "ward of state," sent chills down my spine. Maria Cruz was really in limbo now, belonging neither to the conscious world nor to anyone who'd care for her.

Wayne said, "I got the papers from that safe box like you wanted. But there wasn't nothing I could do for that girl, Mr. Richards."

"I'd hoped she'd be a link to Jay for you."

Something like a chuckle came from the other end of the phone. "Plenty of girls could be a link to Jay, if that's what we're looking for. Girls a lot nearer to home." Then he said, "Suppose you and me goes fishing? In Jay's memory. I'll show you some of his favorite spots. Secret spots. That only the Quanda know."

I took it as a compliment. "I'd like that. Anytime. What did you find in the safe-deposit box?"

"I'll show you. When we go fishing." There was a hint of excitement in his voice.

As I put the phone down, I thought there was one service I

could perform for the abandoned Maria Guadelupe Cruz. Provide her with legal representation. Until her family was found. They'd turn up sooner or later, when the picking season started. Not so very many months away.

Sibby rattled around the office, locking up, and she made a movement with her head at the phone. "Bad news?"

"The girl in Spokane. She's not come out of her coma."

Sibby jingled the bundle of office keys hanging from one finger, noisily, arhythmically, reminding me of the realtor I'd taken a dislike to. "I'm sorry, Noah. Are you going to stay here all night?"

"You want to have dinner with me? I feel like staying in town."

She shook her head. "Sorry," she said again. "Not tonight." I wondered whether Charlie had warned her off.

"Then I'm going to stay and clear my desk," I said.

I didn't go back to Edward's Bay that night. I knew, of course, that it was to avoid any confrontation with Sarah. I fiddled around in the office much longer than was strictly necessary, then walked up the hill and ate dinner at the Italian restaurant on Fifth Avenue. Afterward I checked into the plushly overfurnished hotel next to the restaurant, pulled the thick curtains at the windows, and slept like a log. No sound of surf, no sense of being watched, only the comforting wail of police sirens and laughter from the street below filtering faintly through the curtains. The next morning, I read the *New York Times* over breakfast, got a shoeshine, walked down the hill to First Avenue, and felt part of the real world again.

Belling Sidworth's office was in a building much like ours, brick and stone, high ceilings and tall windows, creaking wood underfoot. But it was much grander than our office, occupying a whole floor, furnished with solid mahogany desks, plush Oriental carpets on the shining floors, and huge photographs of mountains and glaciers on the interior brick walls. The room I was shown into faced First Avenue and was filled with thin morning sun.

Belling Sidworth was a short stocky man, thick in the legs and the shoulders, older than I'd imagined, his face weathered and deeply lined with cracks and crevices like scars. When he shook my hand, his grip was frighteningly fierce. He waved me into the chair on the other side of a gleaming, extremely neat desk.

He said, "You're with Charlie Forsyth? I know Charlie, of course. What has defense law got to do with Harry McKenzie?"

Representing myself as Sarah's attorney wasn't exactly the truth, even though she'd asked me. But if I didn't, I'd have no authority to question Sidworth at all. I decided to lay my cards, such as they were, on the table.

"I'm here as a friend of Sarah McKenzie. There are some things she needs to get straight, and I hope you can help. She's under the impression there's a restraining order on her, preventing her from leaving the country. Is there such an order?"

Sidworth's eyes, buried in the folds and crags of the bronzed face, peered out at me, like an animal waiting to pounce. "You could check with the courthouse, counselor."

"I could. But I'd also like the answer to some other questions, if you'll bear with me. Such as when you expect Harry McKenzie to return. I understand he's climbing in the Himalayas?"

Sidworth said, dryly, "You understand correctly. Harry McKenzie will be gone for another six weeks or so."

Another six weeks? Six more weeks of worrying about Christopher?

"And you're wrong about a restraining order. It was a temporary parenting agreement."

So Sarah had got it wrong. I was cautious, not altogether sure of the facts, "A temporary parenting agreement? I was under the impression that both parties have to sign an agreement like that. Both parents. Isn't that right?"

Sidworth leaned back in the wide leather chair, folded his thick arms across his thick chest. "Mrs. McKenzie should have signed it, but apparently she chose not to. She didn't answer requests to appear before the judge or even answer any of our letters. Your client, Mr. Richards, is a noncooperative parent. As she didn't appear and therefore didn't object, she has, by default, agreed to abide by the conditions of the ruling. Which is not to leave the country with their child until his father returns."

"But it's a very onerous condition. Not unnaturally, she wants to take the child home to New Zealand to see her family."

"Exactly." Sidworth placed two square hands flat on the desk. "The United States has no extradition treaty with New Zealand. If she chose to stay in New Zealand, a court there would almost certainly side with one of its citizens. That is exactly why a parenting agreement is in force. To make her remain in this country."

"I have reason to think it's affecting her health," I said, "and the health of her child."

"Really?" That argument obviously wasn't going to cut much ice with Sidworth. "She should have considered that before ignoring our summons. You should have advised your client better, Mr. Richards."

"She wasn't my client at the time, and I haven't given her any advice on this matter." I paused, feeling my way "When exactly was this agreement put before the judge?"

He sighed, forbearingly. "Mr. Richards, I don't have to offer you information. You can go out and do your own homework."

I placed my own hands on his desk, palms upward, the gesture reminding me of Jay Bishop at the Eagle's Nest. "I don't mean this to be adversarial, Mr. Sidworth, I merely seek information. Sarah McKenzie needs help and advice, and I'd like to be able to give it to her. This type of law is out of my field, and I dislike family disputes. But I worry that forcing her to stay here will do nothing but harm to the child."

"I'm sorry," he said, and stood up, signaling the end of the discussion. He walked around the desk, then paused a moment. "To tell you the truth, Mr. Richards, family disputes aren't my field either. Do you climb mountains by any chance?"

My eyes strayed to the photographs of yet more mountains displayed around the room. Some of them were unmistakably the summit of Everest, craggy outcrops of rock, ice drifting ominously in a thin pale sky. "I'm not brave enough for anything like that."

He smiled suddenly, a charming boyish grin that altered the contours of his face. "I would say it doesn't take bravery so much as compulsion."

"Sarah McKenzie speaks of her husband as obsessed."

Sidworth shrugged. His shoulders were wide and strong, more than capable of carrying huge weights. " 'Compulsion' is the word I prefer. There's a subtle difference in the terms, wouldn't you agree? One sounds fairly healthy; the other doesn't." He smiled again, as though he'd accepted me into his club, whichever one it was, the law or the mountains.

"I try to do my best for my climbing friends," he continued. "We have much in common. They come to me with their problems. Mountain climbers have many problems. They go with the territory, you might say. Usually I write their wills, and sometimes, unfortunately, I end up as executor, taking care of their estates." His eyes flicked to the photographs, then away again. "I've promised my own wife I won't do any more of the big mountains."

He opened the door of his office, held out his hand. His hand was rough and gnarly, like the bark of an old tree trunk. "That agreement between Harry and Sarah McKenzie has lapsed. It was signed over two months ago, to be in effect for two months. Harry's team has been delayed, waiting out the weather. It's blowing up the usual storm on Everest. However, lapsed or not lapsed, I would advise your client not to think of taking that child anywhere. We could make life very difficult for her."

I was sure Sidworth could make life difficult. He looked like a formidable opponent. "I'll tell her that," I said. "I hope Harry McKenzie gets back safely."

The bright inquisitive eyes lost all expression, became blank and cool "And do you think that is what Mrs. McKenzie hopes, too?"

What exactly did Sarah want? Had I any idea? "Have you met her?" I asked, and when he said no, I was disappointed because

I'd have welcomed another assessment of Sarah McKenzie. A personal assessment, by someone other than a doctor. Or an involved neighbor.

On the way out of the office, I paused to look more closely at the photographs on the walls. The pictures were stunningly beautiful, soaring peaks against virgin blue skies, looming rocky overhangs, icy crevasses, white untrodden snow. A high, dangerous world, a far cry from a comfortable law office down in Pioneer Square. A simpler world in some ways.

TWENTY-SEVEN

"JUST MET WITH BELLING SIDWORTH," I MENTIONED CASUALLY to Charlie when I returned to the office. "Interesting guy."

Charlie was standing at the copier, feeding papers into it. His eyes slid to the clock on the wall. I could tell he wanted to say something about the time, but he shut his mouth, with an almost audible snap, thinking better of it. Just as well because I was in no mood for more recriminations.

"Belling Sidworth?" Charlie echoed. "One hell of a man." But he couldn't resist asking, "What were you seeing him about?"

"A personal matter."

He lifted his eyebrows. "Personal?" He lingered another moment by the machine, then followed me into my room and closed the door. "I'd like to remind you, Noah, that all your legal activities come under the umbrella of our partnership. Per the terms of our agreement. You can't just go off half-cocked on your own thing. You're not in a single-handed practice anymore." He paused a half-second. "Is it more of this crazy Indian stuff?"

I struggled with my temper. Some days it was hard to remember I wasn't my own master anymore. Charlie and I had a restrictive partnership agreement that I'd signed to get his help on the Ambrose case; any legal work I performed had to be processed through this office. Even pro bono work. Maybe it should include Sarah's legal problems, but I couldn't and wouldn't discuss those problems with Charlie. Not that I considered myself her legal representative. If Sarah needed an attorney, and she almost certainly did, it would have to be someone other than me.

"Look, Charlie, I asked Belling Sidworth one specific question. On behalf of a friend, as a matter of fact. But it could have been for myself. I have a life, too, you know." I cursed myself for bringing up Belling Sidworth's name in the first place. But he *was* an interesting guy. "And, no, it was nothing to do with the 'crazy Indian stuff.' "

Charlie's eyes were dark and skeptical. "Okay, Noah. If you say so. But obviously you're still dabbling with it. There was a call this morning from Washington, D.C., about that very thing." He produced a pink telephone slip out of the back of his hand, like a conjuring trick. As if he'd been waiting to spring it on me in person. Normally, all phone messages went into our respective in-trays. The time at the top of the slip said nine-fifteen A.M. A name and a telephone number. No message.

"How do you know what it had to do with?" I said. "It doesn't say anything here."

"Beth took the call. She asked what it was about, and as I was standing right there, I spoke to them. I explained we weren't interested in fishing rights or tribal issues."

I sucked in a breath, suddenly enraged. The blood ran into my face, drummed in my ears. "Jesus Christ, Charlie Forsyth! Who the hell do you think you are? You've absolutely no right to interfere in my affairs in that manner. No right at all! I don't care what damn agreement we signed. That was rude, insulting, and unforgivable."

We faced off against each other, chest to chest, nose to nose, the second time in almost as many days we were behaving like fighting cocks. But this time I was angrier than he was, as angry as I remember being for a long time. I wanted to punch that superior smirk right off his handsome face.

He backed away a little. "I gave you the message, didn't I?"

I jabbed a finger in his chest. "If someone calls here to speak to me, don't you ever tell them I'm not interested. Don't you ever speak to anyone on my behalf again."

Charlie batted my finger away, poked at my chest in turn. "You're a self-righteous bastard, Noah Richards. Uptight, sanctimonious, inhibited. An anemic blob on a red-blooded profession. You shouldn't be a lawyer; you should be a damn priest."

I swear I'd have hit him if the door to my room hadn't opened at that precise moment. Beyond Charlie's shoulder, I caught sight of Sibby in the doorway, hand on the knob, jaw dropping. Charlie turned his head and saw her, too. There was a tight stretching silence. You could practically hear the nerves twanging.

"Oh, sorry." Sibby seemed unsure whether to back out or come in. "I didn't realize you two were having a private conversation."

Charlie and I continued to glare at each other for another few challenging seconds; then he swiveled abruptly on his heel, pushed past Sibby who flattened herself against the wall. We heard his feet stamping down the corridor, the door to his room slamming.

Sibby raised her eyebrows, her curiosity obvious and not unnatural, but I didn't bother to enlighten her. "Get me this number," I said, thrusting the telephone slip at her. "Find out who called here at nine-fifteen to speak to me. Tell them I'm back in the office."

I sat down at my desk, waiting for the phone to ring, and my breath came in gulps. But after a few minutes, I began to calm down and suddenly felt good. Like an athlete. As though I'd been running. All the juices flowing, a rush of energy and gratification. Almost as good as sex. I jumped up out of the chair, strode across to the door, and threw it open. Sibby looked startled.

"I need the name of an attorney who deals in family law. You know anyone?"

"What sort of family law exactly?"

"Divorce, custody, that sort of thing."

"There are dozens," she protested, and I recalled those pages and pages in the telephone book.

"I want someone competent, Sibby. Not just any Tom, Dick, or Harry with the biggest ad."

The phone rang at her desk, and she picked it up, rolled her eyes at me, punched the hold button. "Your call from Washington."

"I'll take it in my room." I shut the door, picked up the phone, barked into it. "Noah Richards here."

A male voice at the other end said, "We called earlier, Mr. Richards, but assumed we'd reached the wrong number. We got the e-mail message."

"E-mail?"

"It was from Jay Bishop's e-mail address, but it was this phone number."

Maybe pathetic Pete in Spokane wasn't so pathetic after all. I offered him an apology in my head. I said, "To whom am I speaking?"

The caller rattled off a name I didn't quite catch at first. Brandon something-or-other. I got him to spell it for me. Kurtsheimer. He told me the name of his firm and it turned out to be a nationally known environmental law practice.

"Hang on," I said. "I'll call you back immediately."

It took a few minutes to reconnect to Mr. Kurtsheimer but he was right where he'd said he'd be, with one of the best-connected law firms in Washington, D.C.

"Okay, shoot," I said and knew that was an unfortunate choice of words.

He said, "May I ask what your interest is in this particular project, Mr. Richards?"

But I didn't know, of course, which particular project he was referring to. I said, carefully, "The local Quanda Indians instructed me to investigate the work Jay Bishop was doing."

"That's what I'm talking about. The appeal of the Boldt decision to the circuit court. We're concerned because we haven't heard from Bishop for several weeks. His computer link seems to have been shut off. He hasn't answered his telephone. The e-mail came from his computer, though. It said to contact you for information."

I couldn't think of any way to break it diplomatically. "I'm sorry to have to inform you that Jay Bishop is dead."

There was a sharp indrawn breath. "Dead?"

"Shot, actually. And it wasn't an accident."

"My God! You mean . . . murdered?"

Mr. Kurtsheimer was obviously shocked by the suggestion of murder, reassuring me that despite the prevalence of guns and such everyday deaths, someone out there still found the idea of murder shocking. I told him where Jay was found. I didn't say who found him.

"His family has asked me to find out what he was working on. Can you tell me?"

"It's no secret. Our firm represents a number of western Washington tribes in the matter of shellfish harvesting. Washington State and private owners have been appealing the 1974 Boldt decision, the decision that gave the tribes fifty percent of the harvest. Jay Bishop was one of our externs in the pre-appeal process, and he also helped prepare the report of the court's decision. Are you familiar with it?"

I wasn't.

"This latest decision was very favorable from the tribe's point of view. Maybe the issue will be put to rest, at last. Though we've thought that before. Several times. I'll fax you a copy of the report. It's about to be published in the *Bar News* anyway."

I thanked him, and he said, "I'm really sorry to hear about Jay Bishop. I never met him personally. We communicated only by computer, but his work was good, especially for a student. As a matter of fact, I believe our firm was thinking of offering him a position. He was recommended, I believe, because he was Native American."

Ironic. Jay Bishop, recommended to a prestigious law firm because he was Native American, and maybe killed for the very same reason.

"Was he also working with you on the issue of tribal recognition for the Quanda Indians?" I asked.

"Quanda Indians? No, not that I know of. Tribal status is quite a separate issue."

So Jay had been working on two different projects. Which one had he been killed for? Surely not the fishing rights because that was through the courts now. Except that some people would remain enraged about the decision forever.

After a while, my own rage at Charlie seeped away. The whole ludicrous confrontation suddenly struck me as funny. But I stayed in my room so I wouldn't run into him in the corridor and have to carry on as though everything had been forgotten. The room was peaceful and quiet with the door closed, the phone not ringing, no one interrupting my thoughts. Not even Sibby venturing inside. I thought about Sibby, how I liked her and how she didn't stir my blood, while Sarah, whom I didn't trust, set my flesh and blood tingling.

A knock came at the door, and I wiped the smile off my face. It was Sibby with the fax from Washington.

"You knocked?" I was amazed. Normally, she never knocked, just barged straight in.

"I thought you wanted to be left alone."

"I did. I do. Have you found a family lawyer yet?"

"I made a list. I've heard this woman is good." Sibby handed me the fax and a separate slip with names and numbers, and I accepted them casually, as though I'd been busy doing something other than wait for them for the past hour. Sibby retreated immediately and respectfully. I should lose my temper more often.

Putting aside the list of family attorneys, I studied the fax from Washington. Jay Bishop's name didn't appear on the report, but Brandon Kurtsheimer was one of the authors. The little document was elegantly written, a summation of the circuit court's decision upholding the rights of western Washington tribes to harvest shellfish. Though I was familiar with the original Boldt decision, I'd long ago lost track of what had happened since 1974, but obviously the state and private owners had been appealing the decision ever since. This latest appeal concerned the definition of "fish." "Fish," the circuit court held, applied to all shellfish found on tidelands—including clams, cockles, oysters, and mussels—on private as well as publicly owned tidelands. The court applied the definition to subtidal and deepwater areas, to geoduck, crab, shrimp, sea urchin, sea cucumber, octopus, scallops, and squid. That is, to everything.

It appeared that Native Americans had won hands down.

TWENTY-EIGHT

EDWARD'S BAY NOW SEEMED TOO DISTANT FROM THE BUSTLE of downtown Seattle. When I got back that evening, the house, in its half-furnished state, felt cold and uninviting. I turned up the thermostat, stepped out on the deck to watch the peaks of the Cascades fade into the night. Along the spit and up on the headland, lights sprang up one by one in the houses, a string of pearls reflected in the quiet waters of the bay. Beautiful, but now also melancholic and menacing.

Sarah had once said Edward's Bay "wasn't a real place, just a bunch of houses with nice views." She was right. There seemed no point to the houses, no reason to cover this fragile piece of land that was once the tribes' usual and accustomed grounds and stations with concrete tarmacadam roads and driveways. Who did such land really belong to? To the people who'd bought the land from the Harrisons? To the Indians? To the creatures who lived beneath the water and sand? Could such a delicate slice of the earth ever really be owned by anyone? Chief Seattle, the wise old Suquamish leader, once asked, in the early days of the state, "How can one buy or sell the air, the warmth of the land?" How indeed? It was an impossible, unanswerable question.

Inside the house, the phone rang. I let the machine answer, sure it would be Sarah wanting to know what happened with Belling Sidworth, and I still didn't know how to deal with Sarah. The machine clicked on, and an artificially loud male voice spoke into it. Wayne Daniels. I picked up the receiver.

"Hey, Noah Richards!" he said, the old cheeriness back in his voice. "How about tomorrow for that spot of fishing? We can take my boat out to the point, catch the tide on the turn there."

Tomorrow was Saturday. Tomorrow sounded like an excellent time to me. "That'd be great, Wayne. I haven't been fishing for months."

"I got all the gear and the bait. Pick you up at six A.M."

"You promised you'd show me those documents from the safe-deposit," I reminded him.

"Sure thing, Noah I'll bring them. You'll be interested."

I would be. I heard how he called me Noah for the first time. I turned on the TV for the weather forecast, saw that rain was promised for the weekend, so I went to the basement in search of my old foul-weather gear. The boxes from Springwell were still piled haphazardly, one on top of another, and it took a while to locate the one with the waders and foul-weather gear and the elaborate Eddie Bauer vest with twenty pockets that Janet once gave me as a birthday gift. The foul-weather gear was ancient, the oiled fabric beginning to crack in places, and I couldn't think why I'd bothered to pack it. I'd had it since I was a teenager. I should have tossed all this stuff away and started anew. It's what I'd promised myself, after all.

Back upstairs, on the sectional large enough for eight people, I nursed a scotch and read the court of appeals report again. The list of the disputed shellfish read like poetry: clams and cockles, oysters and mussels, geoduck and crab, shrimp and sea urchins, sea cucumbers and octopus, scallops and squid. The appeal was specifically in regard to the shellfish, but the old tribal rights to fifty percent of all harvestable fish were reiterated. A long and bitter battle the Indians had finally won. God knows how much Jay Bishop had to do with winning this particular battle, but surely it was enough to make Wayne proud. I looked forward to showing him this report that Jay had been working on.

I should also have looked forward to informing Sarah that she was probably free to leave the country, but I reviewed my conversation with Belling Sidworth and wasn't at all certain I could tell her that in good faith. His warning, "We could make life very difficult for her," echoed ominously.

I didn't know what the hell to do about Sarah. I couldn't wait to pass her on to another attorney. I had to show her the list of family lawyers and make her listen to reason. If Chauncey and Hayward were correct, Sarah was a time bomb ready to go off, and even though I'd have much preferred to walk away from the whole wretched mess and leave it to someone else, I had to make sure Christopher was okay. When I went to refresh my drink in the kitchen, I saw the lights on at Sarah's house, and reluctantly, I punched in her phone number.

The phone rang and rang. The unanswered phone made me deeply anxious I listened to the repetitive ringing tone and wondered where the hell she was at seven in the evening with her baby. She could be anywhere, of course. Sarah had to have friends somewhere. She could be in Seattle, gone shopping or to the movies, to the grocery store. She didn't *have* to be running to the hospital with Christopher; she didn't *have* to be inside the house holding her hand over his nose and mouth.

I'd never bought that answering machine for Sarah. I'd never bought her anything. I'd slept with her and now I wanted out, and still it felt as if she were the one who was doing the betraying. I saw the Ford Explorer come out of the driveway at Ralph Harrison's house, saw another light come on at another window at Sarah's. So she was home. Why the hell didn't she answer the phone?

I abandoned the phone, sprinted out of the house and down the road. It felt as if I'd been running this way half my life, this feeling of anxiety heavy in my chest. As I came nearer to her house, I ran faster, up the path to the front door, banged on it.

"Sarah! It's Noah."

Nobody answered, and nothing seemed to move in the house. I had no doubt she was inside. Not only had I seen the light go on, but her presence was almost palpable, that odd unmistakable sensation when someone is nearby. An awful fear for the baby consumed me. I tore round to the back door where I could look into the house through the glass. Nothing. The kitchen was as empty and tidy as usual, shining and compulsively neat. Compulsive, obsessive? One healthy, Belling Sidworth said, the other not.

I banged hard on the glass, rattling it. "Sarah!" I shouted again. "It's Noah. Open the damn door."

I wanted to smash the glass with my fist but had the sense to try the knob first. The door opened easily under my hand, and I almost fell into the kitchen. I hurried down the hallway toward the bedroom. Then I saw Sarah standing against the wall outside the bedroom, still and silent among the shadows at the top of the small flight of stairs.

I slowed in my headlong rush. "What the hell is going on, Sarah? Why didn't you answer when I called? When I knocked?"

She shook her head dumbly and stared at me as if incapable of speech. The phone began to ring nearby, and still she didn't move. I grasped her by the shoulders, my fingers digging into her flesh. "What the devil is going on, Sarah?"

Her eyes slid away from mine. Her voice came out through

stiff lips, in a cracked, unnatural whisper. "Something terrible happened."

Something terrible? Dear God! I pushed her to one side, and she stumbled against the wall, her face white and stricken, as if she'd seen a ghost. "If you've done anything to that child," I threatened, "if you have, by God . . ." I tore into the bedroom.

Christopher's crib was in the corner. He lay on his back, arms outstretched, quiet and unmoving, a small cruciform figure. I couldn't hear the monitor. I snatched him out of the crib, his body limp between my hands. It was a surprise that he weighed so much, a soft deadweight that smelled of milk and talcum powder, I peered into the tiny face, so near to mine, wanted to shake him in desperation, but even as I stared at him, his body stiffened and his eyes opened wide, and his mouth gaped into a square and he began to wail. Very loudly.

Sarah was beside me, grabbing at my arm, her eyes huge dark pits. "Noah, have you gone out of your mind? He was fast asleep." She reached for the baby, and I almost handed him over; then clutched him closer to me, protectively. Now his crying was high-pitched and frightened, his body slippery and struggling in my arms, legs kicking, and I was awkward with him and didn't know the right way to hold him. I stared at him, unable to believe he was okay, but the yelling sounded perfectly normal. He didn't seem to be injured in any way.

"I'm not handing him over," I said to Sarah. "Not until you tell me what the hell's happening."

She stared at me in dismay, her face and the whole of her body rigid and unmoving, hard and frozen and immobile; then she sighed, a harsh painful exhalation. The air seemed to seep out of her, and she collapsed in slow motion onto the edge of the bed, her hands held up in a gesture of defeat. Her mouth folded into a tight line, and she put her hand over it. For another long moment she didn't speak; then she said, "Oh, Noah. It happened. The very thing I was dreading. An avalanche or something . . . on Everest . . . Harry . . . and two others. They were roped together. They were all swept away."

I gaped at her over Christopher's hot screaming head. "Harry? Your husband? That's the terrible thing? That's what you meant?"

"I always knew something like this would happen. I knew it, Noah. In my heart I always knew it would end like this."

I held the baby away from me, his legs beating and his arms flailing, his face red and furious. "Not the baby? It wasn't the baby after all?"

Sarah wasn't listening. "That lawyer called. The mountaineer. A few hours ago. They'd just got the news. He said there wasn't any hope."

I didn't know what to do or say. How to apologize.

She held out her arms for Christopher and I set him on her lap, and she brought him close to her breast and patted his back, absently. Almost immediately he stopped crying. "So I fed Christopher and put him to bed. When you have a baby, you just have to keep doing things, don't you? You can't stop everything when you have a baby to look after. But the phone kept ringing and ringing, and after a while I didn't answer it anymore because I didn't want to talk to anyone. Because I feel so guilty." The words were coming out in gulps. "The last thing I said to Harry was that he'd probably get himself killed, and now it's happened. A self-fulfilling prophecy, isn't that what it's called?"

I looked at her helplessly, sat beside her and massaged her shoulder, an ineffectual gesture of sympathy. "You mustn't blame yourself, Sarah. You musn't feel guilty."

I felt guilty. Guilty of blaming her for something that hadn't happened. I tried to find the right words to comfort her and wasn't sure there were any.

"He knew the risk," I said, to say something. "Anyone who climbs mountains understands the dangers. Isn't that why he did it? For the thrill of it? The challenge? Nothing you could have said or done, Sarah, would have made any difference to someone determined to climb a mountain like Everest."

Her eyes wandered off into the distance. "It seems such a waste," she said.

Of course it was. A terrible waste of a human life on a high distant mountain. For what? Yet I could almost envy men like Harry McKenzie or Belling Sidworth, men who took risks and challenged themselves, met with danger, and usually overcame it. Who obviously counted those few moments in the rarefied atmosphere on top of the world as making everything else worthwhile. I envied the desire to live so intensely.

Sarah gazed at the baby on her lap, quiet now, sucking his thumb greedily. "Now he'll never know who his father was."

"But you'll tell him. One day he'll be very proud."

"Oh, yes. One day." She sounded defeated. "And perhaps you'll tell me what I'm going to do in the meantime."

"You could go home now," I said.

She looked at me for a long moment. "I could, couldn't I?"

She seemed to be trying to smile, but nothing reached her eyes. There were no tears in them, nothing in them, emptied of everything. She was in some sort of shock, but it was impossible to judge whether she was truly devastated or whether she was in some way relieved. And I still couldn't judge whether she was capable of doing those things to her baby that Chauncey and Dr. Hayward suggested.

"You can go home," I said, "if you can assure me you didn't try to harm Christopher in any way."

She gazed at me blankly with dark stricken eyes. "I don't know what you're talking about, Noah. I wouldn't do anything to hurt my baby."

Of course, she'd deny it. Of course.

"You can tell me the truth now, Sarah."

"If only I'd told Harry. He might have come down off the mountain. That was my first idea, to get him off the mountain. I was so alone, Noah. Then all at once you were here, and I didn't feel so alone anymore."

"The baby, Sarah? What about the baby?"

Suddenly she started to cry, great heaving regretful tears, not angry anymore, only remorseful. "I'm so sorry," she sobbed. "So very sorry."

The way she cried made all those awful suspicions rise to the surface again. I couldn't tell whether she was crying for her dead husband or for something she might have done. The uncertainty stunned me into useless silence because I didn't know what to do next.

At last, she said, "I should call my parents. But it's the middle of the night there."

Parents, that's what she needed. Grandparents, that's what Christopher needed. Not doctors and hospitals. Not a stranger like me.

"Call them," I said. "Now."

TWENTY-NINE

WAYNE KNOCKED ON MY DOOR AT EXACTLY SIX A.M.

I'd spent the night at Sarah's house, listening as she talked and cried, cried and talked, revisiting the guilt and regrets about her husband and her marriage. But she told me nothing about Christopher, and I didn't ask again because I didn't want to know the answer now. She said she wanted to wait until it was daytime to speak to her folks in New Zealand, so I took the phone off the hook and listened to her ramblings because there didn't seem to be much else to do for her.

"Noah," she said, at last, "whatever would I have done without you?" Then she fell asleep in the chair, suddenly, like a baby, and I carried her into the bedroom where her own baby was sleeping in his crib, lay on the bed beside her to keep watch for a while. When I knew she was going to stay asleep, I crept away to call

Chauncey to tell him what had happened. "Now what do I do?"

"I'll talk to Hayward," Chauncey said. "We'll take it from here, Noah." (My heart sank for Sarah McKenzie.)

When the dawn began to break and Sarah and the baby were still sleeping, I left a note. *I'll be back later this morning. I'll help with whatever needs to be done. Take care of Christopher. Love, Noah.*

I went back to my own place, made a pot of coffee, and waited for Wayne to arrive.

I filled a thermos with black coffee and my father's old silver flask with scotch and took the ancient yellow foul-weather gear to keep the wind out. Despite the long night of vigil, I wasn't particularly tired, just wrung out, as if I too had lost someone. Sitting silently in a boat would be the perfect antidote for the endless talking night. I thought I could rely on Wayne to be silent.

I expected him to be late. Indians, I'd been led to believe, weren't good at punctuality. But the tide waits for no man, and Wayne Daniels surely knew all about tides. The sun was barely rising over the Cascades, a hazy dawn light filtering through the clouds and across the sound, when he knocked at my door. The cab of his truck was warm and smelled of hot diesel fuel and old boots. Wayne grinned from under his cap.

"Great day for fishing," he said, throwing in the gear, circling the cul-de-sac, and heading up toward the village at alarming speed. "The boat's down at the marina," he said. I wasn't aware there was any sort of marina nearby. "Could have met you there, but, well, you're my guest. It's polite to pick a guest up at the door."

We hurtled through the sleeping village. A mile or so farther on, after the turning to Wayne's house, we passed a large sign announcing Bay Oysters, and I remembered the owner, Jack Partridge, at the meeting at Ralph's, remembered him saying, "Took me years to build up my oyster beds."

Another half-mile and Wayne swung the truck to the right, down a narrow dirt road, to a small dock jutting into a sheltered semicircular cove. A dozen or so boats that had seen better days were tied up at the slips; two more were hauled, listing on their sides; crab pots were piled in a heap near the end of the dock, a skein of nets at another spot. Rusting trailers and an assortment of buoys and boat fenders and general debris littered the muddy parking area; "marina" was a grand name for it, more a junkyard than a boatyard. But when I got out of the truck, the air was salty and sharp, and there was the sweetly familiar sound of water slapping beneath a dock, a gentle bumping of hulls against creosoted wooden pilings.

Wayne pointed to the end of the dock. "That's her. The *Maribelle*. Not much to look at maybe, but she does her job okay."

The planks of the dock were slippery with dew, and everywhere it was so still and quiet that our footsteps on the soft wood rang loud and heavy. Seagulls flapped up from the railings, the beat of their wings distinct, their melancholy cries echoing among the trees. A seal watched from fifteen feet away. I could hear the sound of his breathing, the faint plop and ripple of the water as he slid beneath the surface.

I'd supposed Wayne's boat would be a small dory like the one I'd seen in the bay that first day, but the *Maribelle* was a seiner, at least forty feet long, not beautiful, but functional. Very functional, with all the gear—nets and electric winches and grapnels and radar and depth finder. It was also outfitted, Wayne took pains to point out, with the latest fish-finding device to scan the depths, identify which fish were where, and display them on a brilliantly colored computer screen. He didn't demonstrate the computer until after we'd slipped the dock. The powerful twin diesels throbbed into immediate life with a touch of a button, and he reversed the *Maribelle* out into the cove, chugged forward into the sound. The seal surfaced again and watched our progress from the middle of the small bay. "Damn scavenger," Wayne said.

As soon as we'd rounded the headland, he switched on his new toy. "Just got it," he said. "Isn't it a marvel?"

The bright blue screen flickered and flashed in front of my tired eyes, red and green and orange blips scudding across the monitor. Steering the boat with one hand, Wayne fiddled with the controls of the computer with the other. Dazzling grids and lines and measurements came and went in quick succession. "See, you can set it according to the depth of the water and the size of the fish—salmon, say—and it'll find them for you. Or bottom fish. Lingcod, say. No more time wasted chasing up and down, just wishing and hoping to get lucky."

I blinked at the flickering screen. "I don't know, Wayne. Seems a bit like cheating to me."

"Cheating? It's the latest science. We'd be cheating ourselves if we didn't use it."

Perhaps he was right. "But we aren't going to use it today, are we?"

"Hell, why not?"

I shrugged and unscrewed the thermos. "Fishing is a sport for me, Wayne. Not my livelihood. Wouldn't be any sport with all the guesswork taken out of it." I offered the flask. "Coffee? Or something stronger?"

He gazed at me across the cabin, then out of the cabin windows to watch the water, spun the wheel with one finger and seemed disappointed, his wide mouth drooping, the black eyes impenetratable. "Well, shit, I never knew a fisherman who didn't just want to bring a fish home anyway he could."

"How about a bet?" I suggested. "My fishing nose against yours. If you'll shut off the computer."

"How much?"

"It's foolish of me to bet anything at all, isn't it? You must know every fishing spot around here like your own backyard."

"This *is* my backyard," he said.

"Right. So I'm not risking more than twenty bucks."

"Okay," he said, "done." And he turned the computer off.

Now it was only the simple pleasure of looking for fish, in a boat in the soft morning air.

There was a lot more power beneath the hull than I was accustomed to, but Wayne kept the big engines throttled back and we proceeded slowly and sedately past the headland behind the village.

"Where are we heading?"

"Just beyond Edward's Bay," he said. "Below what they call Lincoln Point. We call it Sumanu. I told you I'd show you some of Jay's favorite spots."

For a while the morning remained hazy and bright, but soon the promised rain clouds came in thickly on a breeze from the southwest, and the *Maribelle* started to buck against the tide and the wind. A steady rain began to fall, but the inside of the *Maribelle*'s cabin was cozy and dry.

"You have different names for all the landmarks round here?"

"Of course. We were here long before George Vancouver ever was."

George Vancouver, in his voyage of 1792, named Puget Sound, the islands, and the mountains for his crew and for colleagues back in England. Even Mount Rainier ended up with the name of a distant Englishman. "Tahoma" the Indians called it. Indian names that still lingered—like Seattle, or Stillaguamish, Swinomish, or Duwamish—had a more fitting sound for the Northwest landscape.

We rounded the first headland. Through the mist I could see Edward's Bay, low and insubstantial on the shoreline. "What was Edward's Bay called by the Quanda?" I wanted to know.

Wayne shrugged his shoulders. "It had no name. It was nothing. Just a sand spit. A place to gather clams."

I remembered Jay Bishop's odd word. "What does Kirowbini mean?" I asked. "Is it Indian? A bird?"

" 'Kirowbini'? Don't mean nothing to me. Not any Indian

word I've heard. Mind you, there's lots of Indian words I never heard. I can't speak the old language anymore. My wife, though, she knows some of it."

I pulled my father's silver flask out of my pocket, took a swig of the single malt whisky. "Did you know Jay was working on the appeal of the Boldt decision in the ninth circuit court?"

Wayne pulled back on the throttle and made a wide arc beyond the spit. I could see my house, or rather the house that belonged to Bigs Harrison, just above the driftwood. A nothing place, a blip on the horizon. Nothing worth dying for.

"The appeal to do with rights to the shellfish," I said. "Not with tribal rights. Did you know about it?"

Wayne shrugged again. "Sure. We knew he was working on that."

"But would anyone kill him for that? What difference would it make? If Jay hadn't worked on that appeal, it would have been someone else. It wasn't as though getting rid of him would get rid of the appeal."

"It wasn't just the fishing rights. It was whether the Quanda will be recognized as a tribe. If we're recognized as a tribe, we get to share in those treaty rights." Wayne spoke patiently, as though he was having trouble making me understand. "That'd mean we have a right to Edward's Bay."

He settled the *Maribelle* off the point, beyond Edward's Bay, a hundred yards from the shore. "This look like a good place to fish to you, Noah Richards?"

I poked my head out of the cabin, examined the swirl of the tide.

"Twenty bucks that we find fish here?"

"Twenty bucks," he said, and I wasn't sure who was betting against whom.

He killed the engine, and the *Maribelle* slopped around in the swell. It was seven A.M., and there were no other boats out with us. The rain dripped steadily and gently out of the gray clouds, not a downpour, just a mild spring drenching. Wayne rooted around in the scuppers, handed me a rod and a box with flashers and bait. "One hour," he said. "If we don't land anything by then, it's your twenty dollars."

I fixed a herring to the hook. "You were going to show me what you found in Jay's safe-deposit."

"Now?"

"Now's a good time."

Wayne reached into the bag he'd carried on board, produced a smaller zippered bag. "You think this'll do it?" He grinned triumphantly.

The bag contained a stack of photocopies, diaries and handwritten notes, duplicate photographs of turn-of-the-century Indians—Quanda Indians, I supposed. All the documents were dated and signed by Jay Bishop, who also noted where he'd found them, and who had the originals. There were interviews with Quanda elders about their past, carefully recorded oral histories. A sociopolitical continuity. I shuffled through the documents; there were too many for me to examine properly there and then, but just to hold them in my hand was exciting.

Wayne said, "If these prove the Quanda are a tribe, we're part of the treaties. Back then, the Quanda weren't recognized. But we know we're a tribe. We've always known. Just because some white men didn't know it a hundred years ago doesn't mean the Quanda doesn't have the same rights as all the other tribes."

I turned the precious slivers of history in my hands. "Jay did a wonderful job. And he wasn't even Quanda."

Wayne shrugged. "If we said he was, then he was. We could say you're Quanda if we wanted. The U.S. government gets to say who's a citizen if it wants. They do it all the time, don't they?"

The logic seemed indisputable. "Someone's got to take a look at all this, Wayne. It seems like a perfectly good historical record to me, but you have to have an expert."

Wayne's eyes flicked to me, his meaning clear.

"Don't look at me. But I'll find you someone who knows about this sort of thing."

"Okay, if you say so. Too bad you won't. So, are you ready to catch some fish?"

I replaced the documents back in the bag, carefully.

For a big man, Wayne was pretty agile around the boat. The jeans jacket was now covered with a yellow slicker and his legs with a pair of large rubber boots, so he seemed even more enormous, but his feet were light on the decking, and he avoided all the clutter as though he knew exactly where to step. Clearing a spot at the stern for me, he leaned over the gunwales and inspected the water. I dropped the hook and ran out the line. The rod was homemade, the reel nicely balanced, the line running smoothly. "Aren't you going to have a go?" I asked.

His teeth flashed. "No. Just going to watch you. Give you advice."

I sat in silence for a while, paying out the line, reeling it back in. The rain dripped off the brim of my hat and down the shoulders of the rain gear, and after a while, I stopped watching the line and stared along the shore at the houses above us, wondering who might be watching us. The morning reminded me of the morning Jay had talked to me on the beach, the mist, the hazy grayness of the day.

I reeled in the line, examined the bait. Not a single nibble. "Someone's twenty bucks are in danger," I said.

Wayne peered over the side again, as though he could read the water. Which he probably could. "We'll try over there," he said, pointing nearer to Edward's Bay. "The tide's running round the spit now." He went forward to the cabin, switched on the engines. I went forward with him, fished the flask out of my pocket, took another swig of the scotch. When I offered it to him, he shook his head. "Don't go for the strong stuff," he said "Stick to beer myself."

Circling the *Maribelle* slowly, he repositioned her closer to Edward's Bay and the end of the spit, cut the engines again. The boat churned in the inrushing tide.

Wayne said, "It's hard to get excited about the tribal thing just now. I think about Jay and how important it was to him, but who'd imagine it'd lead to killing? Except Jay was Indian. Indian life's always been cheap to the white man."

"That was then; this is now. Now an Indian life means just as much under the law as any other."

"Sure," he said "Sure."

Back at the stern, I fixed a fresh herring on the hook, dropped it over the side. Wayne came and sat beside me, his weight enough to tilt the *Maribelle* to one side, very slightly.

"What I always believed," Wayne said, "was, it was the girls who'd get him into trouble. Never thought it would be the legal stuff. Like, he was messing around with some girl down in Edward's Bay. I always thought he'd get hell for that. Not enough to get killed, of course, but enough to make trouble. I told him to keep his hands off, but you know what young guys are like. He was going to be a lawyer. That was good enough for anyone, he said."

"What was her name? Was it Robin?"

"Something like that."

"Why the hell didn't you tell me about her?" I reeled in the line, laid the rod down. "Did you tell anyone?"

"Like who? Who's interested, apart from you?"

"The police, for a start."

"You think they care?" Wayne stared down at the water. "The fish aren't going to bite today. We might as well go in." He stood up, started toward the front of the boat.

At that precise moment, a sharp blow pulverized my right arm, a shattering pain that took my breath away, made me yell out. I bent over in agony, clutched at my wrist, sank down on the thwart. There was a sickening pain in my arm and my hand wouldn't move. The whole of my arm felt as if were on fire. Pulling frantically at my sleeve, I saw a small neat hole in the yellow slicker and stared at it, uncomprehending. I didn't understand what had happened until the unmistakable zing and ping of a bullet came from somewhere nearby, and then I realized that someone was shooting at us. As they'd shot at Jay Bishop.

I slid off the thwart and crouched below the gunwales. "Wayne!" I yelled. "Wayne, watch out." But he didn't hear me, the sound of the engines drowning out my voice, and even as I started crawling forward, I saw him crumple slowly, slumping to the deck, hanging on to the wheel with one hand. The *Maribelle* spun in a mad circle.

I lay on the deck, eye-level with Wayne's back. He didn't move and didn't let go of the wheel. Overhead the clouds rotated and swirled until I was dizzy, the distance to the cabin stretching to infinity, and when I tried to crawl forward on my hands and knees, my arm buckled under me. I collapsed to the deck again, closed my eyes, opened them, and saw right in front of my face, a bullet on the decking, reached out my good hand for it, instinctively, slid it into a pocket of the foul-weather gear. Then I stood up and lurched towards the cabin, my feet slipping and sliding under me. At any moment I expected to be hit again, in the back this time.

Wayne's arm was caught around the wheel, and it took precious seconds to pry it loose, but at last I got hold of the wheel with my left hand so I could straighten the boat. Just in time. The headland was frighteningly close, and we were going straight for it before I managed to turn to port and open water. I had no idea where we were in relation to Edward's Bay, but kept heading away from the shore until I felt at a safe distance. From the shore and whoever was taking aim at us.

Once the *Maribelle* was far enough out into the sound, I throttled back on the engines, and kneeled down to tend to Wayne, a massive motionless heap near my feet. His face was a dirty muddy color, and the sound of his breathing was shallow and grunting, but he was definitely alive. I couldn't see where he'd been hit, and for a moment I tugged futilely at the bulky jacket with one hand, then realized that even if I found the wound, there was little I could do about it. The best first aid for Wayne was to get him to shore and to a hospital as quickly as possible.

When I stood up again my head swam, and it was a moment before I could orient the boat to the land. We were lying about a mile offshore, at least two miles south of Edward's Bay. No use turning around and heading back where we'd come from. There was no one at the marina, and we'd be back in the range of the gun. Going across the sound to Seattle meant taking the *Maribelle* across the shipping channels. I wasn't sure of my ability to keep her on an even course.

I turned the boat south toward Seawards and tuned into the emergency frequency on the radio and prayed it wouldn't be too late for Wayne.

THIRTY

THE DECK HEAVED UNDER MY FEET, AND THE WHEEL DRIFTED to the left and then to the right, but thank God, the emergency call was picked up by the Coast Guard, and they intercepted us before I ran the *Mirabelle* into another vessel. A white boat with a red slash on the bow drew up alongside; like knights to the rescue, young men leapt aboard, seized the wheel, tended to Wayne and to me, put afterburners on the big diesels, and raced to the ferry landing at Seawards. An ambulance waited to take us to the same hospital where I'd gone with Sarah and Christopher. The emergency room was beginning to look altogether too familiar.

I walked in under my own steam, but Wayne was rushed in on a stretcher, the nightmare scenario I'd imagined too often, doctors and nurses running alongside, blood pumping, needles stabbing. They took him straight to surgery.

Filled with pain medication, I was shuttled backward and forward under X-ray machines, and was still lying on a gurney in the emergency room in a morphine-induced torpor, when Dr. Hayward appeared in the cubicle. He peered down at me. "Can't stay away, eh?" he said. "Can we contact someone for you?"

It was an effort to ponder the question. I floated above the world, bound only by fragile strands, a sensation of kindly well-being, drifting painlessly on gossamer wings.

"What about that doctor friend of yours in Springwell? Carlsson?"

I managed to say no. Who needed Chauncey running down to say, "I told you so"? Though it might be nice to have Daphne come tend to me. "What about Wayne Daniels?" I asked.

Hayward shrugged. "Doing okay for someone who took a bullet through his ribs. They've repaired a couple of blood vessels and given him a few liters of blood. Thank God you didn't try to move him. The weight of his body kept pressure on the bleeding. Who the hell was shooting at you two?"

I struggled to stay awake. "Call Roberts of the Seawards police, tell him to get the hell in here and talk to me. Roberts," I repeated.

Hayward patted my uninjured arm. "Okay, okay. Just relax."

"No rush," I muttered. "Who the hell cares if an Indian gets shot?"

They kept me in the hospital overnight, because it took so long to piece my arm back together. By the next day, the morphine had worn off and the mended bones hurt like hell, even done up in a cast. It wasn't as simple to get out of the hospital as it was to get in. There were a myriad of insurance forms to sign, a wait for the orthopedic surgeon to tell me my hand was okay. What I could see of my hand looked fairly awful, black-and-blue and swollen.

They brought my clothes—the old jeans and the sweatshirt I'd worn the day before—and I had to wrestle into them with the humiliating help of a nurse. They also brought the foul-weather gear, and when I rummaged in the pocket, the bullet was still there. I turned it over in the fingers of my good hand. A nice little souvenir. Practically undamaged. Only Wayne and I had suffered damage.

The surgeon eventually turned up and pronounced my arm fit to take home, and I went in search of Wayne. I found him in the ICU, propped up in bed, belly mounding the sheet, with the usual tubes and drips, monitors bleeping away. He was incongruously large and healthy in the sterile white surroundings, his thick coarse skin returned to its normal ruddy shade, his long hair tied back in a knot. His wife sat by his side, her facial expression unchanged, impassive, resigned.

Ignoring the IV running into his veins, Wayne put out his hand to shake mine. "Hi, there, Noah Richards. Hear you saved my life."

"I just drove the boat. And not very well at that."

"Plenty of folks can't steer a boat at all."

He could so easily have bled to death. It was a mercy I was too ignorant to do anything more than call for help. "What was it all about, Wayne? Why on earth was someone shooting at us?"

"Looks like war, don't it? Everyone knows my boat. They knew who they were shooting at, all right. They wanted to keep us off the fishing grounds."

"They? You know who they are?"

Wayne looked at his wife. They both looked at me.

"Just they," he said. "You were there. You got any idea where that bullet came from? Hell, I don't even remember where we was heading at that precise moment."

He didn't have to be so philosophical about it.

"Aren't you mad about what happened—to you? to Jay? to that girl in Spokane? She was a victim, too. If nothing had happened to Jay, she'd be alive and well now."

"Sure, we're mad," Wayne said calmly. "But it don't do to get too excited about it. We'll get even, sooner or later. We got time."

"That's not the way it works. There are laws. They can't go round shooting people and getting away with it."

"No?" Wayne closed his eyes.

His wife said, "I think he's tired."

"How are you planning to get even?" I wanted to know.

But Wayne didn't open his eyes, and his wife merely ceased looking in my direction.

I returned to Edward's Bay in a cab. The herons and the ducks were still there, the sun dazzling on the water, the houses nestling into the sea grass and the driftwood, everything as deceptively tranquil as usual. I picked the mass of Sunday newspaper off the front step, went straight to the phone to call the Seawards precinct, and was surprised to get Roberts on the line.

"Wayne Daniels and I were shot at yesterday morning, more than twenty-four hours ago, and no one's bothered to ask one damn question about it. Why the hell not?"

"Now, counselor," Roberts said soothingly. "We came to the hospital, but Daniels was in surgery and you were flat out. I was planning to interview you when you were more conscious."

"Well, I'm home now and completely conscious."

"Okay, we'll be along. We've been over the boat. We found one bullet, probably the one that went through you. The docs picked one out of Daniels. Both bullets have gone to ballistics, but they're too distorted to be much use."

"Don't kill yourselves with excitement, will you? If you drag it out long enough, there'll be no one left alive to interview."

"Take it easy, Mr. Richards. I don't expect they were shooting at you. You're an honorable upright citizen, aren't you? Why would anyone want to shoot you?"

There was a surreal quality to the conversation. "You better get over here and talk to me."

"We will. Of course, we will. Especially if you can give us a description of who did the shooting. If you can tell us where the shot came from. You know how many shootings there are every year in Washington State? You know how many are solved?"

"At this rate, I can guess it's not many."

"What about motivation?" Roberts asked. "Got any theories?"

Motivation? Theories? Yes, I had a few. I could speculate, but what the hell did I *really* know? I could bandy a few names about, but I didn't think the police were going to take much notice. What proof was there? Apart from a dead man on the beach, one man who'd nearly bled to death, and one smashed ulna.

But there was also one bullet, safe in my possession, that would take a ballistics test very nicely, thank you.

I swallowed a couple of Tylenol. I wanted to get the hell out of Edward's Bay. If I could, I'd have jumped in the car and driven up to the old house in Springwell to lie low. But one hand wasn't sufficient to drive and shift gears on the Saab, so I was stuck for the time being.

I made more phone calls, to the Carlssons, to Charlie Forsyth, to Bigs Harrison. But only message machines answered, even though today was Sunday and should be a day for finding people at home. I lay on the sectional, that foolish and oversized piece of furniture, supported my arm on a cushion, and slid the *Seattle Times* out of its plastic wrapping. A large headline splashed across the front page: Seattle Climbers Killed on Everest.

God, Sarah! Harry McKenzie's death had completely gone out of my mind, as though it had never happened. I'd promised to help Sarah more than twenty-four hours ago. She had to be wondering where the hell I was. I picked up the phone to call her, and she didn't answer either.

I felt like hell; I'd had too many painkillers, and the residue of the anesthesia was heavy in my stomach. Searching for distraction, I turned the pages of the paper to the crossword, stared blearily at the clues, closed my eyes, and slept for a few minutes. I was startled into sudden wakefulness.

I awoke suddenly because the letters of that cryptic word Jay had used as the password in his computer had rearranged themselves in my head.

K-i-r-o-w-b-i-n-i.

It was an anagram. Bird names. *Robin*. The name of the girl at Edward's Bay. And *Kiwi*. What New Zealanders call themselves. What Sarah called herself.

Bird watching. A dangerous sport.

THIRTY-ONE

I'D BEEN A TOTAL IDIOT. SARAH MUST HAVE KNOWN JAY Bishop all along. She'd played me for a fool, suckered me. Duped me.

Whatever it was that Sarah McKenzie roused in me, I'd certainly also felt a degree of responsibility for her. And for Christopher. And I'd felt guilty for taking advantage of her, however old-fashioned it might be. Now it appeared I was the one who'd been taken advantage of, been manipulated ever since the first day I set eyes on her. She'd strung me along with the lonely, abandoned-wife-and-mother act. How many other men had she manipulated? Lured into a web of deception? Two of them were dead, her husband and Jay Bishop.

Rising off the couch in righteous indignation, my legs wobbly, my head none too clear, I staggered down the street to Sarah's house. To accuse her. To vent my anger. To demand some final explanation.

As soon as I reached the house, I knew instantly, even from outside, that Sarah was no longer there. Not from the appearance of the kitchen through the glass door, because the kitchen, as usual, contained no clue, nothing out of place, no sign of human habitation. No, I knew she was gone because there was a palpably empty feel to the whole house, all the life drained out of it, like a dead body. Stepping back, I stared up at the wide bare windows, at the neat deserted look. She was gone. Sarah had escaped home to New Zealand with her baby. The kiwi, the flightless bird, had taken flight.

I tried the handle. It was locked, of course. And then, all of a sudden, I had the terrifying suspicion that she might not have taken the baby with her, after all. She could have left him here, walked away, abandoned him. That would surely fit the picture of a manipulative, vindictive woman, not only ambivalent about her child but destructive to him as well. Dear God!

This time I didn't hesitate to break the glass to get in. I picked up a rock and smashed at the glass until it shattered into a thousand square pieces, thrust my good arm through, and unlocked the handle from the other side; then I reeled across the kitchen and up the stairs to the bedroom. The crib was there in the corner as well as the little mask hanging on the rail, the oxygen cylinder, the black monitor box. But no baby.

I searched the obsessively neat house from top to bottom. Nobody. Nothing. No clue. Not even any signs of a hasty departure. When I was quite certain there was no abandoned baby—a ridiculous idea now that I thought about it more clearly—I searched instead for a high-powered hunting rifle, because that seemed the logical next step. Sarah McKenzie knew Jay Bishop, had lied about knowing him; ergo, she was the one who killed him. Except, despite all my suspicions about Sarah, a picture of her with a gun in her hands was very unconvincing. But why would she lie about knowing Jay?

I scoured the house, throwing open drawers and closets, looking under the beds, in the kitchen cabinets, in the basement, everywhere, and searching for something, anything, that might give an answer to the riddle of Sarah McKenzie. Discovered it at last in the wastepaper basket in the living room, beside the desk. One small piece of garbage in all that tidiness. A piece of paper, a letter, screwed up, half-finished. Addressed to me. Dated yesterday afternoon.

Dear Noah,

I finally got hold of my parents. Christopher and I are flying to NZ tonight. My Dad insisted, and paid for the ticket, a blessing as I don't have enough money for the fare. You know I've been desperate to go home again. I can't wait. I'm confident Christopher's problems can be taken care of in NZ. I admit I don't trust the American medical system too well.

Thank you for all your kindnesses. I wish there'd been time to get to know each other better, but what with the baby's troubles and now Harry . . .

The letter petered out.

I smoothed the creases, read the letter again. And again. It was quite straightforward, not at all complicated, but as with everything else about Sarah McKenzie, it left me confused. The small, perfectly formed handwriting was upright and steady. The writing of someone out of control? The words of someone guilty of harming her own child, of shooting a man in the back?

The letter was addressed to me, so I put it in my pocket, looked around the unnaturally neat house one last time. The neatness still made me nervous. I closed the door behind me and finally walked out with what I supposed was relief. I'd take care of the broken glass, and now Sarah and Christopher would be in someone's else's care. But despite everything, I'd miss them. I'd grown accustomed to their faces.

I limped across the sparse lawn at the back of the house, over the driftwood to the beach, found a patch of dry sand, rested my head against a log, and closed my aching eyes for a moment. Thought about Sarah McKenzie. About Christopher. About Christopher's father, dead on a distant mountain. About Jay Bishop, Indian, activist, lady-killer, dead on this very beach.

Opening my eyes again, I stared across the bay to the headland beyond. Was Walter Drummond watching through his telescope? Walter Drummond or another one of those angry owners? As I gazed across the water, a cormorant flew by, low to the surface, wings skimming the waves, neck outstretched. Another bird. One more bird name came to my mind, one more in the lexicon of Jay Bishop's dangerous hobby of bird watching. If I'd been alert enough when Jay mentioned bird watching that day, I might have recognized the significance of the name of the man at the meeting. Partridge. Jack Partridge. The man who owned the oyster beds. "Took me years to build up my oyster beds," he'd said. "Now I'm told someone who did nothing has the right to help himself to half. . . . I'll be damned before I see that happen." Surely his name wasn't a coincidence. I didn't believe in coincidence.

God knows, there was rage enough about the clashes between new property and old rights, and God knows, there were too many guns within easy reach of hot tempers. So simple to raise the barrel and aim along it, another long-distance act of retribution. As for me, I suppose I'd merely been in the wrong place at the wrong time.

I knew one thing. I wasn't going to hang around Edward's Bay to find out.

But I did just that. Hung around. The sun was surprisingly warm and comfortable on my face, and the Tylenol had begun its work. My arm no longer hurt so much. After a few minutes, I closed my eyes again and drifted off into an uneasy sleep. Dreamed of the people in Edward's Bay, the shadowy figures coming and going in my mind.

I didn't sleep for long. I awoke when the sound of footsteps came near to me, when the light of the sun was blocked from my face. Sitting up too quickly, my head spun again and I raised a hand to shade my eyes. It took a moment to focus on the people standing over me, staring down at me. Three of them. Bigs Harrison and Ralph. And the teenage girl who'd stood beside Ralph at the meeting at his house. A pretty girl with pink cheeks and dark curly hair. The sort of girl anyone could fall for.

Bigs squatted down on his haunches.

"What the devil happened to you, Noah? You look like hell. What did you do to your arm?"

I twisted around to look up into his face. "What are you doing here, Bigs? I tried to call you earlier."

He grinned. "Why? Want to buy the house?"

"I don't think so. It's too damned dangerous round here."

"Geez, Noah. I was sure you wouldn't be able to resist it. I got to sell a few more or I'll be broke. Make me an offer."

I levered myself to my feet. Bigs put out a hand to help me, and we stood face-to-face, too close for comfort. The expression on his face and on Ralph's was exactly the same, surprise and faint bad temper. The girl looked alarmed, her eyes round and startled, her hands clasped together under her chin.

"If you want to sell your houses, Bigs, you need to make sure people aren't going to get guns aimed at them." I lifted my shattered arm in its cast. "See this? It's not your ordinary broken arm. I was out in a boat yesterday morning doing a bit of quiet fishing, minding my own business, out there by the headland." I pointed with my good hand. "Some idiot shot at me."

Bigs said, "No shit? You were shot at?" A frown creased his forehead. "Where from?"

"From somewhere about here, I'd guess."

He raised his own arm and squinted along it. "No way. Someone would have to be much higher up than this to get any sort of aim. Maybe from up on the headland?" He chewed on his lip. "Difficult to tell though, isn't it?"

"I was with Wayne Daniels. In his boat, the *Maribelle*. You know Wayne, don't you, Bigs? Quanda Indian. Wayne was shot, too, in the back, just like his nephew. Jay Bishop. Shooting someone in the back in an act of cowardice, don't you think? And does nothing for the reputation of Edward's Bay."

Bigs stared at me for another moment. All three of them stared at me. "Well, Noah," Bigs said at last, heartily, "at least you survived."

"I'm sure you'll be glad to know Wayne survived, too."

We stood silently on the wet sand for a long moment, the waves slapping slowly and softly. I said, "You heard about the court of appeals decision about the shellfish treaty? The Indians will soon be collecting their share of clams on this very beach."

Bigs shook his head, more in sorrow than in anger it seemed. "The damnedest thing. Those damn Indians want everything, don't they?"

"When exactly did you come down to Edward's Bay, Bigs?"

He glanced at Ralph. "This morning. Why?"

"Just wondering." I looked at the girl. "Is your name Robin?"

Ralph's eyes hardened into cold, gray pebbles. "What's it to you?"

Robin. The other half of the anagram.

Ralph said, "Never you mind what her name is. I'd have thought you'd be more interested in doing something to protect the rights of the property owners around here."

"Is that what you wanted, Ralph? A tame residential lawyer? Nice try." I was suddenly exhausted, weary, unsteady on my feet. "You two know a lot more about guns than I do. What does it take to shoot someone in the back? An investment in a housing development that's in trouble? People not buying expensive houses on the water because the Indians are claiming their right to the tidelands? And what if one of those damned Indians was making a play for a girl like Robin?"

There was another moment of complete silence, broken only by the lapping of waves, the cry of a gull. Suddenly, Ralph exploded into an unnatural bark of laughter and shrugged elaborately. "That Indian made a damned nuisance of himself with the girls. The one who lived there, for example." He pointed to Sarah's house, right behind us. "He was always trying to hit on her at the Eagle's Nest. But she knew better than to have anything to do with him."

A cloud rolled across the sun, darkening the water. Was that it? Not that Sarah knew Jay Bishop, but that he wanted to know her? She hadn't lied at all when she said she didn't know him? Was I wrong about her? Had everyone been wrong about her? In every way? I stumbled over my own feet.

I said to Robin, "Did you know Jay Bishop was using your name as part of a password on his computer? For the work he was doing to prove the Quanda are a tribe. So they could lay claim to this land. Ironic, isn't it?"

The girl gasped, a sharp intake of breath, her eyes widening, a vivid color running up her face, fading just as quickly, leaving it pale and hollowed. The light drained from her eyes so that she suddenly seemed years older. "Jay," she moaned. "Poor Jay. He was a beautiful human being. Sort of noble."

Her father spun on his heel, snarled at her. "Noble? He was nothing but a thief. Stealing our land away from us. I told you to keep away from him. I warned you he was nothing but trouble. Girls like you don't take up with Indians. Especially not Indians who're stealing our land. Our livelihood. Your inheritance."

Robin stared at her father. "Dad?" Her voice rose, mewing like a seagull. "Dad?"

"Go home," he said. "Get out of here."

She clutched at his arm, then put her hands over her ears, blocking him out, wailed again in a thin high shriek, turned and ran, stumbling, along the beach.

And once she'd gone, only Bigs and Ralph were on the beach with me. Bigs stood between his cousin and me, his head yawing from side to side, his face screwed in indecision, then he took a couple of steps away from me, toward Ralph. Stood beside him, shoulder to shoulder. So much alike. More like brothers than cousins.

I said, "Is that how you think problems should be settled? By shooting everyone in sight?" My feet were sinking into the sand, trapping me. "It might have been smarter not to take a gun to someone like me. I flatter myself I'm the type of citizen the powers that be might care about. At least there'll be a decent investigation now."

Bigs's face changed color, lost the ruddiness, went pale about the lips. He clenched his mouth tight and thrust his hands deep into the pockets of his jacket, the material straining. He groaned aloud, as though struggling to remain silent, but the words suddenly spilled out of him. "Shit, Noah, I'd never try to kill you. You're my friend."

But would he have known who was wearing the yellow slicker on Wayne's boat? I was quite ready to believe it was both of them, Bigs and Ralph, together. Or all of them together, all the owners of the land. Easy to imagine a conspiracy, to imagine them cooking it up, ganging up to get rid of the troublemakers, the damned Indians. Deciding who'd pick one off. Making it difficult to prove who'd actually done any of it. I didn't want it to be Bigs, even though he'd been missing from the meeting the day Jay Bishop was shot. Even though he'd tried to pump me for information. I'd known Bigs for such a long time, and I couldn't believe he was capable of murder. Didn't want to believe it. Maybe I was clutching at straws because I understood enough about his hot temper to know he might commit an impulsive act, but Jay's death and the attack on Wayne's boat had been nothing except deliberate and cold-blooded. I hoped he had an alibi for yesterday morning.

My head was spinning again. I sat down quickly on a log, stared out at the sound to where Wayne's boat had been when it was fired on. Then I saw, from the other end of the beach, other figures appearing. Even from a distance, I recognized the swaggering authoritative walk, the uniforms.

"The police," I said. "Coming to ask about this." I raised my arm in its cast. "About Wayne Daniels."

Bigs and Ralph looked towards the approaching figures, at each other. "The police?" Ralph said. "Hell, now we're really scared, aren't we?"

He laughed. Unconvincingly. But he wouldn't laugh when the contents of the safe-deposit box proved the Quanda had a sovereign right to this land. To half the oyster harvests. He wouldn't laugh when ballistics identified the stray bullet still in my pocket. Because an identifiable bullet would at last provide probable cause to search for the owner of the weapon. I'd make sure of it.

But first the weapon had to be found and that could prove difficult. All too easy to dispose of a gun. Especially if you knew someone was looking for it.

"You're going to have to tell what you know," I said. "Otherwise you're all going to be in deep shit, each and every one of you."

Bigs groaned again, as if in pain, and I expected him to tell me who'd done it. I wanted him to tell, for his sake as well as mine, but the answer arrived suddenly from somewhere else, from someone totally unexpected. As the three of us stood watching the police officers approach along the beach, that someone came from the other direction, clambering over the driftwood, running toward us, feet slipping and sliding in the sand. Ralph and Bigs didn't even see her coming. It was Robin. In her arms, cradled like a baby, she carried a long bundle wrapped in cloth, and as Ralph and Bigs turned, startled, she threw the bundle down at her father's feet and tugged at the cloth, spilling the contents out on the sand. A rifle, scope attached. Exposed on the sand, like an accusation.

"I knew where it was," Robin said. "In the Explorer." Tears were running down her cheeks, into her mouth. "You always carry it around, don't you? But I never imagined my own father would do such a thing. Not till now." She pointed at me. "Not till I saw what happened to him."

We stared at the rifle wordlessly, unable to move or to speak. There seemed nothing to say. Ralph and Bigs gaped at Robin, then Ralph sank to his knees and buried his face in his hands. "Jesus Christ, Robin. How could you? How could you do this to your own father?"

Her face was white and she wept, angrily. "How could *I*? How could *you?* How could you shoot someone down like a dog? As though he was nothing. Of no account. How can you think of people in that way?"

The police had reached us by then. Roberts and Jameson. They, too, stood and stared at the rifle as though they'd never seen one before, as though they wished it wasn't there so they wouldn't have to deal with the consequences. Nobody said a word.

Robin looked from one to another of us as if for help and then she dropped down beside her father and put her arms around him. "I'm sorry, Dad. I'm sorry. But I had to, don't you understand? I couldn't let it go. I couldn't have lived with it. It was terribly wrong. You know that, don't you?"

They cried together, father and daughter, and I had to turn away, unable to watch. I screwed up my eyes and peered into the haze, and almost believed I could see the figure of Jay Bishop, tall and lean, still strolling along this beach. As if he owned it.

Which, after all, maybe he did.

EPILOGUE

OF COURSE, I HAD TO MOVE FROM EDWARD'S BAY. I RENTED a condo in the Belltown section of Seattle, with a western view of Puget Sound and the Olympics, and I walked to the office everyday, a mile and a half on city streets each way. I missed the ferry ride and the beach, but the people on the streets, and the local restaurants, made up for it. Sarah McKenzie would have liked it there, I thought.

One day, I asked Belling Sidworth for her address in New Zealand and wrote to her because I had to know how Christopher was. Eventually, she wrote back. Just a postcard, with palm trees and bright blue water. "Christopher's fine," the card said. "He seems quite all right now that we're home in the Bay of Islands. But we still go to the beach everyday. Come see us sometime, Noah."

I turned the card over in my hand. Over and over. The same neat innocent handwriting as on the unfinished letter she'd left behind in the house.

Chauncey said, "You have to hope she got what she wanted. The most important thing is that the child survives his mother's problems."

I know a lot more about Munchausen syndrome by proxy now. It's a very difficult condition to prove. I hope we never have to find out that we were right about Sarah. I hope she knew what it was that she wanted.

The bullets on Wayne's boat matched the rifle Robin delivered to us. It took a long time, but Ralph Harrison was eventually convicted of attempted murder and put away for ten years. He wasn't charged with Jay Bishop's death because in that case there were no bullets for matching.

At first I thought there'd be no retribution for Jay, but he has won a kind of victory. Though it's true that nothing has yet been proved, the Quanda claim is now in the courts. Justice and Interior are involved, old state surveys are being inspected, Indian surveys examined, and the whole of Edward's Bay is in limbo. Ralph and Bigs had to file for bankruptcy. The burden of proof is on Jack Partridge about the legitimacy of his oyster beds and his entitlement to the harvest.

The Ambrose case came to trial. Charlie defended Angel Ambrose and he was quite brilliant. His performance dazzled me. He pled diminished responsibility on her behalf, and she's undergoing treatment at the state mental institution. I visit her every now and then.

After the trial, Charlie and I agreed to part company. Amicably. Belling Sidworth offered me a position soon after I got Sarah's address from him, and we've been representing the Quanda in their pursuit of tribal sovereignty. I didn't miss the kind of cases Charlie and I dealt with, but I did miss Sibby. We still have dinner and martinis now and then.

Lauren Watson never did come back from Minneapolis, but I found someone else to go to the opera with. She's a new friend, and she sings in the Seattle Chorale. A mezzo. I met her at an opera fundraiser when Charlie invited me.

But I often think about Sarah McKenzie. And Christopher. Maybe I will go and visit them sometime. Just to make sure.